HARD TACK

HARD TACK

A CAT MARSALA MYSTERY

◇ ◇ ◇

Barbara D'Amato

CHARLES SCRIBNER'S SONS
NEW YORK

MAXWELL MACMILLAN CANADA TORONTO

MAXWELL MACMILLAN INTERNATIONAL
NEW YORK OXFORD SINGAPORE SYDNEY

Charles Scribner's Sons
Macmillan Publishing Company
866 Third Avenue
New York, NY 10022

Maxwell Macmillan Canada, Inc.
1200 Eglinton Avenue East, Suite 200
Don Mills, Ontario M3C 3N1

Macmillan Publishing Company is part of the
Maxwell Communication Group of Companies.

This is a work of fiction. Names, characters, places,
and incidents either are the product of the author's
imagination or are used fictitiously. Any resemblance
to events or persons, living or dead, is entirely
coincidental.

Library of Congress Cataloging-in-Publication Data
D'Amato, Barbara
    Hard tack:a Cat Marsala mystery /
    Barbara D'Amato.
        p.   cm.
    ISBN 0-684-19299-3
    I. Title.
PS3554.A4674H36   1991
813'.54—dc20   90-26019

            10 9 8 7 6 5 4 3 2 1
        Printed in the United States of America

*To Harold Steketee, the finest possible brother,
also technical adviser for this book*

HARD TACK

PROLOGUE

Chuck's body sprawled on its back on the bunk. Blood lay across his neck like a red bib. Blood spots spattered the teak walls, the light blue bedding, and the lush royal blue carpet of the luxury yacht. Dr. Silverman, standing next to me, put his fingers on the wrist of the corpse, but it was a gesture, I was sure. It must have been as obvious to him as it was to me that death had taken place some time ago.

The knife lay where Belinda had just dropped it.

Easy Girl was pitching* violently in the waves. I was soaked to the skin and so was Daniel Silverman. Wind shrieked over the top of the companionway, using the opening like a whistle. It made a mournful sucking sound down here in the belly of the boat.

We were in the middle of nowhere, in the dark, still an hour or so short of dawn, out of sight of land even if it had been daylight. I have friends from New York who think you can see across Lake Michigan. Ha! We couldn't see land in any direction.

This was a big, beautifully appointed luxury sailboat, a sixty-two-footer. It slept nine. But it was small as a speck out here, and I was scared. Wet, cold, isolated, puzzled, but mostly I was terrified. I can't swim—not that anybody else could swim to land from here, either. I was the only stranger on board. There wasn't a soul I had known before I set foot on this damn thing twenty hours back. And the others were all old friends.

---

* See glossary of nautical terms from Cat Marsala's notebook, pages 226–29.

All friends—except one of them had killed another one of them.

And the most terrifying thing was that this murder couldn't have happened. There had been several people in the galley and dinette area all night. The stateroom door had been locked. It was the only entrance to the room. You could see the door from the galley and dinette. There wasn't anybody on board moronic enough to slip into the stateroom and slit Chuck's throat with two or three other people watching him do it.

But it surely wasn't suicide. Not Chuck. Not this way. And not doped up like he was.

The psychic dislocation, the sheer mental shock of seeing with my own eyes something that was impossible, added to the loneliness and fear I already felt. It was the true source of my terror.

I'm a freelance journalist. My name is Catherine Marsala. If I had not been a writer I wouldn't have been here, staring at a corpse.

When Hal handed me this assignment, it had sounded like a perfectly good idea. Even pleasant. In fact, it was practically a reward for good work done in the past.

Ever get the feeling life tries to trick you?

I did it as a dare. It was a dare from myself to myself, the most dangerous kind and the hardest to turn down.

Hal at *Chicago Today* had said, "Cat, we want a piece on how the other half lives."

"Great. What are you paying?"

He named a figure that was okay, if not princely, and I thought hanging around in penthouses or first-class restaurants or whatever he had in mind at his expense wouldn't exactly be hard duty. Plus, he was talking Sunday section with color pictures. When you're a freelance, starvation is always approximately two articles away. I figured, sure, I'm a professional. I said so.

He said, "Fine. This guy Honeywell's a friend of one of our stockholders. Nice yacht. *Very* nice. You won't be on the Chicago to Mackinac, that's later anyway. We'll use this the Sunday before the race."

"What race?"

"Chicago to Mackinac. On Lake Michigan. The major league race of the summer. Have you been paying attention, Catherine?"

"Race. Yes. You mean the—"

"Yacht. Water. Sail. That kind of thing."

He didn't know that he was driving nails into my coffin. Calmly, I said, "Oh?"

"You'll go on the Fourth of July weekend on the boat that won last year. There'll be eight or ten of the very rich aboard. Get a lot on how you sail a boat. How the very rich live. Are they really different from other people? Do they have class? What *is* class? What do they eat? Do they wear diamonds at the wheel? Brush their teeth in champagne? You know the kind of thing."

I said, "Um."

"What's the matter?"

"Nothing."

"My *God*, Cat. You're not scared of water, are you?"

"No."

"I can always get somebody else."

"No!" I said. Nailing myself but good.

I am scared of water and have been since a childhood incident when I nearly drowned. And although I recently had an experience where falling into Lake Michigan certainly saved my life, I still haven't licked the fear. Plus, I've never understood the attraction of a seagoing camper, when on land you have everything excellent: movies, hamburger stands, rock concerts, the Pump Room, the symphony, a good book by a fire, whatever you like, and none of it tips back and forth.

But Hal made it sound pretty nice.

"It's a sixty-two foot sloop," he said.

Whatever a sloop was. "Not your little dinghy," I said casually. In fact, that made it about twice as long as my whole apartment, including the corner bathroom my landlord valued so highly. The weather had been beautiful, and since it was the middle of summer, I assumed it would go on being beautiful. Silly me.

"You'll sail out of Chicago, around the lower end of Lake Michigan, touching at Michigan City, Indiana, then up to Holland and Grand Haven, Michigan, and back."

I thought, hell, this was a *lake*, not an ocean, so even seasickness couldn't be full-scale.

"Good food and the Beautiful People," Hal said.

The good food is fine with me at any time. As for the Beautiful People, I had spent the past five weeks in the company of four men who were wholesaling heroin, importing the stuff in statues of Sun Myung Moon and in packages wrapped around the roots of Asian orchids and covered with osmunda fiber. *Straight Talk* had wanted an article on Why do they do it? The answer: for money. Surprise. My job was to make that answer interesting. The four men were now vacationing in a federal compound in Minnesota. I figured a change would do me good.

And there was another problem, too. Maybe it's the trouble with holidays. Everybody who thinks they have some claim on you wants you to do something symbolically committing on holidays. My nice, calm stockbroker friend John Banks had invited me to his parents' summer place in Wisconsin for the July Fourth weekend. This would involve long boring cocktail hours with his father, who talked about Eurodollars, and his mother, who regarded me as a little like a scabies infection—pesky, but with time and treatment it will go away.

Mr. Banks was the kind of man who would wear gray flannel bathing suits if he could. Mrs. Banks's idea of a hearty lunch was leek quiche.

Mike, my wilder male friend, who was a reporter, was doing an article on balloon racing for a national glossy. The race would leave Omaha on the fourth and race toward Lake Forest, north of Chicago. Depending on winds, they would arrive in three or four one-day bursts. He was going in a balloon and had wangled an invitation for me. I knew that with Mike's tendency to get high on the adventure alone, he'd be in the bars every night drinking with the balloonists. In three days I'd be driving him home and regretting it all, but I'd never been ballooning. I'd pretty much decided to go with him, not John.

Then the two of them ran into each other outside my apartment while John was leaving and Mike was arriving. This kind of event is a number-one must-miss social goof. John got all strained and silent and aristocratic, and Mike, who announced that I was spending the Fourth of July with him, got all hot and bothered and called John names. I said a plague on both their houses and refused to go with either one.

At which point, Hal's offer arrived. When I told John I was going on the sailing trip, he volunteered to take care of my parrot, Long John Silver. Naturally that made me feel guilty about turning down John's invitation. A nice stew of human emotion!

The final thing that contributed to my undoing was that my mother had set up a family reunion for the Fourth of July at my brother and sister-in-law's house in Terre Haute, Indiana. The town of Terre Haute was planning something special in the way of fireworks. Since my sister-in-law and I together already make something special in the way of fireworks, I thought I would go on a peaceful Lake Michigan cruise.

Ha!

I got to the yacht basin at practically dawn on Friday, July 2nd, the day we were to leave. With the big weekend coming up, I knew all the parking lots would be full, plus the Honeywells' secretary had left me a message that we'd start at 8:00 A.M., but neither reason was why I was early. I was nervous.

My background doesn't include yachts, and my wardrobe doesn't include yachting gear. I wanted to be early to acclimatize myself and try not to feel like the odd woman out all weekend.

I wore tennis shorts and carried a duffel bag, a combo that wasn't too inappropriate as seagoing gear. The bag contained extra tennis shoes, a change of Levi's, and a bathing suit, two locked-room mysteries, *The Judas Window* and *The Three Coffins*, in case the Beautiful People turned out to be The Boring People, extra notepads in case they didn't, and a Police Athletic League sweatshirt in case of cold weather. Lots of extra pens and pencils—I have a mania about having plenty of writing implements. Also a blue plastic Chicago Cubs jacket, the kind the club gives out to fans one day a year. Hal had said I might need something waterproof. At the time, like a fool, I thought he meant in case of rain.

It was 7:00 A.M., and the place was swarming. I can now say I have seen every possible color and style of ice chest, halter top, and sun hat that the world has to offer.

Belmont Harbor is the home of the Chicago Yacht Club. Some years ago the Park District installed concrete moorings shaped like starfish in the little bay for boats to tie up to. At the shore there are still docks, but they are concrete and steel, not the creosote-soaked pilings with a pelican on top that would have been so atmospheric. Not that we have pelicans up here in Illinois anyway, but we have a very nice line of white seagulls, some of which were hanging around in the sky right now, effortlessly riding air currents.

As I looked east into the bay, the water danced with light. It was hard enough to see the boats. I couldn't see any boat names. Being honest with myself, I had to admit that I didn't really want to ask for help. I was intimidated by the whole thing—by the wealth of the boat owners, and even more by my lack of knowledge about boats. And most of all by the real fear that underlay everything this morning. Suppose I got out on the water and had a panic attack, a real, screaming, blue-faced panic attack? I would disgrace myself.

Forget disgracing myself. Suppose I was terrified, and we were way out in the lake? How could I get to land?

I grabbed at the notebook stuck in my pocket like a talisman. I fondled the pens and pencils, my personal rabbit's foot.

Don't think about it. Think about finding the boat. If it was one of the biggest, it would have to have one of the tallest masts, wouldn't it? We investigative reporters know how to deduce things.

Far out beyond the concrete starfish were several tall masts. These biggest boats were tied up to round yellow buoys farthest out from shore. But which was which? Which was the *Easy Girl*? Well, I was not going to be intimidated. I'd find somebody with a kindly face and ask. I shouldered my duffel bag and walked to the edge of the dock, rolling my gait so as to look like an old salt.

Three children erupted from the path behind me and fell against my legs, pushing each other. One clung stickily to my bare left leg. They were about four, five, and six years old.

"Mom said you spilled Coke in the head, and you're going to clean it up," said Four to Five, taunting.

"Am *not*! I get to carry the jenny from the car!"

"I," said the lordly Six, swinging stickily around my calf, "am carrying the jenny. Me and Dad. You get to tape the turnbuckles."

Five said, crowing, "I get to carry the whisker for the jib. Dad *said*!"

I peeled off the adhesive fingers, thoroughly ashamed that I hadn't understood more than half of what they said. In fact, I was lost after the spilled Coke. And they were children! Giving up the rolling gait, I started to walk away when a voice behind me said, "I'm sorry. They're always like that, I'm afraid."

Their mother. A kindly, helpful person, no doubt, just barely glancing at my Penny's marked-down tennis shorts.

I said, "That's okay. Do you have any idea where I could find the *Easy Girl*?"

"Oh." She looked at me with increased respect. I may dress funny, but I was going to sail on the biggest boat.

"Sure! She's right out there."

I sighted along her arm. There was a beautiful boat, white above and emerald green below, out in deep water at one of the buoys. And three absolutely gorgeous men with large shoulder muscles and skimpy swimsuits were manhandling a sail striped orange, red, yellow, and green.

"Aha!" I said.

She laughed. "I see what you mean, but that isn't it. Next to it. Blue below the waterline."

There it was.

I was amazed even at that distance how big she was. Hal had said sixty-two feet, and I had visualized sixty-two linear feet quite nicely. But with the mast, which looked taller than the boat was long, and the cabin and all, she looked as if she could cross the Pacific Ocean without straining herself. She was lovely, white above and cool, cool blue at the waterline. The chrome and brass shone in the sun; every inch was clean and polished. Even as I watched, an arm came up from inside with a cloth and rubbed it along a varnished handrail near the cabin. The hand was followed by the head, bare torso, and finally legs of a young man with reddish brown hair. He glanced around and then went on polishing things.

"How do I let him know I'm here?"

The woman said, "You yell 'Hello, *Easy Girl.*' You can use our loudhailer if you want."

"Well, great. Thanks."

"I'll get it."

I waited, looking out at the boat. So far, I wasn't scared.

There was a rumbling sound behind me, and I looked around. Another young man appeared. He wore cutoff denims—why hadn't I thought of cutting off some pants?—an armless yellow shirt with the number 48 on it, and he had very curly black hair. He was trundling a dolly loaded with three heavy wood crates labeled "Piper-Heidsieck." Well, well. Champagne.

My friend the kindly woman came up to me with a loud-hailer, just as the champagne lad lifted his own megaphone and bellowed, "Ahoy, *Easy Girl!*"

"I guess you don't need this," the woman said, smiling again. "Have a good sail."

"Thanks. You, too."

◊ 2 ◊

Far out at the *Easy Girl*, the red-haired lad jumped over the side. At least that's what it looked like from where I was. But thirty seconds later a little dinghy came swinging around the back—stern—of the *Easy Girl* and headed toward us. The dark-haired boy near me moved to the edge of the dock.

As the dinghy came closer, I could see it had three cross-pieces for people to sit on. With two people on each, it might seat six. It looked like fiberglass and was powered by a small outboard motor. Really small. You could beat egg whites with it if you had a large bowl.

The dark-haired kid took the rope as the dinghy nudged the dock and tied it to a post while the redhead cut the motor and reached for a plastic bag of garbage in the boat. The dark-haired one took the garbage bag and then started handing over the heavy cases of champagne, one by one, very carefully.

The dinghy was spotlessly clean inside. I found this reassuring.

As the third case went into the little boat, the two boys

glanced down the walk behind me, then became, if possible, even more alert. I turned around to find out what they saw.

My hosts, unless I missed my guess.

Coming along the walk was a party of three. One was a man wearing a chauffeur's cap. One was a man of about fifty, firm-muscled and tan, wearing plaid Bermuda shorts, a white shirt, and leather loafers with rope soles. The third was a woman. I knew only from years of experience that she was over forty. She was sleek, slim-limbed, youthful, lightly tanned, with the long stride and heads-up carriage that means either money or a lot of training in looking like money. She wore very crisp, very short white linen shorts and a blue silk shirt knotted at the waist.

I felt like a peon.

All three carried duffel bags, not just the chauffeur. Democracy in action. Their eyes swept briefly over me, in a well-bred, incurious way.

They chucked their bags into the dinghy. The older man said, "Thanks, Jim," to the chauffeur.

"No problem, Mr. Honeywell."

Right so far. My host.

"Now, Jim, you have a nice weekend," Mrs. Honeywell said. "We won't be back before late Sunday night, or even Monday, and we might be delayed beyond that."

"I know, ma'am," said the chauffeur. "Good sailing."

"Might as well use the car yourself, Jim," said Honeywell. The man touched his cap. I almost took notes right on the spot, but it would have been too obvious. Then, lifting his hand in a general wave, the chauffeur strode off up the path. The red-haired kid who had brought the garbage in waved, too, and went off with the chauffeur.

Mrs. Honeywell turned to step aboard the dinghy. Her husband said, "Here's Bill, dear," and she caught herself in midstep.

Bill was a gangling youth, good enough looking, but much

too thin. He was blond and resembled Mrs. Honeywell. With him was a young woman his own age. Mrs. Honeywell kissed her and said, "You look wonderful, Mary." But I caught the look of careful assessment on her face. It was either "Is this girl good enough for my boy?" or "How do I measure up to this twenty-years-younger model?"

I almost had my nerve up to walk over and announce myself, when six people arrived at once. One of them was shrieking "Belinda, dear!" in that high voice some women use to show they're terribly pleased. I was gratified to hear Mrs. Honeywell, whose name I now knew to be Belinda, say in a warm, low tone, "Lovely to see you all."

One of my mottoes is you have to meet life halfway. I constantly get into situations that intimidate me, but I don't have to show it. I had never met anybody here. Financially speaking, these people could buy and sell me, my apartment, my whole building, and my father and brothers as well, and have enough money left over to buy Rhode Island. But by God, they weren't going to see that I knew it or cared.

"Hi!" I said, walking up to Belinda Honeywell and holding out my hand. "I'm Catherine Marsala."

"Wonderful!" she said, and she took my hand and shook it. She smiled as if she were really glad to see me. "It's going to be the most exciting cruise, having you here."

She turned to the others. "This is the reporter who's doing the story on cruising Lake Michigan for *Chicago Today*! I told you all she'd be coming along."

The woman with the high voice said, "Isn't there going to be a photographer?"

"No, Twinkie," Belinda said patiently. "They photographed the boat last week."

"Oh." She was disappointed.

"Catherine isn't doing *us*. She's doing a piece on sailing."

"Call me Cat, please," I said.

"Nice. Okay. Let me tell you who's who, Cat. And then you're all going to be great friends. My orders, crew, are that nobody feels uptight with Cat. Right?"

"Aye, aye," said her husband, chuckling.

"Okay, Cat. This is Twinkie Mandel, my sister-in-law. Twinkie is an expert on gems."

Twinkie was pretty in a very, *very* thin way. And very carefully made up. She wore a pink-and-lavender-striped shirt that I knew at a glance was silk. I could imagine she knew gems—as gifts, to her.

"Twinkie owns and runs the Twinkle, Twinkle boutique on Michigan Avenue."

Okay, so I was wrong. Maybe even hasty. I still didn't have to like her.

Mrs. Honeywell introduced her brother, who turned out to be Dr. Greg Mandel, a Chicago name in the news. Mandel is a vascular surgeon who works out of Hastings Hospital Pavilion and keeps getting headlines with "Chicago's First." First heart-lung transplant, first this, first that. I'd heard rumors that he came from a moneyed background, which meant that Belinda did, too. In person the guy was all eyebrows, teeth, and Adam's apple.

With him was a chunky guy of about forty-five. He looked like an older version of the sailors I'd admired on the green-and-white sailboat. Strong shoulders. Curly sandy hair with touches of gray at the temples. Mmm. His name was Daniel Silverman. Specialty: sports medicine.

A smiling oriental man nodded to us as Belinda went on: "—our friend Takuro Tsunami, who designs boats and, if I may say so, is pretty famous for it. He designed the *Easy Girl*."

"My favorite," he said.

Mrs. Honeywell easily met his graciousness. "Mine too," she said.

"And this is Bret Falcon, the star! Now don't cringe, Bret,

you really are. He's the man who's made such a hit in our musical *Off and On*. His understudy has taken over for a week so he could get a rest. Next to Bret is the man who made him take time off, our fellow producer of *Off and On*, Chuck Kroop. In real life Chuck is a furniture manufacturer, which is one of the reasons we know him in the first place."

Honeywell, I remembered, was the president and major stockholder of Honeywell Furniture, easily one of the four biggest manufacturers in the country. There was a slight lack of cordiality in Belinda's voice when she talked about Chuck Kroop. Like her voice when she talked about Twinkie. Conflicts?

Bret Falcon did indeed look tired. Handsome, and tired. As for Chuck Kroop, he looked a lot like a linebacker. But his muscles had gone to his stomach.

"I flew Bret in last night in the company Learjet," Kroop said. "From New York. Right, Bret?"

"Um. Yes. Just the two of us in this big—um, it was really exciting."

"Behind Chuck, Cat, is my husband, Will. And next to him our son Bill and his friend Mary Shaughnessy. Mary is in her second year at Yale Law School."

Mary said to me, "I've heard of you. You did that great piece in *Chicago Today* on the Greylord judge."

Greylord was the code name for a probe some years ago into judicial corruption in Chicago. Guess what?—they *found* some judicial corruption. My article was on the effect on the children of one of the judges. They were grown children, both lawyers.

"Thanks!" I said, feeling less of an outsider.

Belinda turned to the dark-haired lad, now pushing the champagne into place in the dinghy.

"And this is Emery Langmar."

Emery stood up and gave Belinda a sprightly salute.

"He's going to sail with us. But I don't want you to think

of Emery as a slave. This is his summer job. One that gets
him out on the water in boats, which he loves as much as
we do. In the fall, he goes back to his senior year at Loyola,
studying—mmm—"

"Invertebrates," said Emery.

"I knew that," Belinda laughed. "Now my final order.
First names all. Right? Boats are wonderful, but the living
aboard is much too close for formality." She turned to me.
"Do you sail?"

"I've literally never been on a sailboat."

"Well, you'll soon see."

Then she gestured to the dinghy. "Why don't you and
Daniel and Bill and Mary go out first with Emery? He'll
come back for the rest of us."

I looked at the dinghy.

It was floating on the water, rocking on small waves.

My hand in my pocket gripped a clutch of pencils, hard.
The other hand grabbed my duffel bag.

Emery took my elbow to help me aboard.

◇ 3 ◇

I froze. Emery was standing in the dinghy holding his hand
on my elbow to help me aboard. Dr. Silverman was behind
me, waiting to step aboard after I got out of his way.

Below the edge of the dock, the little dinghy slowly lifted
up and down on the swells. This was my chance to back
out. Probably the last chance.

Damn. I *couldn't* chicken out.

There are times I'd rather die than look like a coward.

I stepped down into the little boat. Emery pointed at the front seat. I sat down quickly. The boat dipped deeper into the water and swayed back and forth as Daniel Silverman stepped aboard. He sat on the front seat next to me. We dipped again as Mary and then Bill climbed in. The boat was getting lower and lower in the water.

What made me think these people knew what they were doing anyway? People always *think* they know what they're doing. People are nuts. They could drown us all!

Emery started the little motor going, and we swept away from the dock. I clutched the side of the boat. Then I noticed Dr. Silverman looking at my white knuckles and clutching hand, and I unclutched it and smiled casually.

The *Easy Girl* had looked large at a distance. As we came nearer, it grew longer and longer and taller and taller, the mast as high above us as a tree. The side of it loomed over us, bright white in the sun. I climbed a short ladder and stepped aboard, too awestruck to be scared.

The pure white of the cabin was blinding in the morning light. The wood of the mast and deck glowed like copper under a coating of shiny varnish. The brass fittings looked like solid gold.

Dr. Daniel Silverman and young Bill Honeywell were casting ropes off the buoys. The red-haired lad apparently was staying ashore.

I took out my notebook, a gesture that always made me feel better. More in control.

Quickly, I jotted down who was aboard. There is absolutely *no such thing* as having too much information for an article. I might need to contact these people later.

Will Honeywell, about fifty. Furniture manufacturer. Owner of the boat. Old family money. According to John

Banks, right now their stock had taken a bit of a dip in the market.

Belinda Honeywell, his wife. Maybe forty-five. I'd read they'd been married twenty-three years. They were socialites in a quiet way. She organized the occasional charity ball.

Bill Honeywell, their son. About twenty-one.

Mary Shaughnessy, Bill's friend. Law student.

Dr. Greg Mandel, surgeon. Belinda's brother. Big name in Chicago. I'd guess him at forty-two.

Twinkie Mandel, his wife. Thirtyish.

Bret Falcon, Broadway star. Twenty-eight?

Chuck Kroop, financier, mogul, and so forth. Forty-five. I didn't know anything at all about him, hadn't known he'd be aboard.

Takuro Tsunami, engineer. Forty.

Dr. Daniel Silverman. Physician. Forty-five to fifty.

Emery Langmar, able-bodied seaman. Twenty-two?

Cat Marsala. Me. Mid thirties.

There were twelve of us. Well, that was fine; thirteen might have been unlucky.

Will Honeywell, at the wheel, put the boat in reverse, cleared the buoys, then shifted to forward. The lines of dozens of boats at their moorings turned majestically past us, like the spokes of a wheel. We joined a parade of watercraft heading east toward the channel, toward Lake Michigan, into the morning sun.

Pencil at the ready, I approached Honeywell.

He started to chuckle happily. "I hear you've never sailed."

"Never."

"Not *ever*?"

"Never ever. Why?"

"Well, this is going to be *fun*. You just ask anything you want."

I was half charmed at his delight, half apprehensive. I mean, I know everything there is to know about enthusiasts. The first time I ever went skiing, my friend Mike assured me that if I just *paid attention* to his lessons on the baby slope in the morning, I could handle the black diamond slope in the afternoon. Fortunately, nothing was broken. Just a bad sprain. "Okay. Why," I asked, "don't you use the sails?"

"Why no sails? In a confined space like this, you don't have enough control with sails. The wind's light right now. You lose control when the wind's low, plus the high-rise buildings around here turn the breeze in different directions. It's too unpredictable. When we get out on the lake, we'll get up the sails. By the time we're out of sight of land, we'll have plenty of wind."

"Out of sight of land?"

"Mmm."

"We're going out of sight of *land*?"

"Well, sure! We're making our first landfall at Michigan City, Indiana. The shortest way is to cut across the bottom of the lake. Didn't you know?"

"Um. I hadn't actually thought about it. I guess I pictured us kind of traveling along the shore of the lake. Looking at towns and boats and sand dunes, and—you know?"

I felt a hand on my arm. It was Dr. Silverman.

He said, "Come on. Let me show you around. Everybody else has had a chance to stow their gear."

"Come back in ten minutes," Will called as we walked away. "We'll be clear of the harbor."

Out of Will Honeywell's earshot, I blurted, "If we go out of sight of land, how will he know where we are?"

"You've heard of compasses?" Silverman was laughing.

"Sure, but there are a lot of empty miles out there." There were, too. We were still in the channel, going very slowly, but ahead was open water. "You can't be that accurate with a compass."

"Oh, yes, you can. Very accurate."

Now, I was not as naive as I sounded. I was well aware, as anybody who's completed seventh grade world history was aware, that ships navigate over hundreds of miles of open ocean. What was really bothering me—but I couldn't quite say it to Daniel Silverman—was that Will Honeywell was a weekend sailor, not a professional navigator. Most of the time he was in an office, being a businessman. Piloting the ship of commerce, some of my friends in the journalism biz might call it. Anyhow, here I was placing my life in his hands.

"Why's it called the *Easy Girl?*" I asked, falling back on my job for a sense of security. I pulled my notebook out.

"He makes Easy Boy recliners. But boats have to be named after women."

"Like hurricanes used to."

"Yes."

"*Easy Girl* sounds like a woman of easy virtue."

"It does at that. Will probably thinks that's funny."

Carrying our duffel bags, we walked toward the cabin. There was a door to an opening leading down. "Are these the only stairs?" I asked.

"It's called the companionway."

"Oh, aye, aye. Companionway." I put down my bag, took out my notebook and wrote the word. "Is this the only way down and up?"

"No, but it's the only convenient way. Come on."

The companionway was a stair, but with open risers like a stepladder. It led down into a sort of hall, on either side of which were the kitchen and dining area. It was astonishing how much room there was. The dinette table was attached to the wall, and on either side of it was a bench that could seat three. The benches were upholstered in royal blue. You could feed six at a sitting with no crowding.

Across from the table was a completely appointed kitchen. No ice chests and six-packs here, like my father takes fishing. No can of worms in wet peat moss. There was a propane-powered refrigerator bigger than the one in my apartment. Backing it up was an insulated pantry that could take a chunk of ice and be used as a second cooler, or left without ice and used as an ordinary place for storage. I looked in. It was filled, literally packed, with champagne, beer, wine, and every kind of soda pop known to civilization. Also several cantaloupes and two watermelons. I made a note. The Beautiful People eat well. This should be news to everybody, right?

The stove operated on propane, too. Emery was making coffee, but he moved aside to give me space and said courteously, "Look around."

"Thanks. Looks like you have everything you need."

"Oh, this is *great* to work in. You should see some boats!"

"This is a little bigger than some boats."

"You got *that* right. But this is well designed besides."

You could embroider that on a sampler. There wasn't a wasted inch. I looked in a couple of the cabinets over the stove and sink. Being nosy doesn't bother me. One cabinet held scotch, bourbon, rum, angostura, vodka, slivovitz, and Lord knows what behind them. All the brands you see advertised in full color in *The New Yorker*. Another held cornflakes, bread, salt, pepper, spices, even flour and baking powder and vanilla. There was a deep drawer under the stove. Potatoes and onions. We certainly weren't going to starve.

Daniel Silverman was sitting patiently at the dinette.

"See this?" he asked.

Over the dinette was a little shelf that held condiments that were in current use: ketchup, mustard, salt, pepper grinder, tabasco, bitters. He gave the shelf a push. It swung back and forth on hinges, like a playground swing. Also it had a lip all the way around the edge.

"That's so they won't fall out?" I said.

"We'll be on water," he said, watching me. "There are going to be waves."

Now I noticed the lip around the edge of the dinette table.

"Plates try to slide off, do they?"

"Not often."

"Mmm. Right."

"Come on. Let me show you the rest. Now, this is called fore, because it's toward the front of the boat."

"I got it. As in fore and aft."

"You bet. There are sleeping quarters for five up here. That's the head."

He pointed to a door on our left, which immediately opened. Twinkie Mandel came out, wearing a two-piece, silky fuchsia bathing suit. The top of it was held together by a gold ring maybe two inches in diameter between the breasts. The pair of triangles that made up the bottom part was held together by similar gold rings, one over each hipbone. There wasn't a wasted inch here, either.

She wore matching fuchsia sunglasses with pink lenses.

"Hi, Twinkie," said Silverman. He was so cheerful, I knew at once that he didn't like her. I took some satisfaction from this. Women who can spend an hour each morning on their makeup make me feel itchy all over.

"Daniel," she said softly. "Come up on deck. It's going to be a beautiful day. And Catherine," she added without enthusiasm.

"We will," I said. "Thanks."

She emitted a high-pitched, social laugh and went up the companionway. Silverman pointed again at the room she had left. "That is the head."

"Funny, it looks just like a bathroom to me."

"Funny."

"Why do people have to use all these ridiculous nautical

terms? We have perfectly good words for bathroom and kitchen. We don't need galley and head."

"It'll enrich your vocabulary," he said. "Plus, in some cases, it's clearer. Port is always port and starboard is always starboard. If you were facing the stern and trying to say turn right or left, a man facing the bow would think you meant the opposite directions. If you were amidships and looking out over the port rail, the bow would be right and the stern would be left. In a crisis, you don't want to give a command like 'Turn left,' and the man at the wheel turns right."

"Okay, okay! That goes for port and starboard. But not for head."

"Then think of it as more fun."

"What's this?" I put my hand on the wall panels.

"Teak."

"Oh." Basket-weave strips of teak covered all the walls. The floor was carpeted in royal blue plush, groomed to perfection. There were no stains, no worn spots, not a piece of lint or speck of dust on anything. I made a note.

Silverman led me forward to a room that came to a point at its front end.

"Are we in the bow?"

"Yup. These are called V-berths."

The beds had an aisle between them, and like the room, they tapered to a point. Several roughly folded sails lay on top of them.

Silverman pointed to a skylight above us, a square of translucent fiberglass. "You wondered if there was any other way to get down here."

"Actually, I wondered if there was any other way to get *out*. In case of—um—fire in the galley. Or sinking. Or whatever."

"This is it. It's a hatch for letting sails down. Or getting them up."

"Don't people sleep here?"

"Sure. Once we're moving, most of the sails'll be out of here."

"Oh."

As if for my personal benefit, the hatch was opened from above, and the cute kid, Emery, and Bill Honeywell looked in.

"Hi," said Bill. "Want to pass up that main?"

Silverman picked up the edge of one of the sails and fed it up through the opening to the two kids.

"How did you know which one he wanted?"

"It was the biggest, and it's not striped."

Underneath the berths were cabinet doors, hinged on top so you could lift them up and down. I assumed side-hinged doors could flop open and chop at your ankles when the boat was crashing into twenty-foot waves. I looked inside. They were crammed with duffel bags and sleeping bags.

"Stuff your duffel bag in here."

I did so. He pushed his in also, gave the whole lot a hefty shove, then let the door fall.

"Who is Chuck Kroop?" I asked.

"Furniture maker."

"Like Will?"

"Not exactly. He makes a cheaper kind of furniture. School and office chairs. Desks. And he's selling a lot of it. He's having a lot better year than Will right now. Takuro designs for some of Chuck's lines."

I was making some rough sketches in my notebook. It's a lot quicker to draw a picture sometimes, than to try to describe certain kinds of things in words, especially because, when you first start working on an article, you can't anticipate what you're going to need later. You just don't know what direction the piece is going to take. It's a little like shooting film for a movie. Ninety percent of what you do winds up on the cutting room floor.

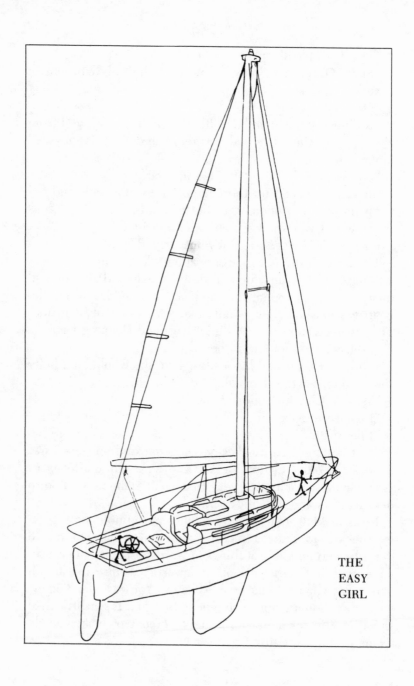

THE
EASY
GIRL

Silverman led me to a door right across from the head. Inside was a tier of three bunk beds, one right above the other, with a clearance of only two feet between them. The beds lay along the long axis of the boat, the better to maximize space. The distance between them and the door was about three feet. There was room to stand and get dressed, and nothing more. The bunks themselves were covered in royal blue velvet, and on the facing wall was a poster from the seventies, framed in glass, saying POVERTY SUCKS.

The carpet was plush, the walls were teak, and the brass was brightly shining, but the bunks were stacked up like coffins. I couldn't keep the dismay out of my voice when I said, "This is it?"

"Too Edgar Allan Poe?" he asked.

Hey, right on the money! I nodded. And I looked at Silverman with new eyes. Once in a while, a person will really be on your wavelength, really read your mind. "The Premature Burial" had flashed through my mind, with visions of my waking up in the dark, trying to sit up, and figuring I'd been buried alive. I was enormously relieved that he had understood. I guess until now these people had been strange to me—polite, in fact really nice, but a little foreign. Suddenly, Daniel Silverman was beginning to seem like a friend.

Up close, I realized that he had to be older than I had guessed. Put him at fifty or fifty plus a touch. Nearly twenty years older than I. Older than what I would call my "possibles" range. But the more I observed him, the more I thought, Why be rigid about this kind of thing? Especially now, when I was annoyed with John and Mike.

He led the way aft, through the galley and dinette. There was more space in the rear of the boat, because a boat is wider in back.

There was a room to the left from where I was standing—

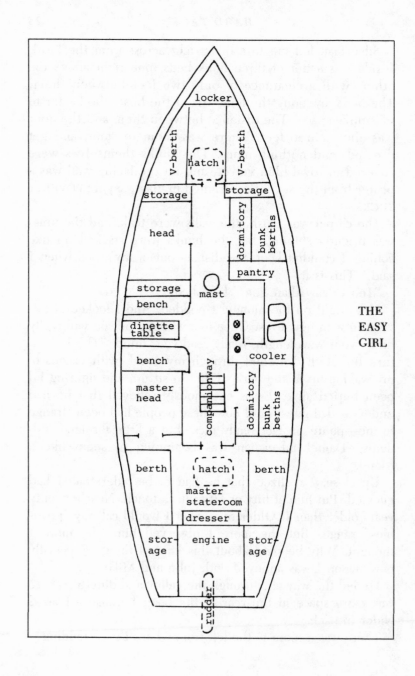

THE
EASY
GIRL

damn! he's right. It's a lot clearer to say starboard. It was
a bedroom corresponding to the one we'd just seen, but
with two berths and more floor space. Where the third
berth had been in the fore cabin, this one had cabinets.
I looked in them. Life preservers. Rope. Flashlights. Mys-
terious nautical objects of unknown use, including one that
looked like a giant aluminum pie pan. The berths were
wider, too.

"Mine!" I said.

"Kind of depends who gets here first," Daniel said. I
didn't know what he meant, then.

Belinda Honeywell came out of a door at the end of the
hall.

"Hello, Cat," she said. "Feel at home yet?"

"Not really. But very impressed."

"I guess that's the next best thing. Come in and let me
show you our room."

It was the largest bedroom I had seen on board. It occu-
pied the full width of the hull. The floor was covered with
the same royal blue carpeting, but it went halfway up the
wall behind the two beds. The beds were parallel to the axis
of the boat, like all the berths aboard, but these were notice-
ably wider, and still there was good space in the middle of
the floor. Between the ends of the beds was a small dresser
and mirror. On either side of the mirror were cut crystal
light fixtures. The light fixtures were not turned on because
plenty of light came in a translucent hatch in the ceiling,
which was slightly ajar for air. I wanted this room, but I
couldn't have it.

Opposite the beds was the door into the private head.
Master head? Head master? This bathroom was tiled in light
blue.

"Is this the very rear of the boat, then?"

"Oh, heavens, no. There's quite a lot of the cockpit
behind this, and under the cockpit is the auxiliary."

"The inboard motor," Daniel said. "It's behind that wall." He pointed at the wall with the dresser, mirror, and lights.

I became aware again of a faint rumble underfoot and a low-pitched hum. I had got used to it.

"It's probably very reliable," I said.

Belinda laughed again, and I smiled at myself, too. Then, completely unexpectedly, something hit the boat and we tipped over on our side. I screamed "Look out!" and clutched at Silverman. By the time I realized what I had done, we were level again.

"Sorry," I said, peeling myself off him. He didn't seem to be in a hurry to get rid of me.

"Wake of a boat, probably," Belinda said, smiling. She took my arm. "You'll have to get used to a little motion, but we're perfectly safe. Let's go up on deck. It's easier to see that everything's under control when you're up there."

We walked back into the galley. She gestured toward a plate of miniature Danishes, and I took one. Hesitated half a second and took another. You burn a whole lot of calories when you're nervous.

"We've got every safety device known to man," she said, helping herself to a single grape from another plate. Is this how she keeps her figure? I asked myself. Belinda led the way to the stair, saying, "Including radio, of course, and the Coast Guard is never more than a couple of hours away. Plus, the hull is virtually unsinkable. Even if we tipped all the way over on our side, the weight of the keel would pull us right back up again."

"But we aren't going to, are we?" I said.

"Never have yet," she said, leading the way up the stairs.

I looked across the deck and gasped. We had cleared the end of the Belmont Harbor breakwater. The two flashing red signal beacons had fallen behind us.

Just a few minutes before, we had been sailing in a sort of pond, with the feeling of being enclosed by the city of Chicago. Now we were in open water. The buildings were suddenly too far away, a backdrop to the west—the ornate Tribune tower, scalloped Marina City, the huge black coffin shape of the John Hancock, all framed underneath by the cement breakwaters.

The boats that had left the harbor with us were still in a ragged line. As I watched, the line was breaking up. The tight queue became a loose flotilla, then a scattering, then dots diminishing in size on a blue field of water and sky.

We were headed east into the sun.

It was now about nine-thirty in the morning. The day was warming rapidly. We native Chicagoans only needed to see the bronze color of the early light to know that it would go over ninety today, the air conditioners spitting at us from the high rises, the melting street tar grabbing at our heels.

I stood amidships, thinking how Olde Salt "amidships" sounded. Will Honeywell was at the wheel. When I looked forward from the boat, light was reflected from the water. Sky and ripples and all were silver and blue. But when I walked to the rear—aft—and looked behind us, the light sank into the water, showing it green and deep.

The structural lines of the buildings became indistinct, swallowed up in the bright reflections of sun on the glass windows. The city shimmered, dissolving gradually into sparkles of light.

"The channel here is two hundred ninety-six degrees," Will Honeywell said to his brother-in-law, Greg, and Daniel and me. Daniel and Greg nodded. "Emery and Bill, you can run up the main," he said. The two boys jumped up. Honeywell glanced around to see what other crew was available to him.

"Greg? Do you and Belinda want to get the spinnaker? Or anybody else who enjoys doing it."

"We enjoy it," said Belinda, and she and her brother went to the forward hatch.

By this time the boys had the mainsail attached to the ropes, and they paused to glance at the skipper. He nodded and they raised the sail. It popped and crackled in the breeze like rifle shots. At the same time, Honeywell cut the engine, the ship glided on momentum, the sail reached the top of the mast, Daniel took the winch that controlled the mainsheet, the boom swung out until it was almost at right angles to the boat, and Honeywell said, "Fine. Hold her there."

The sail stiffened, taut with air. Utterly silent, we swept along the surface of the water.

Hardly aware I was doing it, I walked forward and stood in the bow, holding on to the metal railing of the bow pulpit. Slices of water rose like dolphin backs on either side of the bow, almost without splash or sound, and fell away alongside the hull. Ahead was open water, blue, deep, and so clear we could have been flying in blue air above the earth.

I stood in the bow, stunned at the swift motion and the silence. Modern man, I suppose, has learned to equate speed with noise, and I was entranced by this swift, silent run.

Daniel came up and touched my arm.

"I like it," I said.

"I could tell."

"I love it."

• 4 •

Daniel said, "Even so swiftly may one catch the plague."

"Well, it isn't as if I'm going to take up sailing," I said.

"It's expensive."

"How much does a thing like this cost?"

"This boat? Oh, in the neighborhood of eight hundred thousand, nine hundred thousand dollars, I guess, Cat."

"That's a ritzy neighborhood."

"Definitely right side of the tracks."

"Let's see. I manage to save about sixty bucks a week, on an irregular basis. But call it regular. Sixty into eight hundred thousand—mmm—is thirteen thousand three hundred thirty-three weeks, or—um—"

"Two hundred and fifty-six years," Silverman said.

"That long, huh?"

"Yup."

"I'd be too old to get much out of it."

"After a hundred years or so, you'd have enough for a down payment."

Hoo, boy! Naturally, I immediately began thinking that, as a guest on board, I didn't have to worry about insurance, or hiring help, or winter storage, all that stuff. I could walk home after the weekend sail with no residual responsibilities. Sour grapes? What's the matter with sour grapes? Sour grapes keep people sane.

Over the next hours I picked up dozens of nautical terms,

many in self-defense, since the rest of the party used them
constantly. For convenience, pretend I knew them then.

I was leaning out over the oncoming water, supported by
the bow pulpit, when Daniel said, "Hate to bother you,
Columbus, but they're coming up with the spinnaker. We'd
better move."

Greg and Belinda hauled up an enormous red-white-and-
blue sail. Mary got up from where she was sunning on the
deck and asked, "Want me to help?"

"Sure," Greg nodded.

Mary slowly raised the top of the spinnaker, while Belinda
held tightly on to the rope—for some perverse reason called
the sheet—attached to its starboard corner. Greg took a long
spar, fixed one end to the port side of the spinnaker to hold
it rigidly out from the boat, then attached the boat end of
it to a ring in the deck. As Mary raised the sail, the great
red, white, and blue stripes opened to the wind with a huge
crisp puff, snapped full, and bellied out ahead of the boat
in the shape of half a sphere.

Immediately, we picked up speed.

"Daniel, I think I should go talk with Will Honeywell—" I
began.

Silverman smiled. "Sure. Don't forget your notebook."

I liked Daniel. He was mellow and gently funny. Of
course, the last thing I needed in my life right now, with
Mike and John playing tug-of-war, was another romantic
entanglement. But I wasn't dead, either.

I flipped a page in my notebook. Briefly, I wondered why
Will had agreed to have me aboard. All the rest of these
people were his friends. It had to be constraining to have a
stranger with a notepad along.

Now, I am not a gossip columnist. Thank God. Nor do I
ever do those sneering kinds of "investigative" reporting.
The sort of thing where the reporter says, "The committee
to reform prison conditions met at Northwestern University,

then adjourned for a lunch of quiche, white wine, and chocolate mousse." Implying, of course, that they were dilettantes, plus insensitive enough to lunch on foods the prisons never served the inmates.

My piece on sailing was not going to be slanted, as Hal would have known when he hired me. I write what seems real to me—how the waves feel, what the boat looks like, what sailing people eat. Would I mention the price of a boat like this? Yes, but told straight. Let the reader draw conclusions in accordance with his or her own beliefs.

I would be especially careful because my own background was blue-collar. My people, like most people, probably, were schizoid about wealth. They had a sneaking belief that the rich were different. But at the same time they were sure the rich were just like everybody else—except luckier, or maybe less honest.

But Honeywell couldn't know what I would write. Like anybody in the public eye, he must have been victimized at times by reporters who twisted his words or, in doing a warts-and-all portrait did only the warts. It was brave of him to have me aboard.

Chuck Kroop reached the cockpit the same instant I did. He said, "Will, how about giving me a turn at the helm?" He said it in that jovial tone of voice that told you he was sure you would agree with him. I could tell that Honeywell wasn't pleased. After all, he'd just got the *Easy Girl* under sail, after half an hour of carefully edging out of the harbor. And now that it was fun, Chuck Kroop wanted to take over.

"Sure, Chuck. That'll give me a chance for a cup of coffee."

You can say one thing for the rich. Some of them are awfully good at being polite. He even offered to bring Kroop a cup.

"Naw. I've got a beer."

I was right that Will was just being polite and didn't want coffee. He came and stood near me.

"So. How do you like it?"

"Except for occasional fits of terror, I love it. I didn't realize it would be so—so—"

"So airborne, maybe? That's the beautiful thing about sailing. And you're using only the power that's out there all the time, waiting for you. You go out in a motorboat, all you do is drive around. Like a Sunday driver, only on water. Slamming over the waves. There's no *skill* involved." He glanced back at our wake. "Chuck, aren't you drifting a little off course? We should be east southeast. It's one hundred seven and a half degrees."

"Hell, hardly! We'll pick up the smokestacks at Michigan City easily. You can't miss them."

"I like to get it right, though," Will said.

"Only thirty-three miles. What could go wrong?"

But I could tell from looking at the wake that Chuck Kroop had straightened it out.

Nice that Will could smell a deviation from course so quickly. He appeared to be an extremely competent man.

I glanced up from the wake to look back at Chicago. It wasn't there. Thinking we might have turned, I looked to port, but there wasn't anything there, either. Or starboard. Or anywhere.

There was nothing but water and sky in any direction.

My stomach lurched. The boat that had seemed so large in the harbor shrank in my mind to a minuscule dot in a trackless expanse.

Will saw my face.

"Believe me, Cat, we know where we're going."

"I do believe you." Well, I was beginning to.

"It's easier here than most places. This is one of the few big bodies of water on earth where magnetic north and true north are pretty close to lined up."

"Gee!" I said. I changed to a sharper pencil. "Gee, great, except that I don't know why that's important. Will you tell me about it?"

"You bet!" he said.

It was dazzlingly bright on deck. The sun shone on the white of the boat and glinted back at us from the water. I could see the breeze in the sails, in the royal blue burgee of the Macatawa Bay Yacht Club that stood out forward from the masthead, and in the American flag that rode forward from its brass standard on our stern. But I could hardly feel it.

I mentioned this to Daniel Silverman, who said that since we were riding along with the wind, it did not blow past us as fast as it would have if we had been standing still.

Silly me. I should have thought of that.

The deck was not really hot underfoot, but warm, as if the boat were a living thing, and my skin was heated by the sun. I went down to the galley to scare up a beer. Down there it was really warm, probably mid-nineties, and I stopped to sympathize mentally with sailors in the tropics in the days when boats were wood, not cool white reflective fiberglass.

That thought became so depressing that I took two Coors instead of one and went back up on deck. Daniel was lounging amidships, leaning back against the side of the cabin trunk, his feet protruding over the coaming, his deck shoes damp from the spray. The white hair at his temples was very attractive. I let myself sink down next to him, but kept my feet back farther from the edge.

"You can have one of these, if you insist," I said, "since I now consider you my friend."

"Thank you."

"What'cha doing?"

"Basking."

"Well, you've certainly chosen the hot side. If we went over to port we could get out of the sun."

"Port, indeed. You've certainly mastered the lingo."

"Us professional wordsmiths are quick like that."

Dr. Greg Mandel slouched by, stepping over Silverman's outstretched legs. He carried a glass beaded with moisture, which he gulped at after getting past Silverman. His bushy eyebrows looked sweaty.

"Hey, Greg. How you doing?" Daniel said.

"Um, sure."

"No, Greg, what I said was how are you?"

Now, Mandel was a heavy hitter in experimental heart and blood vessel surgery. Plus, he kept a research lab going, and he was no wimp at getting appropriations, either. Mandel couldn't be a dullard. What was wrong with the fellow? My nose plus my eagle eye said it wasn't drink.

Greg stared vacantly at Daniel for a few seconds. Daniel said, "Greg, is there anything wrong?"

"What? What's wrong?"

"That's what I said. Greg, this is me. Daniel. Are you in there?"

Mandel blinked, then smiled briefly, baring big, blocky teeth. Very briefly. "I'm sorry, Daniel. Just tired. I wasn't really paying attention."

"Go," Silverman said. "Lie in the sun. Rest."

Greg smiled sheepishly and stumbled off. I raised my eyebrows at Silverman.

"Something on his mind, I guess," Daniel said.

"I guess."

Bill Honeywell and Mary Shaughnessy lay on top of the cabin roof. They weren't exactly nuzzling. After all, they had been very carefully brought up. But they were sunning very, very close together. They talked quietly, desultorily, laughing a little now and then. At one point Bill seemed to be reciting something, song lyrics or poetry. Their soft murmur was very much like the susurration of the water slipping past the boat, their laughter like the occasional gurgle of a wave, the remnant of the wake of some unseen boat.

Forward of us there was livelier socializing. Takuro had taken over the supervision of the sheet, relieving Belinda Honeywell, who now lay on the foredeck in the sun. Takuro watched her as she dozed there, golden and relaxed. She had brought a big red sun hat for shade, but she was lying on top of it, face up to the sky. Twinkie had been sunning ever since we waved goodbye to the John Hancock Building. Bret Falcon, Broadway star, he of the good build and commanding profile, had taken up a well-selected spot. Right between the two women.

He wore only wraparound silver sunglasses and the briefest of men's bikinis, pure white, with some classy openwork on both side seams. The white went well with his tan. A store-bought tan, the reporter in me said, because the fellow had been tied to eight performances a week, including two matinees, and could hardly have been hanging out at the beach.

"And how long has that been?" Twinkie asked Bret. They were engaged in a conversation about his life and appeared to have arrived at his early twenties. Bret certainly warmed to the subject.

"Oh, then I went to New York. People say you should get experience in one of the smaller cities first, like San Francisco or Chicago, but I just couldn't see why."

"To get your feet wet before you hit the major critics, I suppose," Belinda Honeywell said. So she wasn't asleep.

"Sure! But there's plenty of off-Broadway houses where you can do that. I acted in some places that were so grotty, the critics pretended they couldn't find 'em. But you're right there in the city, and you can audition for major companies."

"You've really paid your dues, Bret," Twinkie said admiringly.

"I sure as hell have."

"And now you can cash in."

"Maybe. You never know with a movie. Movies are different. Plenty of Broadway stars fail in movies."

"Not you, dear. You photograph beautifully."

"That's not the whole battle," he said, accepting the compliment without a flicker of humility. "When you're onstage, you're in control. Not even the director is going to run onstage in the middle of a scene and yell 'Hold it! I don't want it done that way.' But with a movie, six months later when it comes out, you can discover that all your best scenes have been cut."

"They shouldn't be allowed to do that!"

"They can do absolutely *anything* they want. An older friend of mine, a man, got an important supporting role in a movie. When they were done filming, he thought he'd put in the best work he'd ever done. During the shooting he had a death scene that brought tears to the whole crew— the director, the cameramen, gaffers, lighting—everybody. A perfectly ultimate performance. He took all his friends to the opening. I mean, he was feeling great. Looking for a big future. And when it came on screen, *he wasn't in the movie!* They'd cut him."

"The death scene?"

"No. The *whole role!* Cut him while they were editing, because it was running too long."

"Omigod! What did he do?"

"Nothing he *could* do. He went back to the stage. He says he'd never do a film again, no matter what."

"Well, they sure can't do that to you. You're the star!"

"Right. Well. I hope it'll be okay. Plus, they have a good director lined up. I figure a great director is more likely to appreciate great acting."

At this note of none-too-subtle self-praise, Belinda glanced at Bret with a half smile on her lips. Twinkie, however, was nodding sagely, not an easy thing to do when you're lying flat on your back on the deck of a boat.

Takuro, keeping half an eye on the spinnaker, walked back and forth along the starboard side. He stared down into the water and appeared to be studying the way the wash that came back from the bow moved along the side of the boat. In the course of this, he came in our direction.

"Are you working when you should be relaxing?" Daniel asked.

"What? Oh—" Takuro smiled sheepishly.

I said, "Want to sit with us?"

Takuro sat.

"Whenever I get on a boat, it's kind of a busman's holiday," he said. "But it's not work. In fact, my work is more like play."

"Definition of a happy man," I said.

Takuro smiled and sipped his beer. "Yes, I think so. I'm very lucky. This is the most exciting time in the entire history of the world to design boats."

"I thought boats hadn't changed much in hundreds of years!" That seemed rude, so I started to backtrack. "I suppose new motors—"

Takuro wasn't annoyed. Spurred on, maybe. "Motors are the least of it. This is the first time in centuries there's a real revolution in shipbuilding. Two reasons. Aerospace analysis, which we now use to find the best shapes to move through a fluid medium. And space age materials."

"My oldest brother has a fiberglass canoe," I said. "It's practically indestructible. Fell off the car once."

My oldest brother is not the last of the big spenders, though he has occasionally been called the credit card that walks like a man.

"Exactly! Can you imagine what a 1700 shipbuilder would say if he saw fiberglass! He'd think it was a magical substance. To build a ship he had to first find an oak tree.

Then cut it. By hand, of course. Saw it. Plane it. Age the wood so it wouldn't warp. Fit it into the hull. And when you got it in the ship, cut, aged, sanded, sawed, planed, assembled, and caulked, it was still vulnerable to shipworm, warping, barnacles, dry rot, wet rot, swelling, shrinking— Lord!

"The thing about space age materials isn't just that they're easier to work with and don't rot. You have totally different potentials. They can be thin and yet strong. Pliable and still spring back to their original shapes. Lightweight but rigid. You can choose ones that conduct heat and ones that don't. They stand up to salt water and dry without cracking. So the number of shapes you can play around with has just, just—" he waved his hands—"just exploded!"

"Stop and breathe!" Silverman said.

Takuro laughed. "Think of polystyrene and urethane foam. You can pack the stuff in anyplace for flotation. The average small boat built today *can not sink!* Imagine that! Nobody seems aware of it, but it's revolutionary."

Chuck Kroop laughed hugely down in the galley; then his heavy feet came up the companionway. I looked back to see who was at the wheel. Will Honeywell. That was fine with me.

Chuck came forward, feet well apart as if he were on heavy seas. "Cat and Daniel and Takuro," he said, proving he remembered everybody's name. The fact that Takuro had been talking meant nothing to him. "Isn't this great!" he said, as if he had invited us personally.

"Great," Takuro and I said in unison.

"Sure is," said Silverman rather dryly.

"Where's your camera, Tak?" Chuck asked.

"My camera?"

"Sure. All the years I know you, you never carry a camera."

"I guess that's right."

"I thought all you Japanese people carried cameras. Maybe two or three. One on each shoulder and one in the middle. And light meters." Big booming laugh from Chuck. Takuro thought about it. "No," he said. "That's tourists."

"Tourists?"

"Tourists. They like to take pictures home. I'm not a tourist. I live here."

"Well, tell me this, then. Do you take a camera when you go there?"

"There?"

"Japan."

"I've never been to Japan."

"Never *been?*"

"I don't take that many vacations. When I do, I go to Florence."

"Florence?" Chuck shouted.

"Sure."

"When you could go to *Vegas?*"

The three of us stared at him.

Chuck rumbled away. "My favorite womenfolk!" he caroled, descending on Belinda, Twinkie, and Bret, oblivious of the fact that Bret was telling Twinkie about his early years in innovative Shakespeare. Belinda smiled courteously and Bret sat up.

"Hello, Mr. Kroop," he said, respectfully.

"None of that, my boy. Call me Chuck. Should have started it long ago. Although, I don't know. The minor members of the cast might have thought they could get familiar, too—hmm."

"They're all very profes—"

"Anyway, you and I have had months of profitable association. May it turn into years." He lifted his beer in salute.

"Yes, sir. Chuck," Bret said.

"Our next miracle will be the film of *Off and On*. And then—who knows?"

"Right, Mr.—Chuck. Who knows?" Bret said enthusiastically. Why did I get the feeling he was acting?

Chuck settled down next to Twinkie and Belinda. He had lots of black hairs on a white belly that bulged over his orange bathing suit.

"Tell me, Bret," he said. "All the time I know you, I guess we've been too busy for a good talk. Is Bret Falcon your real name or a stage name?"

"Oh, a stage name, of course," Bret answered so nonchalantly that anyone with a soul would have known he didn't want to discuss it. "About the film of *Off—*"

Anyone but Chuck. "So what is your real name, Bret?"

"Bret Falcon is my real name. I had it changed legally." At this point even a bag of cement would have guessed Bret didn't want to talk about it.

"Well, then, what was your *original* name?"

Twinkie giggled at Bret. She knew perfectly well he was stalling.

"I don't like to use it," Bret said, giving up all hope that Chuck would take a hint.

"Surely you can tell *us*, son. We're your friends!"

This, of course, was the inescapable appeal. Plus, Chuck was a major backer of Bret's play. Bret was caught, and he knew it. He tried to pass it off as a good joke.

"Dwayne Dummer." He chuckled manfully. "How about that?"

"Dummer!" Chuck guffawed. "Dwayne Dummer!"

Twinkie laughed with him. Belinda didn't. Bret laughed, but then, he's an actor.

"Kid," said Chuck. "You were smart. You made a helluva good move changing that name." He roared again.

Belinda said, "Chuck, it *was* his name, you know. I don't think it's so funny."

"Belinda, you gotta learn to get more amusement out of life. Dwayne Dummer! Ha! I can just see *that* on the marquee."

Belinda went below to see about lunch. Takuro went too, because he had a special dish to prepare. Daniel, Mary, Bill, and I all offered to help. Twinkie and Chuck didn't. Belinda thanked us but said with Emery they would have three in the galley, and three was absolutely the upper limit of people who could work there. Chuck shifted nearer to Twinkie and put his hand on her thigh.

Daniel said to me, "It's getting hot. Want to get on bathing suits?"

"Okay, if I can find a place to keep my notebook."

When we passed through the galley, I could see what Belinda had meant. Takuro had a long, razor-sharp roast knife in his hand and was slicing marinated beef into thin strips. Emery worked at a wooden board, set at an angle over the sink. There was a huge fish on the board, and as I watched, he brought a heavy cleaver down with a great *thwack*, hacking a steak from the fish. The *chunk!* sound reverberated off the walls. Belinda herself wielded a small vegetable knife, cutting melon into squares.

"You see?" she said. "If there was anybody else in here, we'd all be sliced to ribbons."

I changed in the cabin in the bow, the one with the V-berths. "Hey, Silverman," I said, coming out. "Aren't there nine berths aboard? Two in here, three in that dormitory there, and two in the master stateroom and two in that room next to it."

"Mmm. Right."

"Well, we've got twelve people. Where do they all sleep?"

"In sleeping bags laid on the bunks. No problem. After all, there'll never be fewer than three people on deck at night to handle the boat."

"At night? We sail at night? I thought we'd tie up at a dock and all go to sleep."

"Sailing at night is the most fun of all."

"Sure. I guess so."

"What's the trouble?"

"They have—the boat has lights, I suppose. So other boats can see us?"

"Yes, Cat. They have lights. And all the lights have to be in good working order, every single one of them, or you get your ship to a yard and have them fixed. The Coast Guard is very serious about boats having running lights at night."

"Good."

"That's too many pens," he said.

I had the notebook in the left side of my bikini bottom. The pens and pencils, just eight of them, were stuck in the cleavage of the bra for a quick draw. Well, where would you put them?

If they called this lunch, which they surely did, I couldn't wait to find out what they called dinner. They laid out a buffet on the counter in the galley: Takuro's beef on skewers for appetizers, which had been marinating at his house for three days and which he had brought as a kind of thank-you, salmon steaks grilled and served with capers and slices of lemon, a big bowl of watermelon, cantaloupe, and papaya cubes, hot rolls with sesame seeds, coffee, and white wine well chilled.

I made notes and then stuck the notepad in my bathing suit bottom. Which made me realize I had never researched a story in a bathing suit before.

Greg Mandel and his sister, Belinda, sat down to eat at the dinette table. Most of the others filled plates, took a cup or a glass, and went up on deck. Bill Honeywell had replaced his father at the wheel, and Mary made up his plate and hers and took them both up there, where they ate and snuggled together. The rest of us spread out around the foredeck in positions of repose.

You would think, with twelve people on a sailboat, the place would be crowded, but it wasn't. Twinkie and Chuck and Bret hung around the sheets to the spinnaker, ostensibly to help out. But the wind, still from the west, was dropping, and I couldn't imagine they expected a problem. Takuro, Daniel Silverman, and I sat amidships, and Takuro talked about the importance of keeping the cabin roof low, so that the person at the wheel could see over it. And the competing need for headroom in the galley and dinette below.

It was about this time that I realized something. Most of our group meandered around, more or less chatting with everybody over the course of time. But Dr. Greg Mandel and Chuck Kroop never exchanged a word, as far as I had seen. In fact, it seemed to me that Belinda arranged things to keep them apart. For instance, right now she was sitting below having lunch with Greg.

However, it was not my business. I was grateful again that I wasn't a gossip columnist.

Will Honeywell came and sat with us. I was content to watch the gulls overhead diving for fish and crying with frustration when the fish got away. They sounded like cats mewing. I was content to soak up the sun and eat my lunch and drink my wine. Come to think of it, I'm always content to eat. I said to Will Honeywell, "This is exactly the right way to live."

He smiled, settled back on his towel, and slowly nodded twice.

• 5 •

In midafternoon the breeze dropped away completely. The sky was almost white, a clear light blue at the zenith, with just a hint of copper to the east, where Michigan lay invisible. In the west, far down on the horizon, were clusters of white, rounded clouds, like a white forest seen at a distance.

The red-white-and-blue spinnaker hung in folds. Will ordered it taken down. He said you couldn't tell where the next breeze might come from, and he didn't want it to catch the spinnaker suddenly from the wrong direction.

For the same reason, they reefed the mainsail. Bill brought out a crank. This he inserted in a hole in the boom close to the mast, and turned. The whole mainsail started to sink slowly, rolled up inside like a window shade. In a few minutes there was nothing left of all those square feet of canvas but a tiny triangular tip sticking out near the mast.

I made a note of it.

Twinkie asked Will, "Weren't we going to have dinner in Michigan City?"

"Yes, and we'll make it, too. We can motor in if we have to. We can't be more than ten or eleven miles out right now."

"Then let's swim," said Bill. "Mary'd like a swim."

I looked around. The boat stood still. I was hot. Everybody was hot. The lack of breeze, the sun reflecting from the white deck and from the water all around—I felt grilled. But would they swim in the middle of nowhere? With nothing to put their feet down on? There was no land in sight, no other boat, nothing to see but the sky, the water, the sun, and the *Easy Girl.*

"It's okay with me, as long as you take precautions," Will said. A man after my own heart. "Anyone who can't swim well has to wear a life jacket. Period. Nobody farther than fifty feet from the boat." He grinned at everyone, softening his tone. "Sorry to be Captain Bligh, but we've never had an accident aboard the *Easy Girl,* and we never will have if I can help it."

Emery ran to get the ladder, which he hooked over the coaming and tied on. Bill removed a section of the lifeline at the same spot. It was the place on the port side where we had stepped aboard the boat from the dinghy.

Bret Falcon stood on the deck, looked around, possibly to see whether any of the women were watching, took a deep breath that puffed up his chest nicely, and dove in.

Twinkie hurried over to watch when he came up.

"Wow! It's cold!" he yelled.

"About sixty degrees," Bill Honeywell said laconically.

"Not bad for this far out," Belinda said. "The warmer surface water usually blows over to Michigan."

I turned to Will. Twinkie was already easing her body down the side, shrieking, and Mary and Bill had leaped over her in flat, racing dives.

"Is this safe?" I asked.

"Oh, sure. With precautions, of course."

"Like everything in sailing?"

"That's about right. Let me show you something."

We were standing in the cockpit, and he took me to the stern, to lean over the transom. Affixed to the outside of the stern were two bright yellow life preservers. He patted one.

"These are always within reach of the person at the wheel. You see? If somebody goes overboard, the man at the wheel jerks this out fast and throws it backward. If the boat is moving, you can't stop it instantly. The life preserver is on a hundred-foot line and floats back from the boat, staying near the person in the water."

"I like it."

"So—if we got a sudden wind, I would throw these overboard first thing."

"But why would we move in a wind? There's no sail up."

"Oh, even a boat by itself with no sail catches some wind. It wouldn't start moving fast, but it might pull away from a weak swimmer."

"You're not going to swim, are you? You're staying to watch?"

"Absolutely. I promise."

Still, I hung back.

"How strong a swimmer are you?" Will asked.

"I can't swim."

"At all?"

"At all."

He blinked, as if he'd never met a person who couldn't swim. Maybe he hadn't. I didn't know what to do, and was thinking seriously about getting out one of the books I'd brought when Daniel touched my arm. He carried a pink-and-yellow life jacket.

"You'll float like a cork," he said.

"Oh. Okay."

I crept little by little down the ladder. The water felt icy cold.

"That's the painful way," said Daniel, and he dove. He came up eight feet out, shaking water out of his hair. "Not bad at all."

By now I had got as far as my armpits, so I struck out away from the boat. I noticed Emery standing on the coaming amidships, holding a round life preserver, which he evidently meant to throw at anybody in trouble. Honeywell wasn't taking any chances. He himself was watching the flag and the burgee at the masthead for the first sign of a breeze.

I floated like a cork. True. No problem. Then I looked down.

Over the bulge of the life preserver, I could see my feet dangling down. They hung there as if they were suspended in space. Below them, the water went on down and down and down.

And down and down and down.

I pictured myself sinking through that clear water. Down, falling slowly, turning over and over, slowly. Hair trailing like seaweed. Sinking beyond the sun's rays, into the twilight, deep down. Then darker and darker, sinking slowly into eternal gloom. Settling softly into the sandy bottom in the dark, cold—the dark cold—

My teeth chattered. I thought I was going to be sick.

Somebody grabbed my arm.

"Cat! Hey!" It was Daniel.

I couldn't speak, my teeth chattered so violently. I tried to control it, but I couldn't. He put his arms around me and hugged tight.

"See, it's okay," he said. He hugged tighter, burying my head under his chin. "You're not alone. I'm solid. You're floating. You can't sink."

Still, I shook. Still, he held me. "Don't look down. Look at the boat. Look at the sky."

I pulled my head back and looked at the sky.

"Now take a breath." He let me go, but kept an arm around my waist. I held onto his shoulder. "Take a slower, deeper breath," he said.

It helped.

"Again."

After a minute, he said, "Do you want to go back in the boat? I'll help you if you do."

Boy, did I want to! I said, "No. I'm gonna stay here."

"Tell me if you change your mind."

"I'll just—I won't look down."

He studied me a couple of seconds. I was challenging myself and he knew it, of course. And went with it. Not bossy, not demanding. A good man.

Belinda came to the edge of the deck with an inflatable ball and two nets on floats. She threw the ball to Daniel and dropped the nets overboard. Then she jumped in, Chuck Kroop after her, making a big splash, and Takuro after him, diving like a pro, no splash at all. Greg Mandel, who had got into the water while I wasn't watching, yelled "Water polo!"

"You take one team," Belinda shouted at Greg, "and Daniel can captain the other. Chuck, you and I and Bill can go with Daniel—"

Was she keeping Greg and Chuck separate again? Twinkie, Mary, and Takuro got on Greg's team. Bret decided to go with Twinkie, so I wound up with Daniel, who had joked that they might use me for a goal post if they didn't have an even number of people.

Twinkie and Belinda were goalies. So it was Mary, Takuro, Twinkie, Greg, and Bret against Chuck, Bill, Belinda, Daniel, and me. Daniel and Greg Mandel both showed absolutely ferocious hitting arms. You'd have thought the ball would rip open when they surged up out of the water and blasted it. Maybe surgery requires more strength than I realized. Twinkie reached to fend the ball away from her goal, lost the top of her suit, shrieked, missed the ball grabbing for her suit top, and pulled the suit up, giggling. This was really a stellar performance, since they were all treading water, and she had nothing to stand on. Oddly, the same thing happened every time she reached for the ball. Bret showed nice form, swimming on his stomach and slapping the ball toward the goal accurately with one hand. Mary and Bill, on opposing teams, lunged for the ball at the same moment and bumped their heads together. They fell into each other's arms, laughing, and forgot to tread water, sank,

and came up coughing and laughing and sneezing. Meanwhile, Takuro deftly flipped the ball away from them and
made a goal, right past our goalie, Belinda, who was usually
alert but was laughing along with Bill and Mary. I made a
major coup when, in a confusion of slippery bodies, I seized
the ball and submerged it beneath me. Then, looking around
innocently, as if I didn't know any more than the others
where it had gone, I made my way to the goal. Twinkie
shrieked when the ball bobbed up underneath her. She lost
the top of her suit again, and I made a goal. My team
cheered me.

I never once looked down into the water.

With no bottom to stand on, the game exhausted people
quickly. They had to keep afloat and high enough in the
water to get the ball. Twinkie, who didn't have much pad-
ding and had spent a lot of energy in dramatics, got cold
first and climbed the ladder.

Then we discovered that no one had been keeping score.
A little friendly bickering took place as Chuck and Belinda
and Bill and Mary rehashed the major events, trying to
decide who had won. Daniel finally remarked that it was
better not to know, and since by then half the swimmers
had left the water, it ended like that, everyone pink and
invigorated, laughing and content. Bret Falcon was the last
out of the water. When he got to the rail he leaned back and
shook the water out of his hair, looking like Prince Valiant.

Emery had hot coffee ready on the stove. He remarked that
there was some instant cocoa somewhere, but nobody took
him up on it. There was a lot of good-natured back-chat in
the rooms, with several people of different sexes trying to
get dry in the same small area. But most everybody simply
dried the exposed skin, took a mug of coffee, and went back
out on the warm deck to let their suits dry off in the sun.

I sat in the sun and made extensive notes. Water polo out of sight of land was exactly the kind of detail I needed for the article. It seemed that this piece might be one of the easy ones that almost write themselves.

Daniel said nothing about my panic attack. Neither did I. I was ashamed of myself.

It's amazing how time passes when you're lolling around on a yacht in the sun. The very next thing I knew, it was the cocktail hour.

I heard the clinking of pitchers and stirrers and ice cubes and decided maybe I'd been asleep a little while. I was lying on my back on a towel. Up on the bare mast the club burgee hung limp. Then, as if my gaze had disturbed it, it stirred. I looked, and it flapped gently once more.

"Will!" I called, sitting up. "I think we've got a breeze."

But it was Belinda at the wheel. She had been talking with her brother, Greg, who stood near her with a plastic highball glass in his hand. She looked up the mast.

"Great! You're right."

Will Honeywell turned out to have been lounging not two feet away from me, with his legs dangling overboard. He smiled. "We'll make a sailor of you. I can tell."

"Maybe."

Greg moved forward to the boom and ran up the mainsail. Belinda called for the spinnaker, since whatever breeze there was seemed very light.

"I think it's moved a little north of west," she called to her husband.

Chuck and Bill Honeywell got the spinnaker. They had the whisker in a different position, Chuck struggling to put it into place. When they got it rigged, even I could see that the spinnaker stood out a little differently from the way it had in the morning. Chuck tied off his sheet. He turned and planted his feet, evidently convinced that he had done enough work for the day. "Emery!" he called.

The kid poked his head up from the companionway, starting up the stairs.

"Yes, sir?"

"Get me a highball, willya?"

"Right away."

I glanced at Belinda. For a second I thought she was looking at me. But she wasn't—it was Will, next to me, and she raised her eyebrows at him. Neither one said anything, but it was pretty obvious that they felt ordering someone else's employees about was very bad form.

As Emery came up with the highball in its clear plastic glass, ice clinking, garnished with a twist of lemon peel, Belinda, at the wheel, caught his eye. She smiled at him and mouthed the word, "Thanks."

Unaware, Chuck took his highball and flopped down near Mary. Bill, who was left to watch both spinnaker sheets alone, frowned slightly.

From where I was lying, head fore and feet aft, it was easier to look at the stern and Belinda in the cockpit than anywhere else. As I watched, she crooked her finger. I turned to look at Will, assuming she was communicating with him again.

"No, silly. Not him, you."

I got up briskly and jumped down into the cockpit. Slipped on some water left by the swimmers and fetched up sitting on one of the water polo balls, then rolled off. Plop.

"No harm done." I laughed.

She laughed and said, "Good girl, Cat. You're fun to have around." Then she beckoned me over, took her hands from the wheel and put mine on it.

"Me? But I don't know how."

"You will in a minute. Go ahead. Steer."

"All right."

"The breeze is five miles an hour, tops. What can go wrong?"

Everything, I thought. "I don't know what can go wrong. That's why I could be dangerous." But I put both hands on the wheel and stood, head up, watching eagle-eyed over our bow.

"I'm not going to abandon you," Belinda said. "If you get worried, I'll take over."

But in fact, it was easy. The breeze was light and didn't shift or zoom in from odd places, somebody else had set the sails and set them properly for the quarter the wind was in, so it was utterly baby stuff, but I felt good anyway. She pointed at the compass.

"We're heading east southeast. ESE. You see that."

"Yes."

"Now turn, just ever so slightly, to port. No, a little more than *that*. Don't worry. We won't capsize."

I turned. The compass swung in its watery plastic case and said E.

"See? Now take us back."

I found ESE again. And held her there.

"If there were big waves," she said, "coming over your bow, say, starboard, they would swing you slightly to port each time. And each time you would just compensate."

"Yes, I see."

The breeze was from the northwest, we were heading just south of east, and the sail was in the position I think they call a beam reach.

"Now, did you notice that when you turned east, the sail wasn't quite as tight?"

"No. I didn't."

"Well, try it again. And watch."

I did. Heading due east, the sail wavered a little.

"What we do if we want to go east in this wind is just pull the main in a little. That puts it in the same position relative to the wind that it was when the boat was going more to the south."

"I think I've got that. What I really don't understand is how you tack upwind."

"Well, we can't do that now, or we'd wind up back in Chicago and miss dinner besides. But you can see that tonight."

"What do we do tonight?"

"Head for Holland and Grand Haven. You can tack to within about forty-five degrees of the wind, and that's just what we plan to do. Head due north into a stiffening north-west breeze."

"Oh," I said. "Goody."

◇ 6 ◇

It was five-thirty when the tallest smokestacks of Michigan City, Indiana, began to rise out of the lake. We were still a few miles off, but Belinda took the wheel back from me. This made sense. There was now a scattering of other boats and one very large freighter in sight, and I didn't know anything about right-of-way. It's not like driving a car; out here they play by different rules.

She had me get out the chart. She said they always did that coming into port, regardless of how familiar they were with the place, except for Chicago, since they were *too* familiar with that. The chart was a very large sheet of heavy paper rolled up, and I had to weight down one corner with my drink and hold the others with my hands and elbow.

Belinda told me to study the chart and see how much information it told you about the port. "Compare it with what you're seeing."

She was right. The smokestacks were exactly where the chart said they'd be, and in the same pattern, one in front, with a fixed red light on it, and a cluster behind. The flashing-red and flashing-white channel markers were there, too.

The chart gave the depth of the water, fifty-five feet where we were now, but shoaling up quickly to thirty, then fifteen, then six, except in the channel.

Bret Falcon leaped to the bow and shouted "*Land ho!*" striking a pose like Errol Flynn in *Captain Blood*—with wraparound sunglasses, of course. He was kidding, but he must have realized that on him it looked good.

Then he started singing "Sailing, sailing, over the bounding main." It's a singsong sort of tune, but he did it Broadway-baritone style, with rousing emphasis, as if he were calling all the rabble of Paris together to march with him to defeat Burgundy. The power of his voice was amazing. And no matter how silly the words, they blew me away when he belted them out. I realized something I had not really absorbed before, what with Bret's being the same size as the rest of us and all. This man was a star.

We were near the diagonal breakwater now. Slowly the main breakwater crept into view behind it, a long, low, concrete structure almost perpendicular to the outer one, lying along the bend of the channel and with a second bend at the end, just as the chart said. I looked closer at the chart and saw that the water behind the outer breakwater was only seven feet deep, but that the channel was eighteen feet all the way in, past the marina and up to the freight yards.

"This thing's wonderful!" I said to Belinda, and to Will, who had joined her. "I could do it myself."

"Well, not this time," he said. "But you can probably tell me what we're going to do now."

"Take down the spinnaker, reef the main, and start the auxiliary engine," I burbled.

"Quick study," said Will, really pleased. Most people with a consuming hobby are eager to convert you. I'd had an enthusiastic woman try to convert me to breeding beagles once, but that hadn't been a take.

Bill Honeywell, Emery, Dr. Mandel, and Mary were standing by the spinnaker and main.

"Take down the spinnaker!" Will called. "Reef the main." He was intentionally using my exact words. It was a nice gesture. If I had come out looking to see whether rich yachtsmen had class, Will had class.

He started the engine.

It all went like a countdown. The sails vanished. The engine purred, and the instant we were ready to enter the Michigan City channel, we were under power and moving smoothly along behind a big motor yacht.

There was an incident as we motored in that surprised me a little. Chuck had finished his second or third highball, leaning negligently on the cabin trunk. He popped a small ice cube in his mouth and tossed the plastic glass over the side. I was not pleased, but Mary Shaughnessy looked at him as if he were a child and said, "Don't do that" in a very firm, almost hostile, tone of voice.

I was surprised because, up to now, Mary had hardly said a word, if you don't count whispering and talking softly with Bill.

"Why not?" said Chuck, just to be belligerent.

"It's littering. That stuff never breaks down. It just hangs around and washes up on the beaches."

"Ah, everybody does it," said Chuck.

Of course, this is the time-tested defense for any sort of stupid behavior. Mary didn't fall for it. She had the perfect answer, and it stopped him cold.

"*You*," she said, "should know better."

As this is halfway to being a compliment, he did not know what to say. In fact, it occurred to me that Chuck was maybe not too bright. He turned around and saw Takuro and me looking at him. Somehow he must have thought we felt Mary had spoken to him too sharply, because he barked at us: "It's okay. I think it's cute when girls have strong opinions."

At this, Mary's eyes turned up in her head. Bill Honeywell passed his hand nervously over his hair. Then he took Mary's hand and they went below.

The restaurant was exactly what you'd expect at a marina: you walk up creaking, creosoted planks to reach the front door. The railings are hawsers, knotted around wooden pilings eighteen inches in diameter, roughly the kind of thing you would use to make sure the *Queen Elizabeth II* didn't drift out to sea. The door is made of tarred planking, and for a window—you guessed it, folks—a brass-framed porthole. Inside it's so dark your eyes take fifteen minutes to adjust. On the tables are kerosene ship's lanterns, circa 1870. Hanging from the ceiling are ship's wheels, studded with light bulbs so dim that you can barely see the bulb, much less use its light to illuminate your menu.

Dividing the reception area from the tables in this particular restaurant was rigging, the kind they used to climb up to see if they'd found any whales yet. As the young woman in a navvy's garb led us to our table, all of us bumping into each other and chairs in the dark, we passed another room divider, setting off the bar from the rest of the place. It was made of a trawling net, studded with cork floats the size of typewriters. It did very little to muffle the sounds of revelry from the bar.

The table we were shown to, previously reserved for Mr. Honeywell, was separated from the rest of the area by a brass rail and a peculiar object: a column of wood a foot thick, brass-bound, with a brass-rimmed compass set into the top of it.

Protruding from the wall over our table was a figurehead like the old sailing ships used to have. But not just the head. It was the whole upper body of a well-nourished young woman in clinging blue draperies, carved from a piece of oak the size of a Toyota.

I was about to say this place was fun, when Twinkie said, "This place is terribly ersatz."

And of course it was, if that was important. But since she was a guest, it didn't seem very polite for her to say so. Twinkie looked at Bret for support.

"Plastic place, do you think?" Bret said doubtfully. He wanted to please her, but he didn't want to offend Will, either. Belinda seemed to have stiffened.

"Watch it with that word 'plastic,' " said Dr. Greg Mandel. "Chuck here's built a fortune on the stuff. Plastic dinette sets from Paramus, New Jersey, to San Luis Obispo."

"Now, wait—" Chuck began, and Belinda said, "Chuck, he's not—" but Daniel was louder than everybody for once, and he headed off the argument.

"Sure, it's fake," he said. "Why not? The scenery in a play isn't real, either, and it's all the more fun because somebody made it exaggerated. You don't seriously expect an authentic old English sailing ship to be beached in Indiana, do you? It wouldn't make a very convenient dining room if it was. Or very sanitary, either, I expect."

"No, you're right," Bret said. He didn't know whether he was being argued with or agreed with.

"And you certainly don't want a genuine roadside stop—burger, fries, and a Coke. I like hawsers and pilings, and I like the lady over your head. I say, enjoy!"

Right on, babe, I thought. We're with you.

"My sentiments exactly," said Will. The waiter was poised at his elbow. "What'll you have to drink?"

So we all had drinks. We'd just had a two-hour cocktail hour on board, but who's counting? I noticed that Daniel, who had had a scotch on board, ordered ginger ale, but I didn't think anything of it at the time. It's one thing to notice and another thing to understand.

We were at a big round table. Belinda had got herself and Will between Greg and Chuck, confirming my suspicions, but nobody else appeared to notice. We were very jolly. The drinks came. We laughed over all sorts of idiotic things. The fact that nobody could remember the score of the water polo game. The fact that everybody was starving again after a huge lunch.

I pointed to the compass on the stand next to us.

"What *is* that?"

Everybody laughed. "It's a binnacle," Will said.

Takuro said, "In the old days, it was a capital offense for a seaman to tamper with a binnacle. Their lives depended on it."

"So they kept it on a pinnacle," I said.

"You wouldn't want barnacles on your binnacle," Daniel said.

Everyone was laughing again.

Takuro said, "You have to be finical about your binnacle."

"Don't be cynical."

"Too clinical."

"A barnacled binnacle would have too many particles on the pinnacle."

They were giggling and roaring, and so was I, for that matter. The truth was, we all felt like the very devil of fine fellows. We had sailed all the way here from Chicago over open seas, never mind that it was only thirty-five miles with a gentle breeze. We had hit our port of call precisely. We'd swum and sunned and were a little sunburned—not badly, just enough to tingle a little—and we all felt just fine. They went on with the jokes, sillier and sillier, until the steak and lobsters came. At which point Bill Honeywell said, "I can't remember what I ordered," and we laughed some more at that. Then they tucked into dinner as if threatened by scurvy. And so did I.

We were eating our surf and turf when a couple dressed in the finest of designer denim passed by. The woman got two feet away and then did a double take and turned back.

"Are you," she said with awe, "Bret Falcon?"

Bret stood up. He said yes he was. He said it very nicely.

"I *knew* it." She grabbed the man with her. "I knew it!"

"You sure did." The man with her nodded courteously to us and turned to leave.

The woman was the tanned, hazelnut-brown type you see in marinas and golf clubs, leathery and wrinkled, but she looked as though she'd had fun. She went right on talking.

"We saw you in *Off and On* when we were in New York last month. You were just as good as everybody said. Just *won*derful! The reviews in the *Times* and *Variety* were absolutely right!"

"Well, thank you very much," Bret said. He was still standing and didn't know how to get rid of them and sit back down. "These gentlemen are the producers of the show. Mr. Honeywell and Mr. Kroop. They gave me my big break."

What had been happening was this: the longer the woman stood there, the more men got up from their seats. First Bret, because he'd been spoken to, then Will, probably because he was the host. Then Daniel and Takuro about twenty seconds later. Then Bill. Then Greg Mandel. Finally, Chuck Kroop.

By this time the woman's escort could see there was plenty of disruption being caused. He said, "Awfully good performance, Mr. Falcon. Good luck in your career. Now, let's not keep these people on their feet." He moved determinedly away. His wife had to follow.

"Goodbye,"she said regretfully. "Take care of that beautiful voice."

I wondered at this remark until I realized her own voice had a marked whisky baritone.

"God! What a bore!" said Chuck, flopping back down.

Will said, "Hey! It's people like that who buy tickets and keep the show running."

"Obviously, but we don't have to entertain them personally."

"That woman is going to tell all her friends she met Bret, and she's going to suggest they see the show."

"Suggest, hell! Demand! Oh, well." He turned to Bret. "Get used to it. After my next move, you're going to be a household word."

Takuro, mystified by this, looked from Chuck to Bret. Chuck's primary business was furniture, not plays. Plus, the play was doing well without a "next move." I felt tension at the table, as if it were a sudden change of air pressure.

"I don't understand," Takuro said to Bret. "Aren't you staying in *Off and On*?"

"Yes, I'm—"

"I'm flying him back for the matinee Wednesday in the Learjet," Chuck said. He leaned back and smoothed a hand down his paunch. "But our boy here is going to be a major film star. You don't ever really make it big just by making it on the Broadway stage."

"What about Geraldine Page?" Bret said. "What about Julie Harris and—"

I liked him for arguing that there was life outside of Hollywood. But his voice was swamped by Chuck's. Bret might reach the back row in a fidgety matinee audience, but Chuck's was the voice that made machine shops fall in line.

"They're minor league!" he said. "When they go to

Hollywood, what becomes of them? Supporting players! And when it comes to the big bucks, *no contest!*"

Mary Shaughnessy and Bill Honeywell had established their own quiet spot, where they talked, withdrawn from the rest of us. So I was surprised when Bill said, "But Mr. Kroop, you've made millions from the Broadway production."

I hadn't even known he was listening.

"Couple million. Couple million," Chuck said negligently. "Over two years. Know what *E.T.* made the summer it came out? Fifteen million a week! Top Broadway plays take in maybe four hundred thousand a week. Gross, no net. Difference?"

"Yeah," said Bill sullenly, "that is a difference."

Bill's mother looked at him, wondering at his tone. So did I. The kid was usually the height of courtesy.

"People," said Mary Shaughnessy, "should not make fifteen million a week. There's no way they've earned it."

Okay. Bill was uneasy with the talk about big money because Mary didn't like it. Belinda could see this clearly enough, too, and I'm sure she anticipated a debate about social policy, graduated income tax, socialism, estate taxes, and God knows what all else, because she tried to head them off.

"I wonder how many of you have to work Monday," she said. "We thought we might try to see the fireworks at Holland and go on to Grand Haven afterward."

If this was a subtle effort, Chuck did not respond to it. Not responding to subtlety was definitely chronic with Chuck.

He said in a great, big, fatherly voice, "Well, kids, you don't get sixty-foot yachts selling encyclopedias door to door." Which is true. But in this company, not nice.

Mary and Bill both started talking, but Will had thought of something that *did* deflect Chuck.

"I still say we ought to take the Charisma Productions offer."

"Not on your life!" Chuck bellowed. "What they're offering isn't diddly squat compared to what we could make if we own the whole thing."

"*Could* make. That's the point. They know how to produce movies. We don't. They know how to distribute movies. We don't. Even when you know how, it's a damned big gamble."

Takuro asked, "This amount, this diddly squat, is certain? No risk?"

"Oh, it's certain. They just pay us for the property," Will said. Chuck cut him off.

"They pay us zip! Zilch! Two, four. That's what they want to buy us out for. Two, four."

"Two, four what?" I asked. I didn't understand.

"Two million four hundred thousand," Chuck said. "Have you ever *heard* of such a thing?"

Well, I hadn't, actually. But while to him I guess it looked microscopically small, to me it was more money than I could mentally grasp. I'm kind of in the range of dithering over whether to buy a six-pack of beer or splurge on a bottle of Gallo.

Will was silent. I was beginning to pick up on some of the things I had come on this trip to learn. How did these people, really rich, seriously rich people, behave? What did their money mean to them?

I had done my homework on the Honeywells before I left home.

Will was old money. His father's father had founded his furniture business, and while Will had been something of a genius building it up and modernizing it, there had been money in his family for generations. Old money doesn't talk about money.

According to Daniel Silverman, Chuck was new money. New money apparently talks about money. It doesn't think money is vulgar. It thinks it's excellent. Chuck believed that the money he had made was a confirmation of his intrinsic worth as a human being. Which was why Will's next remark and Chuck's next remark were right in character.

"We were very lucky with *Off and On* in New York," Will said. "It could have flopped. Hey!—I know the show was good, and Bret was wonderful. But good shows can flop. It happens all the time. There are no guarantees in theater. We were very lucky, and we might not be so lucky with a film."

"Dammit, Will! That show was a success because we *made* it a success. We picked the property, and we got the right team together, and then we marketed it right. A movie is no goddamn different."

Chuck, having had almost overnight success with his furniture company, riding the crest of a trend toward cheap, light, movable, indestructible furniture for schools and offices, thought his success meant he couldn't fail. Will, on the other hand, knew about the ups and downs the furniture business had taken in his grandfather's day and his father's day—the 1929 crash, the quick changes of fashion after World War II. He knew about riding out recession and changes of taste. He knew about irrationality in the marketplace, overextending when times seemed good, and simple bad luck. He knew there were no guarantees.

"Two million four hundred thousand dollars," Mary said to Chuck, "for doing nothing?"

"Doing nothing? You *kidding*? For developing the play in the first place. For taking the risk! For making it a hit! You think that doesn't take work?"

"I think it doesn't take two million four hundred thousand dollars worth of work."

"Well, it really isn't that much. Will and I have to split it." Chuck guffawed so loudly at this sally that other diners looked at us to see what the joke was.

I heard Mary mutter to Bill, "Brings it down to what he would call one, two."

"Stamp money," Bill said, and they both giggled. I could tell from the motion of their arms that he had taken hold of her hand under the table. Belinda smiled at them.

"Can't you compromise?" Daniel asked Will.

"Charisma wants to buy it outright. That's fair, I think. You can imagine they wouldn't want two coproducers hanging around with different ideas from theirs. And personally, I wouldn't want to have an interest in something if I didn't have any power over decisions."

"Now wait a minute—" Chuck said, but Daniel, playing peacemaker, said to Belinda,

"How'd two furniture people get into plays, anyhow?"

"Chance," she said. "Will and Chuck and I and Chuck's ex-wife, Adriana, were in San Francisco at a furniture convention. We got bored with the convention and went out on the streets. We went into a place where we heard music, but the topless women bothered Adriana. So we went into a place with young comics, but Chuck didn't understand them—"

"I under*stood* them," Chuck said. "They just weren't funny."

"—but they weren't funny. So we went to the next thing along the street, which turned out to be an underground theater. I don't mean the material was bizarre; the actual theater was in the basement. One of those places where you go down damp cement stairs full of rubbish and sit on the floor. Adriana thought it was dirty. Not the play, the floor."

"It was dirty."

"It was dirty. But it was a surprisingly charming musical comedy. You expected something incomprehensible. Actors making believe they're sponges or songs about what it's like to be a big toe. We talked with the author and the composer. One was selling tickets and the other was the usher. We got to thinking—we're in New York a lot, as it is, for business. Why not do a little play, maybe off Broadway?"

I made a mental note, being too polite to take out a note-book during dinner. Rich people can say "Why not do a little play?"

Will said, "But what happened was, next time we were in New York, we looked at Off Broadway theaters. And you can't make a profit in them. The costs of mounting a show in a small house are less than in a big house, but they're still so high that you need more than a hundred and fifty or two hundred seats to break even. There are Off Broadway houses where you could play to capacity crowds every single performance and still lose money. It's like selling all you can make of a product and still running in the red. So we went to a Broadway house.

"We hired a theatrical management company," Belinda said. "And a director. And he picked the choreographer and the musical director—"

Chuck interrupted. "But not until we'd talked with them and saw we could work with them. Belinda, I think you're playing down the amount of research we did. We didn't just hire a director and he brought in all his friends. We checked everything out and made all the decisions ourselves."

"And the show went on, and all lived happily ever after?" Takuro asked.

"Well, no, it wasn't that easy," Belinda said. "Halfway through rehearsals the director fired the choreographer. The choreographer had been having an affair with one of the supporting actors, who then went into a nervous fit and developed hives. The new choreographer didn't have enough time to fix things. We had to open in Boston because we had paid for the tryout theater, so we did, and got ghastly reviews and lost a quarter of a million dollars in three weeks, and the musical director quit in a huff because the director cut the one song he had added to the show. The day we moved the set and costumes to New York, there was a fire in the theater. The scenery didn't burn, I'm glad to say, but we had ozone

machines on for the next two weeks of previews to get the
smell of scorched leather and burned carpeting out."

"We were thinking of calling the show *Fire Sale*," Will said,
"if we had to open smelling that way."

I said, "Or *Smokey and the Baritone*."

As we made our way to the door, several other customers
waved at the Honeywells or stopped them to talk. Will and
Belinda seemed to know everybody. I suppose that's natural.
The owners of yachts the size of Will's must be few in number.
They probably tie up at all the same marinas around the lakes.
Note for article: yacht owners are a small, gossipy club.

One of them said, "Cold front coming in."

Will rubbed his hands together with glee. "Great!"

Outdoors it was still an hour or so to sunset. In Michigan
City in July sunset is about a quarter of ten. The day was late
and golden. The boats in the marina were the color of straw,
gilded with gold highlights, and the masts were brassy against
the darker eastern sky.

For just a second before I stepped back onto the boat, I
had a moment's qualm.

"They're predicting strong winds tonight," Takuro said. "We
ought to make good time."

Well, I had to get back aboard or look like a chicken.

Far in the west, still below the level of the sinking sun, the
cloud line had grown larger. A few of the clouds reached above
the others with heads flat and anvil-shaped, piercing white in
the light of the sun that was setting down above them.

· 7 ·

When we'd left the boat to go to the restaurant, the lifeline had been festooned from bow to stern with drying towels and bathing suits. When we got back from dinner, all this had disappeared. Down below, all the bathing suits, dry and neatly folded, were waiting on the dinette table for their owners to claim them. I glanced in the head, and there on the rack was a big pile of towels, fluffy and dry. Royal blue, by the way. Emery must have spent the whole time in the marina laundromat.

Emery also had a pot of hot coffee steaming on the galley stove and the brandy bottle out, ringed with brandy glasses. It was hard to say whether he was an overworked slave or a highly competent and appreciated craftsman. He looked happy. His crisply curling dark hair was neatly combed. He was dressed in a blue-and-white striped fisherman's jersey, and he was smiling as he took real cream out of the refrigerator.

Belinda was at the wheel, driving one-handed and holding a coffee mug in the other, backing away from the dock as Bill and Emery cast off. When she first started the engine it had sputtered a bit, then caught. Some people on neighboring boats waved, and one shouted that they would see us in Grand Haven. Another said something about racing us to Big Sable Light, whatever that may have been, but it didn't matter, because Will called back that we were cruising, not racing.

Will pointed out that the wind was coming from northwest and we were going out of the channel to the northwest, and that was why you had to have an auxiliary engine. "Plus, you can't tack in a channel that's a hundred feet wide with a boat that's over sixty feet long," he said. That seemed obvious enough to me. I must be learning something.

Emery went back to ask Belinda what the problem starting the engine had been.

"I don't know. It just took a couple of times to catch." She took a sip of her coffee. "This is good," she said. He smiled.

"I'd like to take a look at the engine," he said.

"You're right. Greg, would you come and take the wheel?"

Greg Mandel went aft to the cockpit and took the helm, while Emery threw open a trapdoor in the cockpit floor. I walked back to take a look.

They kept the engine just about as spotless as they kept the head and the galley. I must say that I found that reassuring.

With the trapdoor open, the noise of the engine was much louder, as loud as any outboard motor. Takuro must have been good at his soundproofing. Belinda stood back to let me look in. It sounded to me as if the thing was running smoothly now. After a minute or so, I got out of their way and went back to Will in the bow.

"That smells like diesel, not gasoline," I said. I had done a series on truckers and truck stops the previous fall.

"It is. I'm more comfortable with diesel. Gasoline is just too explosive. There are too many boat fires for my taste."

"Mine, too."

"Your chances of drowning while sailing are less than being killed by a boat fire."

"You certainly keep the engine clean."

"People let gasoline accumulate in the bilge water, they

smoke around it, spill gas—you'd be amazed what people
will do in a boat."

"Not after seeing what they do on land."

From the galley, I heard the radio tuned to a weather
broadcast. Cold front coming and rising winds. Small craft
advisories. But how cold could it get in the middle of July?
At the moment there was only a nice breeze, a little stronger
than we had during the day, but not really windy. In the
west, though, the anvil-topped clouds had grown taller.

Thunderheads.

Chuck came strolling along the foredeck, side by side with
Twinkie Mandel, toward the bow, where Will and I stood.
She was wearing her dinner outfit: a silk blouse the color of
spring violets, designer pants in white, and her dinner jewelry, amethysts in a choker for her neck, amethysts in cres-
cent shapes for her ears. Chuck's hand patted her on the
rump as they walked. I knew that Greg Mandel was at the
wheel and therefore looking forward. He must have seen
them, and he may have seen me glance at them. So I was
careful to resist the impulse to look at him to find out what
his reaction was.

Chuck put his arm around Twinkie's shoulders. That was
better. More of a buddy-buddy gesture.

Half a mile from the marina we were out of the dogleg
channel, outside the breakwater, and in thirty feet of water.
Belinda asked Greg, still at the helm, whether he wanted
the main.

"Sure. Run her up."

July Fourth weekend or not, there was far less boat traffic
here than in Chicago. Of course, some of the traffic would
have been daysailors, small boats now comfortably in their
home port or tied up for the night in a marina. Lucky devils.

Takuro and Belinda ran up the main. Belinda had pulled

in the sheet, so that when the main got to the top of the mast, the boom was in the place they wanted it, and except for a couple of snaps as the sail filled, there was no swing.

But as the wind filled it, the whole deck tipped over. I grabbed for the lifeline, put one hand on the companionway rail, planted my feet wide apart, and fixed my eyes on the life preserver.

The wind was from the north northwest. The boat was heading a touch east of north, or beating, as they called it, with the sail hauled close, the boom running almost along the long axis of the boat. The speed was amazing.

Takuro and Will came to see if I was all right.

I asked Will, "Why are we going so much faster? The wind's not that much stronger."

"This afternoon we just had push," Will said.

"Well, sure, isn't push what you want?"

Takuro said, "Push is simplest, but it's not the fastest. The way we're running now, we have lift. Like an airplane wing. An airplane wing cuts the air into two slices. The slice moving over the top has to move faster because the top of the wing is curved, and that provides the lift."

"But we don't have a wing."

"No, but the sail is like a wing. We're being lifted forward."

I looked at the sail. It was just a piece of cloth. "I don't believe it."

"Maybe not, but see how well it works." He looked with some pride at the boat cutting through the water, swiftly and cleanly.

"Um. Right."

I studied the sail, trying to see it lift, then gave up. The wind was getting stronger. We were going so fast that Michigan City was already lost behind us. Somebody put our lights on—the running light in the bow, the stern light, and the anchor light on the masthead. It was not dark, for the sun had not yet set, but they looked cheerful just the same.

Gradually, I came to believe that the whole boat was not going to capsize. I even walked around, but crabwise, holding one object, like the lifeline, and letting go just long enough to grab a rail or a cleat farther along.

With the boat running so fast, everybody came out on deck to watch. Even Emery, who stood near the companionway steps with his hands on his hips and a big smile on his face as we plunged forward into open water. Will Honeywell's hair blew back from his face. He looked like a seafaring explorer.

The audience was assembled. The heavens produced a finale that has long been playing to appreciative people.

The sun had been behind a thunderhead, leaving the sea and sky a predark purple. Now it slid out under the cloud. Magenta and flame washed over the waves, the sails turned bloodred, and a splash of carmine ran out along the bottoms of the massed clouds. From gaps between the clouds, flaming rays shot out to the top of the sky, where they faded to an infinite purple. Time stopped, the day at an end, the night not begun. Then, sinking, the sun flattened on the horizon. It sank faster, becoming half a sphere, a flattened oval coal of fire, then a spark that flickered on the water and was gone.

And all at once, flickering between cloud and horizon, was lightning. It was an ice-green glow, quickly gone. Then another. Then none.

It was so far off, it might have had nothing to do with us at all.

Greg asked who would like to take over the wheel. Bill said he would. Mary followed him into the cockpit, which could have surprised nobody. Greg told them, "We're heading due north northeast unless the wind changes." Mary and Bill both nodded.

Greg shouldered his way past everyone and went below. As far as I could tell, he did not even glance at Twinkie and Chuck. They stood in the bow, Twinkie laughing her high-pitched laugh at Chuck's remarks.

Then she turned to Bret, who was doing his Captain Blood imitation again. Believe it or not, she must have asked to feel his muscle, because he held his arm up and made a fist and she squeezed his biceps. Chuck turned and stalked away, back to the cockpit.

"Mary!" he said, all enthusiasm.

I don't think she liked him very much, but she smiled politely.

"Want to come below and have a coffee and rum?" he asked.

This was a dilemma for her. The man was Bill's parents' guest, their friend, fellow furniture man and co–play producer. Mary turned with raised eyebrows to Bill, who said, "Sure. Go ahead. I'll play sailor for a while."

A well-brought-up lad.

"Thank you," Mary said to Chuck. "That would be nice. It's getting cooler out, isn't it?"

Also well brought up.

"You bet it is," Chuck said. He put his arm over her shoulders protectively as he led her to the companionway.

It *was* cooler. After a hot day, it was now maybe seventy-five degrees and falling. And the stronger breeze carried away body heat. It was getting darker, too. I was more aware of the wind whistling in the rigging and the sizzle of water rushing back from the bow.

Daniel came up from below, wearing a windbreaker.

"Expecting sleet?" I asked him.

"Cat, there are two kinds of wind on Lake Michigan. There's the kind that goes down with the sun and the kind that doesn't. The first one's more common by far. We've got the strengthening kind."

I looked at the horizon. It was mostly dark, indigo with a rose glow high in the west. Why wouldn't the glow be at the horizon? It took me a little while to tell: the clouds had filled in. The whole western horizon was solid with them.

I was standing amidships, letting the wind blow through my hair as we sped along into the blackness. I felt like a helluva brave person. I was enjoying the solitude when Chuck came stomping up from the galley. He came over to where I was and stood there, puffing and snorting. After a few seconds he turned toward me and smiled and reached out to pat my rear. I looked him in the eye and said, "Don't even *think* about it."

His hand fell. His eyebrows rose. But he didn't say anything.

Takuro stood in the bow, his slight, elegant frame whipped by the wind, peering into the water as he so often did. Near him was Will Honeywell, feet wide apart, head thrown back. He appeared to be sniffing the wind and finding it good.

Twinkie Mandel and Bret Falcon were amidships on the starboard side, leaning on the cabin trunk. Since we were heeled over that way, they must have been uncomfortable. Bret leaned back against the cabin roof, hands spread out on each side of him, his whole body forced back against the tilt of the boat. His face looked happy. But Twinkie, who was trying to maintain the same position, was handicapped by the fact that she had to keep fooling with her hair. Whenever she reached up to pat it back into place against the tug of the wind, her back slid sideways on the slippery fiberglass surface. It must have worried her. Her weather side was beginning to lose curl.

She had changed to her evening sport togs: a black sweater, red pants, and jet earrings.

Bill was still at the helm. Daniel Silverman sat next to him in companionable silence.

Abruptly, Mary marched up the stairs and stomped over to Bill. She spoke briefly to Bill, then he and Daniel turned and looked forward at Chuck. Mary jerked her head sideways at Chuck. She did it again, more angrily. Bill shook his head. He dropped the wheel and put his arms around her waist. Daniel jumped for the wheel as the boat swung into the wind, the boom started hurtling toward the deck.

Bill scarcely noticed. He hugged Mary. They walked over to the companionway and down the steps.

Oho, I thought. Daniel wrenched the wheel back into position.

I slipped into the cockpit.

"Need a friend?"

"Sure, if it's you," Daniel said.

"What happened to Mary?" I asked.

"Chuck patted her."

"Chuck pats everybody."

"This was a place she was keeping in reserve."

· 8 ·

The spinnaker had been rolled and tied in the bow up against the lifeline when we finished with it in the afternoon. Now it was starting to move. It lurched a little bit every time a wave hit our bow. I saw Will push it a couple of times with his foot, just testing. Then he went to the companionway and yelled, "Emery!"

Emery popped up instantly, a wet rag in one hand. "Yes, sir?"

"We've got to get the spinnaker stored."

"Yes, sir!"

Emery leaned back and tossed the wet rag someplace below. Knowing him, it probably landed right in the sink. Then he walked forward with Will.

Emery leaned over and unscrewed the handles of the forward hatch and pulled up the translucent hatch cover. Will, meanwhile, had stopped to say something to Takuro, who was staring intently at the mainsail. Chuck, still sulking amidships, chose this moment to be assertive.

"Hey, Emery!" he said. "Get me a bourbon!"

"Umm." Emery straightened up, indecisively. He looked at the hatch, then at Chuck, then at Will.

"Come on. You can fuss with that sail anytime."

"Well, I'm—Mr. Honeywell wanted—" but Will was still talking to Takuro, so Emery hesitated. He could be back in half a minute. Of course, so could Chuck if he'd gone to get his own damn bourbon.

"Okay." Emery hurried back down the deck.

His head was just disappearing into the companionway when Will turned back to the sail.

"Emery! What are you doing?"

Emery's head came back up. It swiveled in a short arc, from Will to Chuck.

"Um—"

"I told you we have to get that spinnaker stowed. It's washing loose."

"But—"

"Let's get to it!"

Chuck just watched, rather pleased if anything, not making a move to help Emery or explain why the kid had been hurrying away.

"Mr. Kroop said I should get him a bourbon."

"Oh." Will stood for a second, expressionless. "Well, go ahead." He waited another second or two, then strode over to the companionway. "Bill!" he shouted. "Bill!"

"What?" Now Bill's head came up from below.

"Get up here a minute!"

Bill did.

"What did I do?" he asked.

"You could lend a hand once in a while. Emery's got too much to do."

Bill just stared at his father. He had missed the whole exchange and had no idea what had happened. After a second he gave a small nod.

"Sure. Let's get to it." He sounded a lot like his dad.

"Come here, then, and give me a hand with this spinnaker."

"Okay."

The spinnaker by now had come partly unrolled. Together they manhandled it over to the hatch Emery had opened. The breeze caught at the edges of the cloth and whipped them back and forth with a crackling sound. While Will steadied the bundle so it wouldn't slip overboard, Bill pushed one end of the spinnaker into the hatch opening. Then they gave the whole body of the sail a push and it slithered into the hatch.

"Down the hatch!" I said to Daniel, taking innocent delight in suddenly finding out where an expression I often used had come from.

He smiled.

Apparently there had been somebody in the forward cabin, because we heard a voice call "Hey! What the hell?" from below the hatch. I suppose a big wet sail in the neck could be a surprise. Bill stuck his head in the hatch opening, explaining or apologizing.

By this time Emery was back, handing a clinking glass to Chuck. He accepted it with a nod.

"Nice guy," I said to Daniel.

"A peach,'" he said.

I sat next to Daniel in the cockpit, feeling the momentary halt of the boat each time a wave slapped the port bow.

"How are you doing?" he asked.

"Just fine."

"You sure?"

"Yes, I'm sure!" I didn't mean to snap at him, but I was feeling proud of myself. I wasn't seasick, and I wasn't scared, and by God, I didn't want to be reminded of being scared. How could I tell him I was more frightened of chickening out?

"All right, all right," he said. "But let me know if you feel panicky."

"I'm perfectly fine!"

He let me simmer down; then he said, "Have you ever been on a boat before?"

"Sure. In a way." I didn't want to talk about it, but I didn't want to lie to him, either. "Actually, not voluntarily."

"Ever?"

"That's what I said!"

"You're doing good."

The bow of the boat cut cleanly through the swells. But there was an increasing amount of spray. Twinkie and Bret had gone below, where their hairstyles would be under less stress.

You had to watch your footing carefully on the slick deck. My tennis shoes weren't too slippery, but I could see why the experienced sailors wore a squeegee type of sole.

I decided to go below and get on my waterproof Cubs jacket.

I went down the companionway steps into the galley. There had been major changes since I was down there an hour before. Mugs stood all over the dinette table, some of them half full of coffee and rum. The coffeepot was on the table, too. So was the rum bottle, and we'd only need to heel over a couple more degrees to pitch them right off onto the floor. Emery was on his knees soaking a big blotch out of the blue carpeting with a towel. Belinda was rinsing mugs in the sink. Twinkie was sitting at the dinette, whispering in Bret's ear, not helping at all with the cleaning up. I went over and picked up a couple of mugs. To Twinkie and Bret I said, "Are you done with these?"

Twinkie nodded, as if I were a waitress. Since the instant I met her, she had hardly acknowledged my existence. I took the mugs over to Belinda at the sink, leaning back as I walked to compensate for the floor being canted up on the dinette side and down on the galley side.

Belinda said, "Thanks, Cat."

"No problem. I'll get the rest." I felt sorry for her, with no one but Emery willing to help.

"Who's at the helm?" she asked.

"Daniel."

"Oh. That's good."

Maybe a little bit of irony had slipped into my voice when I asked whether they were done with the mugs. Whatever,

Bret must have had an attack of guilt. Before I got to the
dinette table, he had the rest of the mugs in his hands and
was stepping over Emery, who was still blotting the spot,
to take them to Belinda. At that instant, Chuck came thun-
dering down the stairs. Bret, unaccustomed to the tilt of the
floor, was startled by Chuck's sudden appearance, hesitated
for a second with his foot in the air, and put it down on
Emery's hand. Emery lurched, the boat lurched at a wave,
Bret fell on top of Emery, and the mugs went skittering
across the carpet, spraying coffee and rum. Emery said,
"Yipe!" and flattened out under Bret's weight. Two of the
mugs rolled against the galley wall, which was the lowest
side of the room, and shattered.

Nobody moved.

Then Belinda scooped up the broken mugs and dropped
them in the trash can. "Thank goodness," she said. "I never
liked gloomy brown mugs." She wiped her hands. "Now roll
over, Bret, and let's see if Emery's all right."

Bret rolled over and Emery sat up. "I'm not hurt."

Bret told him he was sorry. Emery said it was not Bret's
fault anyway and no harm "done. Chuck apologized to no
one, but said to Twinkie, "Come up on deck."

She looked at him as if he were a bird dropping that had
gotten into her caviar, and said, "Do you think everybody's
going to jump when you say jump?"

Twinkie reached out to pat Bret's hand, which was now
grasping the table edge for support as he rose. But she was
talking to Chuck. "*You* go up on deck. Go bump into somebody up there."

"I didn't bump into anybody." He nudged Emery's foot
with his toe. "This character is just clumsy."

"Then go up and—and fish!"

I heard Belinda, behind me, burst into a laugh. I spun to
look at her. She had covered her mouth and was making
giggly noises behind her hand.

Chuck stomped off down the hall and slammed the door to the head behind him.

The instant he left, Greg Mandel came out of the aft dormitory, like a new character coming onstage in a play. He had changed to a sweater and Levi's and carried a waterproof jacket. I wondered if he had timed his entry, waiting until Chuck had cleared out. Methodically, he sat down at the dinette across from his wife. His mouth was set in a straight line, and he didn't say a word.

Bret, meanwhile, got himself vertical, picked up the rest of the broken mug pieces and deposited them in the waste-basket. He walked back to the table and hesitated. You could almost see the questions going through Bret's head. He didn't want to sit down next to Twinkie, like before, not with her husband right across the table. He also had serious doubts about sitting next to Greg, who looked hostile. His eyes flicked to the companionway stairs, but running out was too obvious.

He sat down next to Greg.

I got a rag from the sink and went to wipe the dinette table.

"Do you think we all ought to get on waterproofs?" Bret asked Greg, by way of starting a polite conversation.

"Only if you plan to go out on deck," Greg said. It sounds like an innocuous statement, but he said it with a sneer in his voice, as if certain people were either too scared or too lazy to go out and help.

Twinkie said, "Well I certainly don't plan to. Almost everybody here knows more about sailing than I do. I'd just be in the way."

"That and the hairdressing bill," Greg said.

Twinkie ignored the jibe. "They don't need inexperienced people running around the deck and falling in the lake and throwing everybody into fits."

In a way, I had to agree with her.

I rinsed the rag in the sink, wrung it out and rinsed it again. Belinda looked at the three around the dinette table and shrugged. She picked up a dark blue windbreaker and asked me, "Want to go up and see the weather?"

I said yes, eagerly. I'd had enough of the tensions of the people below.

Everything was new—darker and wilder. Before, there had been a strong breeze; this was wind. The spray from the bow shot back horizontally over the deck. We were heeled over farther. I must have become accustomed to the angle while I was below. Our starboard side was practically under water. You could look down and see white water run past, sucking and curling, just inches below the coaming.

Daniel was still at the wheel, a funny, pleased half smile on his face, his eyes squinted into the distance ahead. I had seen Will look the same as the wind built. Maybe it's sailor's euphoria.

Will, Bill, and Takuro were in the bow, staring ahead into the night.

Belinda said, "Don't you just love this?"

"Yes." I was surprised. "I guess I do."

It *was* exciting. I was not frightened. The sense that the boat itself was in control, that the *Easy Girl* balanced all the forces of nature that acted on her, was exhilarating. The boat took in all the powers that converged on her and converted them to speed. The sail was white and tight against the darkness. The wind whistled around the mast and sheets.

Our lights did not really dispel the darkness. They were more for safety, I supposed, so that other ships would see us. The stern light and running light did make the deck more visible, and they picked out the white water that foamed back from the bow and ran alongside.

We were pitching more than before. The waves were rising, and we rode higher up and dropped farther down into the trench after each one. Belinda walked toward the bow, and I followed, keeping a careful eye on where I placed my feet on the wet deck and noting the position of the lifeline along the side, in case I should have to grab it to keep from going over. The water beyond the boat was black and empty. The thought of being lost overboard in these miles of open space—I put it firmly out of my mind and concentrated on watching where I was going.

The group in the bow moved aside to let Belinda and me have a go at the excitement of standing in the pulpit. She stood as still as a figurehead on an old sailing ship, leaning forward into the wind. Her hair blew out behind her, damp from the spray. She drank in the night and the rushing air.

Finally, she stepped back to give me a turn in the bow pulpit. Placing my hands securely on the metal railing, I leaned bravely forward.

A wave was mounting toward the boat. Because the light carried only ten or fifteen feet out from the craft into the water, the wave came into sight out of nowhere. It came curling up gradually, then threw itself at us. The bow of the boat rose, partly slicing through the wave, partly riding up over it. We hung there a second as it passed under us. When it passed amidships, the stern tilted up and the bow and I fell down into blackness.

I felt as if I were alone, as if the boat were not there beneath me and I was holding only the thin metal rail, falling unprotected into the dark.

As the bow reached the bottom of the trough, there was a sickening deceleration, a momentary halt. I had an instant to brace myself and my stomach, when I saw the rise of the next wave coming at us. The bow bit into the upward slope.

I rode up that one, then down. Then the next one up and down. And up and down and up and down.

There was something wrong. I didn't feel quite as well as I had a few minutes before. Turning away from the rail, I said, "I think I'll go find a ginger ale."

"That can be good for a touch of seasickness," said Will. "Takuro, will you take watch for a while? I want to go around and tell everybody that from now on each person on deck has to wear a life jacket."

"Sure."

"I'll be back and relieve you."

We went below. Greg was still sitting at the table with Twinkie. Both were silent. Bret wasn't there. I passed Emery, asking if I could get a ginger ale out of the cooler, and he pointed at the refrigerator. I popped the top at the sink, in case it fizzed over.

My eye fell on the magnetic knife rack. If Emery's kitchen had not now been so shipshape, I would not have noticed. The long, heavy roast beef knife Takuro had been using to cut beef strips wasn't there.

Did they use it for cutting rope in emergencies, I wondered? It didn't seem at all likely. This was a boat with the proper tool for every use.

There was a snarl from the dinette. Chuck stood next to the table. Greg had snarled. Chuck said something I couldn't catch, though I sure tried hard. Then Greg said,

"Just get out of here."

"Let her say so, if she wants me to leave!"

Greg stood up. "Move!"

Chuck turned away, muttering a few words, of which I only heard, "—back."

"Where's the big knife?" I asked Emery.

"I don't know. I was wondering about it."

"Maybe they use it for something else?"

"Maybe. But I doubt it."

"Strange."

"*I* didn't lose it," he said.

I looked at the ginger ale in my hand. It didn't seem as appetizing as I had thought it would. Chuck had gone up the companionway steps. I stood at the bottom of them, feeling the coolness of the air coming down, the cant of the floor under my feet, the pitching of the boat forward and back, the spray that now came over the boat with enough force to spatter a few drops in the open companionway. There was an increasing sigh of wind over the hatch above.

I held the ginger ale out to Emery. "You want this? I haven't touched it."

"Yeah. Sure."

The boat jarred into a still bigger wave as I handed it over, but we didn't spill a drop.

Great. There was human tension aboard, a storm rising, and now we had a large knife missing.

◦ 9 ◦

When it came, it was out of nowhere. Not the storm, the fight. We heard shouting from the hatch. And with the wind whistling in the rigging and the waves hissing past the bow, the voices had to be *really* loud.

I was standing in the bow with Daniel. Mary and Bill had just taken the wheel.

Greg stormed up the companionway steps, his body half-turned, looking back down. He was yelling "—arrogant, stupid bastard!"

Chuck crashed up after him, and he was in the middle of a sentence, too. "—took care of her, she wouldn't!"

Greg spun around.

"You—you—you!—to talk about sensitivity!" He was nearly incoherent, stuttering with fury. His voice cracked.

"When you haven't got—you hunk of brainless *meat*! God! Talk about your football days as if they were something! A hulk big enough and fat enough—they put you in the line for people to run into!"

Chuck slipped on the deck, trying to swing at Greg. Greg went on shouting.

"Stupid, slow, and thick! You've always been a brainless shit! Everybody knew it!"

"You never had to compete at a damn thing!" Chuck yelled. "With your rich father and your—your— You never—I started a company! It takes brains and a—it's a goddamn competitive world—"

Greg had a grip on his breathing, but he didn't have enough sense to quit talking.

"You were just lucky! Shit, you get enough people starting enough businesses, and a few of 'em will hit it right out of sheer dumb luck. And they'll spend the rest of their lives thinking they're *geniuses*! Just like you!

Daniel and I had come aft. Chuck turned red and was swelling up. I saw Twinkie in the companionway, just watching. Belinda was coming up behind her.

"Okay," Daniel said. "Greg, come with me. We'll go get some coffee."

He took Greg's arm, but it was too late. Chuck had reached detonation.

Watch out for the large, pink, porky types when they lose their tempers. They blow all at once.

Chuck shrieked like a factory whistle. His eyes were bulging out and he leaped at Greg. He hit him sideways, with his full weight behind his shoulder; then he reared back and punched him in the stomach.

Bill left Mary at the wheel and came running. Greg was doubled over from the stomach punch, but he broke away from Daniel and straightened up and slugged Chuck in the jaw. Chuck was either too angry, too solid, or too stupid to feel it. He bellowed again and hit Greg in the chest with both fists, held like battering rams. Greg's feet went out from under him, and he fell back, sliding downslope on the wet deck all the way to the lifeline.

Neither Greg nor Chuck was wearing a life jacket.

Greg's legs slithered under the lifeline. One foot dragged in the foaming white water.

Chuck kicked at his head, trying to push him overboard.

Greg had one arm over the lifeline stanchion, but the rushing water was pulling hard at his legs. Chuck kicked his arm.

Daniel took a grip on another stanchion and grabbed for Greg's shirt. So did Bill, but he couldn't get a grip, and his feet kept slipping.

Belinda shrieked, "Will! Takuro! Emery! Will! Will!"

Mary left the wheel and leaped for Chuck, but he shrugged her off easily. The boat, with no one at the wheel, and having a weather helm, came up into the wind. The boom swung from starboard over the deck just as Bill Honeywell straightened up, and it caught him on the side of the head. He went down like the dead. In the buffeting wind, the boom swung back and forth amidships, in an arc of about six feet, threatening to kill everybody on deck.

Daniel, yelled at me, "Get the wheel, Cat! Dammit! Get the wheel!"

I jumped for it. Not sure what to do, I had nevertheless heard a lot about north this evening. I grabbed the thing and tried to bring the bow to starboard, at the same time reading the compass. It told me we were heading northwest.

"Watch the boom!" Daniel yelled as Takuro, Will, and Emery rushed up from below.

I had wrenched the wheel over, amazed at how it tried to fight me in the wind, and the boom swung over, narrowly missing Will Honeywell, who saw it coming and ducked. The boom cleared the deck. The compass dial floated to north and I fought to hold it there.

Greg still hung from the lifeline stanchion. Chuck dove at him, but Daniel fended him off. Slowly, he pulled Greg up the wet deck. Greg, shaking, got his feet under him.

Mary and Belinda bent over Bill, who lay supine on the deck.

Greg reared up and rammed Chuck. They locked together and wrestled back and forth over the slippery deck, pushing, clutching, falling over the cabin trunk rail. Will tried to pull Chuck away and was thrown back against the mast. Takuro dove for Greg, and Greg hit him. Daniel circled the fighters, looking for an opening, not rushing it.

Greg dropped and grabbed Chuck's legs, and twisting and pushing, tried to pitch him down the companionway steps. Chuck got one leg loose and kicked Greg in the neck. Greg fell back over the cockpit coaming and onto my foot. Chuck leaped down after him. Greg brought a right fist up into Chuck's face, but Chuck caught him first with a left, then a right, and as Greg's consciousness faded from the blows, put both hands around his neck and started to choke him.

Daniel was in position. Leaning over Greg's shoulder, he pulled Chuck's right hand away from Greg's neck, holding it in a left-hand grip that made Chuck wince. Then he gave Chuck a right to the jaw that sent him flying backward and onto the port deck where he lay, out cold.

Greg, no longer supported by Chuck's strangling hands, lurched forward, fell over the cockpit coaming, and slipped under the lifeline. He slid rapidly down the starboard side toward the water.

I grabbed at his foot and tried to hang onto the wheel with my other hand. It was too far to stretch and I just wasn't strong enough. I couldn't hold on.

"Daniel!" I yelled.

He was already there. He got hold of the back of Greg's jacket at the small of his back and held on. The jacket bunched and stretched. Greg's face was in the water, hanging down from the low starboard side.

I thought of bringing the side up by steering into the wind again, but I wasn't a good enough sailor to know what the consequences would be, and I didn't want the boom swinging around the deck.

The thought only took a split second. By then Will and Takuro were there, Takuro first because Will had stopped to look at Bill. Takuro took a firm stance in the cockpit, took hold of Greg's right leg and pulled.

Daniel pulled, too.

For a moment nothing happened. Then Greg came slipping back up over the edge and all three flopped onto the cockpit floor.

By now Chuck was sitting up on the deck.

"I'll kill him," he said.

Will Honeywell stood over him, one hand on his shoulder, pressing down. "No, you won't," he said.

"Yes, I will. I'll kill him. I'll just get my breath back. Then I'll kill him."

Daniel stood up slowly. His ribs must have been badly bruised from hanging over the coaming holding Greg's full weight. He didn't mention it, only shifted his shoulders, as if he were in pain. He glanced at Greg, who was not moving but didn't look dead, then went back to where Mary and Belinda were still huddled over Bill.

"Let me take a look at him."

Bill was unconscious. Daniel put his head to Bill's chest. Then he sat back and opened up one of Bill's eyes. Belinda and Mary knelt there, frozen, the spray whipping back from the bow over them, all unnoticed. Belinda's face was strained with fear as she stared at her son.

Emery had been standing around nervously through all this, weaving back and forth from one foot to the other. You could see his problem. He wanted to help, but punching out one of his employer's guests was not something he could bring himself to do. And surely it wasn't in his job description.

"Emery! Go forward and keep watch," Will said. "Wait! Get a life jacket on first, but move it!"

Emery moved.

"And tie onto the lifeline!"

Daniel said to Mary and Belinda, "There isn't enough light up here. Help me get him below."

He cocked his head at Chuck and Greg while looking at Will and Takuro. The question was obvious: could they keep those two apart?

Will nodded. Takuro said, "It's okay."

Chuck was still blinking from Daniel's blow, so it seemed safe.

I said, "Will? You're better off at the helm. What do you say we switch?"

Will smiled grimly. "All I wonder is which is more dangerous to let go of while we switch. Chuck or the wheel?"

I kept two hands on Chuck's shoulders. I just wasn't large enough to hold him if he wanted to move, but I could surely slow him down. I watched them carry Bill down the companionway, Daniel protecting Bill's head and neck. They laid him out at the foot of the steps. I could see them from up here. Daniel asked for a flashlight. Belinda got one for him faster than you can say "electricity."

Daniel opened one of Bill's eyes and flipped the light past it. He did the same with the other eye. He said, "I don't think we have a serious problem."

Bill blinked. Then he made a noise. Belinda and Mary were thrilled and looked at Daniel with gratitude, but personally I think Bill was just irritated with having his eyelids messed around with.

He tried to sit up.

"Not yet. Lie still," Daniel said. Bill stopped struggling. "Can you answer some questions?"

"Um—sure," Bill said, thickly.

"What day is it?"

"Tues—Friday."

"Good. Who is this over here?"

"My mother."

"And who is this?"

"Mary."

"Do you remember my name?"

"Sure. You're Dr. Silverman."

"Okay. You'll do. Let's move him out of the way of the stairs. But Bill, I want you to lie still for a while. No heroics."

"All right."

Daniel came up the stairs. He stepped down into the cockpit, where Takuro was minding Greg Mandel. Twinkie by this time had got herself into the cockpit, too, but she was doing nothing helpful or sympathetic, as far as I could see.

Greg was still lying down.

"He's breathing, isn't he?"

Takuro smiled. "I would have called you if he weren't."

"Right."

Daniel felt Greg's neck. Greg must have been conscious for some time, because as Daniel finished his half-blind assessment, Greg said one word. "Bastard."

His voice was a croak, but carried enormous conviction.

Daniel correctly interpreted this as referring to Chuck, not himself. "Let's get you below now," he said.

I was watching this scene too closely and not minding my charge. As Greg reached the companionway stairs, Chuck surged up out of my grasp and shot toward Greg, punching him in the back and precipitating him down the stairs. Greg fell onto Twinkie, who was already halfway down the stairs. She screamed but managed not to fall.

It was a good thing they had moved Bill away from the bottom of the steps.

I jumped Chuck from behind, feeling guilty for letting him loose, took a firm grip on his hair with my left hand and pulled his right arm up behind him in a painful lock.

"Go slowly down the stairs," I ordered.

We were quite a procession: Twinkie teetering on her inappropriate shoes, Greg leaning on her, then Daniel, Takuro, and Chuck, with me literally on his back. We staggered into the galley, since Bill and the two women took up most of the dinette floor space. Mary stayed with Bill, but Belinda hurried over.

"You can let go now," Chuck said.

"Not on your life."

Chuck had a certain reasonable way of talking, in between attacking people and promising murder.

"This is ridiculous," Belinda said. Speaking, I'm sure, for most of us.

"I *will* kill him, though," Chuck said, calmly.

It happened again. I wasn't cautious enough, because Chuck was speaking quietly. He jumped at Greg with me still on his back like an incubus. Lightning fast, Takuro slipped between Greg and Chuck. Chuck was big and heavy and under way he had a lot of momentum. Takuro was slight. Chuck hit him full force with his shoulder, like a football player, and unbelievably, Takuro stood his ground. There was a lot of steel under that slim exterior.

Enraged, Chuck slapped him forehand across the face, as if to swat him out of the way. His nails opened two tracks down Takuro's cheek. The wounds bled; Takuro did not budge.

By this time I had both hands in Chuck's hair. I pulled his head back, hard. His face was toward the ceiling, so he couldn't see to attack anybody. He clawed at my hands, but Takuro pinned his arms and he stopped, grunting with pain.

All this time, the boat was riding up, then swooping down over the waves. The floor tilted up in front, then dizzily down. Plus, it was permanently canted to starboard by the wind pressure on the mast.

Daniel said, "Is there any place we can lock this idiot up?"

"Oh, no!" Chuck roared. "You're not—"

"The master stateroom," Belinda said, accepting that

something had to be done. "Except—the door and the lock aren't very strong. He could break out pretty easily. It's really a sort of—privacy lock. Not a brig."

Chuck thrashed frantically in our grip. I could feel the crackling tension in his muscles.

"One of you'd better come up with a suggestion," I said. "He's wild and he wants to kill somebody."

"There's a medical kit," Belinda said. "It's got some sedative or anesthetic, I think."

Daniel said, "Get it, Belinda."

"No!" Chuck howled. "Wait! I'll tell you what. I *won't* kill him."

His glittering eye and gritting teeth told me differently. Daniel, too, I guess. Daniel looked him in the eye, as if he were a rational human being, and said, "I'm sorry, but we just can't take your word for it. Not tonight." Daniel's voice was somber with real authority. "I'm sorry, Chuck. I really don't like this. But we've got a rough night ahead. We're going to need three people on deck at all times. And we don't have enough able-bodied men to guard you and still run the ship. Not with you and Greg acting like madmen. I can't trust you not to push him overboard. And in this weather—"

Chuck stared. He knew Daniel meant it. Then he started throwing his body wildly back and forth in our grip. Takuro held on like a sales tag on towels.

Belinda came back with the medical kit. It was big. Daniel opened it. I was amazed. I'd been expecting one of those little things with a packet of Band-Aids, a roll of gauze, a bottle of disinfectant, and maybe a thermometer. I should have known the Honeywells wouldn't do things that way. There were a dozen labeled vials, two packages of sterile sutures on prethreaded needles, a blood pressure cuff, tourniquet, disinfectant, packages of several different tablets, charcoal and ipecac for poisoning, an otoscope, splints, and odds and ends I didn't know the use of. If the Honeywells were in midocean and somebody needed an appendectomy, no problem.

Daniel picked up and studied several vials of liquids before he found one that pleased him.

"Valium," he said.

I hadn't known Valium was injectable.

My prisoner held still for a second, then jumped, but I was ready for it this time and just held on.

Daniel checked the cap for a tight seal and read the expiration date. Suddenly Chuck picked both feet up, leaving Takuro and me holding his whole weight. As we buckled under it, he jammed his feet on the floor and pushed up, crashing the top of his head into my nose. Holy jeez! White and yellow stars exploded in front of my eyes. The pain was astonishing.

I screamed "Shit!" but held on blindly. I didn't see it happen, but Takuro must have let loose, dropped, and tackled Chuck's ankles. Chuck fell like a tree, with me on top of him, and Takuro jumped on both of us. Chuck flipped over to his back. Takuro lay on his legs. I wormed my way over and sat on his chest.

My nose was bleeding like a slit wrist. But I could see again.

Greg had simply stepped back and had not been hit. He was blinking foolishly. He didn't seem to be taking it all in.

Takuro said "Hurry up!" to Daniel.

But Daniel said, "No. I have to figure out the dosage. He's been drinking, and I have to allow for that, too. I don't want any respiratory depression."

Takuro and I exchanged glances. Both of us thought any kind of depression at all was exactly what Chuck needed.

Daniel couldn't be hurried. We sat on this writhing mass of mixed muscle and fat while he checked the strength of the stuff, the tightness of the seal, the integrity of the vial itself—Lord only knows what else.

And all the time Chuck was yelling, "I'll kill him! I'll kill him! I'll *kill everybody!*"

With me sitting on his chest, I don't know where he got the breath.

Finally—I'm thinking, hurry up, hurry up—Daniel picked up a disposable hypodermic syringe and tore the paper off. He filled the barrel and methodically eliminated air bubbles. He approached Chuck's arm.

Chuck shrieked and doubled up, throwing Takuro off entirely and flipping me onto his legs. But I've got to say for Daniel, once he's ready to go, he goes. His reactions must have been trained in emergency rooms on wild drug-overdose patients. He sat on Chuck's stomach, ripped up his sleeve, swabbed his upper arm with disinfectant, plunged in the needle, and had it back out, all in maybe three seconds.

Chuck still thrashed around.

"It didn't work," I said.

Daniel said, "You've been watching too many spy movies." He raised his wrist and looked at his watch.

Little by little, Chuck's struggles were less violent. Little by little, his body seemed to flatten out on the floor.

"You bastards," he said.

A little bit later he must have realized he was drifting off. "You wait," he said in a dreamy voice. "I'll rest a little bit. *Then* I'll kill him."

Daniel got out the sphygmomanometer and checked his blood pressure.

Chuck started laughing, a little gurgle that was oddly frightening. It went on and on, getting fainter and fainter until we couldn't hear it at all.

• 10 •

"Tilt your head back, Cat, and pinch your nose," Daniel said.

"Pinch your own damn nose," I muttered. But not loud enough for him to hear. As it was, he was as busy as Spiderman at a comics convention. I tilted my head back.

Daniel listened to Chuck's heart, flashed the light in his eyes, watched him breathe. He counted his pulse, then did the blood pressure again.

"We'll move him to a bed," Daniel said.

I said, "The master stateroom. Then we can lock the door."

Greg blinked. "What if he breaks out?"

Belinda stared coldly at her brother. "You certainly could have behaved better this evening, Greg. There's no reason you couldn't have ignored whatever he said."

"It isn't what he *said*."

"Well, it's too late now."

Daniel took Chuck's blood pressure a third time. He listened to his heart again. Finally he seemed satisfied.

I had wondered where Bret Falcon, matinee idol, had disappeared to throughout all of this. Now he came out of the forward head, dead pale—I mean, seriously fish-belly pale—and sweating, his curly hair damp on his forehead. He didn't even glance at the bodies strewn all over the floor, but went straight to the table and sat down.

Seasickness. Yuk.

Daniel picked up Chuck's shoulders, and Belinda and I each took a foot. Even that much was a load. What a tub of guts! We slung him on one of the berths in the master stateroom.

"If you push him over a little," Belinda said, "I can wedge some pillows next to him and he'll be less likely to roll out of bed."

"You mean it's going to get even rougher?" I asked.

"I don't know. I don't know." Belinda ran a hand through her hair. She looked distraught, and small wonder.

We gave Chuck a shove, not as much of a shove as I'd have liked to give him, she placed some heavy bolster pillows around him, Daniel took a last listen to his heart, Belinda turned out the lights, and we went out the door.

She started to lock it.

"We shouldn't leave him in the dark," she said, hesitating. "If he wakes up groggy in the dark in a pitching ship—"

Daniel said, "He won't wake up soon. But still—you're right."

"Okay." She went back in and the light went on.

She came back out, locked the door, and handed Daniel the key.

"I think we ought to have a couple of keys around, just in case the boat runs into an emergency."

"Which we won't, right?" I said.

Belinda smiled and looked younger again. "No. But *if* there were a fire, or if we capsized, each of us, you and I and Daniel, should be individually responsible for getting him out. He's no bargain sometimes, but we couldn't let him drown."

"Right."

"There's another key in the galley drawer, and I'll give one to you, Cat, and Daniel. If you lose your key, remember that the door opens inward and you can break it down with your shoulder if you have to."

She patted my arm and added, "But you won't have to."

*   *   *

Daniel told Greg to put an ice pack on his neck. Greg muttered hoarsely that he was a doctor, too, and could think for himself. Daniel told him not to take his crabbiness out on his friends, then ordered Twinkie to get a towel and ice and get to work on Greg. Surprisingly, she did. Then he checked Bill and gave Mary permission to get him to bed. My nose had stopped bleeding at last.

He and Belinda and I went back on deck.

It was darker, if possible. My watch said three minutes to midnight. We stood looking forward into nothing. It was so dark, our lights were absorbed by the blackness, sucked away into the void.

Then there was a lightning slash, a sizzle, and I went blind. Instantly, there was a crash. I staggered into Daniel.

"Where'd it get us?" I shouted.

"I don't think it did. Boats aren't usually damaged by lightning." He was perfectly calm. The clod.

Another flash, blinding white. There were pink spots in front of my eyes. I closed and opened them, but the spots didn't change. The crash of thunder was immediate, and the air smelled of ozone. Then, in quick succession there were three flashes, with great bolts of lightning that stood like columns between the clouds and the water. The thunder was simultaneous.

And then the rain.

All at once we were in a deluge. I could scarcely see anything but the spots, which were now blood red turning purple. After a few seconds, I could see our running light and more lightning, farther off to the north. The running light was a globe of moving drops, a shimmer of falling rain that stayed in one place. The rain was so dense that the light did not reach through it to illuminate the boat.

We heard Will calling from the cockpit.

Daniel, Belinda, and I groped our way back there, leaving Emery alone, still manning the bow watch. A bolt of light-

ning showed Will standing up at the wheel, his mouth open
to the rain, singing: "Fifteen men on a dead man's chest—"

He cut it off as we more or less fell into the cockpit.

"We need the radar reflector up right away," he said.
"And reef the main partway."

"We'd better get slickers," Belinda said. Will already had
one on, probably from the cockpit locker, since he had never
left the wheel.

"No, get the reflector up and the main reefed first. We're
in the shipping lanes and we can't be seen in this weather.
And we've got too much sail up."

"Aye, aye, sir!" said Daniel cheerfully. Something in his
tone told me he thought we should have done it earlier. Of
course, we'd been busy with a few little problems.

"I'll take care of the main," said Belinda.

Daniel said, "I'll go below and get the reflector and pick
up three slickers at the same time."

"I'll help," I said.

"Not on the foredeck you won't, Cat," Will said. "I don't
like those shoes you're wearing. There's an old saying, you
won't be washed off the foredeck if you stay in the cockpit."

"I want to help."

"In this weather, we should have a second person in the
cockpit. If anything happens to the helmsman, the boat
won't be ungoverned. I'm electing you first mate."

Well, there I was. First mate. Will started singing again,
the rain lashing his face, the spray whipping his hair, one
wet hand on the wheel, the boat riding up and down over
the waves.

"Fifteen men on a dead man's chest. Yo-ho-ho and a bottle
of rum. Drink and the devil had done for the rest. Yo-ho-
ho and a bottle of rum."

He was loving it. It was as if the very skin of his face was
drinking in the wind and rain. I would have been happier,
though, if I hadn't seen an actual bottle of rum in his other

hand and realized he was drinking that in, too. I wondered where he had got it. Another item from the cockpit locker, I supposed. I had not pegged Will as a problem drinker, and I think I was right. But this kind of night he loved. He was happy, really happy. He was *celebrating*.

He took another swig from the bottle. I thought I could see the level go down.

He was still in control of his faculties. All the same, maybe first mate was an important position after all. If Will quit on me, would I know what to do?

Belinda cranked the mainsail down to its reef points, a position where it had about half the total amount of sail area exposed to the wind. The roller made it possible for her to do it alone.

Even a tyro like me could feel the effect on the boat. It struggled less against the wind, and the impact, the sheer punch, when a gust hit was a lot less. Of course we didn't go as fast, either, so the force with which we met a wave and rammed through it was less.

Daniel was back with the slickers and a thing that looked like a large metal pie plate. He and Belinda messed around with a rope near the mast for a couple of minutes. They fought with the dish as the wind tried to take it out of their hands.

And all the time the lightning flashed and sizzled.

Then the reflector started up the mast, Daniel pulling the rope and Belinda watching the thing rise. She said a word to him, lost in the wind, and he tied down the rope.

They came aft to where we sat. Belinda eyed the rum bottle but didn't refer to it directly. She said, "Maybe we could all use some sandwiches."

I was not hungry. I was feeling queasy.

"Not for me."

Daniel said, "I'll go down for some. And, Belinda, you or I ought to switch with Emery soon. It's hard to be alert for more than half an hour or so with rain driving into your eyes."

"I'll take over from him," she said. "I like it up front. Cat, you'd better get on dry pants and a shirt if you're going to stay out here in the wind. Even the slicker won't keep you warm if you're wet."

Well, I surely was going to stay up here. Every time I went below, I got more seasick.

When Emery came back from the bow, I went below with him to get my dry clothes. In the V-berths in the bow the bunks were covered with damp spinnaker, and there was no place for anyone to sleep. While I struggled into a dry shirt and pants, the boat bashed me back and forth from wall to bunk.

The head was free of Bret for the minute, so I hurried in and out. Bret sat at the dinette, his chin in his hands, looking miserably seasick. Just the sight of him made me feel worse. Mary had got Bill into the two-berth room near the master stateroom. Greg and Twinkie sat across from the deathly Bret, Greg leaning back against the wall. Twinkie was greenish white, which is not at all trendy or even pleasant with a red and black ensemble. Even as I watched, she got up and ran to the head and slammed the door.

I started feeling really rotten. Emery was making coffee again—I think he could brew a pot in his sleep—and the smell of it made me feel sicker. He had also opened some canned liver spread to make sandwiches. The odor and look of it made me feel absolutely dreadful. I bolted up the stairs into the open air.

Daniel, Will, and Takuro sat in the cockpit singing "Yo-ho-ho and a bottle of rum" at the top of their lungs. The wind howled, and the waves beat so hard on the hull that down below I had not even heard them.

I could see Belinda in the bow, haloed by the yellow running light, the flapping slicker not detracting from the straightness of her back and the somehow gallant way she liked to ride into the waves. She was ten or fifteen years older than I was. I hoped I'd keep as much enthusiasm at her age.

Behind me came "Drink and the devil had done for the rest," then at absolutely top volume, "Yo-ho-ho and a bottle of rum."

I held on to the lifeline, trying to think about the people on board, the weather, anything but my stomach. I was too sick to be scared. The boat went up one wave, tipped up its rump and plunged down, just like a roller coaster. Then up again and down again. Up and my stomach stayed down. Down and it stayed up. Up and down. Up and down. Up and down. My head felt cold. There was sweat on my forehead. Up and down. Up and down.

No need to say what happened next. But better here than down in the head. Time stood still. I wished I had drowned. I didn't care.

The next thing I knew was an arm across my shoulder. Daniel was saying, "Very courteous, Cat. You used the downwind side. You'll become a real sailor yet."

"I don't ever want to see waves again. Not even the ripples when an olive falls in a martini."

"You're just temporarily upset."

"How can you talk this way when I'm dying?"

"You aren't dying. You're already feeling better."

Damn it, he was right. Don't you hate that in a friend? I straightened up a bit.

"I can give you some Dramamine," he said. "But if I do, you'll have to go below. It slows your reactions."

"I'll stay here. I'm all right."

If I had put the storm out of my mind while sickness used my whole brain, the storm had used the time to grow stronger. Waves rose up at the bow, crested with foam so white, it looked phosphorescent, so white I could see it from thirty feet away, even in driving rain, even though our lights were weak. Waves lifted, leaped forward, slammed into the bow. A layer of water a foot deep sloshed over the boat. It slammed past Belinda, washing up to her knees, then struck the front of the cabin roof, eddying up to the base of the mast. The rest, parted by the cabin roof, raced down the port and starboard decks and spilled into the stern as the boat rose on the wave. Only the cockpit was free of water, because of its high coaming.

"I'd better make sure Belinda has a safety harness on," Daniel said. "From now on, nobody should be in the bow without one."

I watched him go forward. A wave smashed into the port bow and Daniel, having gone up the starboard side of the deck, was thrown to his knees near the cabin trunk. Water swept down the deck, washing over him. He must be wet to the skin. I resented his treating me like a baby, sending me to the cockpit, out of harm's way. Then I wondered whether I would have known enough to walk on the starboard side. If I were washed overboard out of sheer inexperience, it wasn't going to add to anybody's enjoyment of the weekend. Especially mine.

Daniel got to his feet cautiously and forced his way against the wind and water. The boat came over the crest of a wave and pitched forward, threatening to tip him down to the bow. He held on to the lifeline, then let gravity take him forward to Belinda. They fiddled around with some apparatus I couldn't see from here. There must have been a tethering device holding her to the boat. That had to be the safety harness Daniel was talking about.

She needed it. I had got used to the idea that waves came in cycles, a set of large ones followed by enormous ones.

But the next wave was a real monster. This was a wave from hell.

The spray of its crest hurled itself across the bow, flattening Belinda and Daniel in an instant, covering both with foam. It parted on the cabin roof and came sizzling back past me, a wall of water three feet high, hissing around the lifeline, billowing over the cockpit coaming and into Will and Takuro's laps. While the boat was poised for an instant on top of the wave, I dove headfirst into the cockpit.

"Daniel went to check on Belinda?" Will yelled.

"See if she had a harness!" I screamed.

"No need. She *always* wears a harness in a storm."

Unbelievably, just when I thought we were sinking, he and Takuro started singing again. Will took another slug from the rum bottle. Takuro and I exchanged a glance. About then Daniel precipitated himself into the cockpit. He was totally drenched and his waterproof hat had blown or washed away. His hair was stuck flat to his head, and the skin of his fingers was wrinkled, like a person who had stayed in the bathtub too long.

◇ 11 ◇

Then the *real* storm hit.

The lightning was so continuous and the darkness so brief that the eyes could not accommodate to the dark before the next flash. The lightning was green-white, and the eyes afterward burned a blackish red, like dried blood. We could not have seen a ship the size of the *Queen Elizabeth II* bearing down on us.

The thunder shook the boat. I was frightened, getting more so, and trying not to show it.

The waves coming at us were doing something new. The wind was so strong that, as the crests rose up, the froth at the top blew out forward, shooting ahead of the wave across the deck.

"Can we get to a port?" I yelled at Will.

He couldn't hear me. He put his hand up, cupping his ear. The boat shuddered as she hit a wave, and the wheel turned in his grasp. He put both hands back on it in a hurry.

"Can we get to a port?" I screamed at the top of my lungs.

"Wouldn't—be safe!—near a port!" he yelled. "We could smash into the breakwater!"

"How strong—is—this—wind?"

"About full gale!"

He acted delighted, and hanging on to the wheel a bit more carefully, he tipped the bottle up to his mouth. The rum was gone, all but a drop. I saw the last drop vanish.

I was worried. And while Takuro and Daniel, and Belinda in the bow, I suppose, did not appear to be seriously frightened, Takuro was behaving very cautiously. He appeared to be looking forward, but in fact he was watching Will out of the corner of his eye. I've done that myself a lot in interviewing people. You look unconcernedly elsewhere and catch the person working up a deceptive facial expression.

Will reached behind himself and brought out another bottle. I saw Takuro's lips part as if he wanted to speak, but he closed them again.

"The wind's moving further west!" Will shouted. "Just a touch."

"Right!" Takuro shouted.

Will yelled at me, "See? So I'm riding almost due north now. Can't bear up any farther into the wind."

Will took a big swig from the second bottle, a terrifying tableau illuminated by lightning.

The wind was increasing. How could it possibly get stronger than it already was? Where did it *come* from? Was there still some place on earth where everything was quiet?

At the same time, I realized that more and more of the lightning flashes were east of us. Fewer of them were hurled directly at the boat. Great! Let Zeus try to sink somebody else for a while!

But the wind was stronger. Looking down, I could see my hands shake. Daniel leaned against the coaming. Takuro kept his eye subtly on Will. Will began another chorus. "Fifteen men on a dead man's chest—"

"Yo-ho-ho and a bottle of rum," sang the four of us. I was trying to keep up a good front. "Drink and the devil had done for the rest—"

"Yo-ho-ho—" Will sang and fell flat on his face in the cockpit.

The boat swung wildly to port. In the bow I barely saw Belinda lurch sideways and fall to one knee at the bow pulpit railing. The sail slapped once like the crack of a giant rifle. Takuro leapt to the wheel and righted the boat in an instant. The sail firmed.

Takuro, now captain, said, "Daniel, will you and Cat take Will below?"

"Sure thing," Daniel said.

"After that somebody better relieve Belinda," Takuro added.

We got Will out of the cockpit. It was heavy business, and slippery. Will was solidly built and moderately tall. Without being fat, he probably weighed a hundred and eighty pounds.

Daniel and I slid him over the coaming and half carried him to the hatch. The pitching of the boat tried to pull him away. Wind was lashing wave spray back at us. Our slickers flapped straight back in the gale, letting water in on our legs.

I called "Emery!" as loudly as I could while still holding on to a slippery, nerveless body that was trying to slide down to the starboard side. I hooked one of Will's arms into the companionway opening while Daniel kept a grip on the legs. I called "Emery!" louder.

I heard a voice say "Coming."

Daniel left. I saw him work his way forward against the spray and wind, a tall figure, bent over.

Emery stood on the bottom step of the companionway, his face about level with Will's, and looked at his sodden employer.

"You take his shoulders," I yelled. "I'm losing my grip on him."

We manhandled Will down the steps, bumping his rump a little as we went, but not hard. We kept getting thrown back off balance by the impact of the waves against the bow.

Finally we laid him on the royal blue carpet at the bottom of the stairs.

"What are we going to *do?*" Emery asked, desperately. "His room's in use."

Emery, obviously, felt the only place for the master was in the master stateroom.

"We'll put him in the dorm thing. He's not gonna know the difference."

Bret and Twinkie watched us with dull eyes, and we trundled him forward to the room with the three berths. We rolled him into the lowest one, neither of us feeling up to lifting him farther. He mumbled a little as we tucked him away. It sounded like "yo-ho-ho."

When I got back to the galley, Greg was sitting with Bret and Twinkie. Twinkie was scared.

"What the hell were you people doing up there?" Greg said. "I was in the head and you threw me against the wall. I could have cracked my skull."

"Will collapsed."

"Collapsed, hell. He's drunk."

"We have a limited number of people running things up there," I said. Not as an excuse, and actually we had enough staff. I wanted to see what he was like, whether he'd offer to come up on deck, lend a hand, and get soaked and cold.

"Yeah," he said, partially acknowledging what I meant. "I wish I didn't have this splitting headache."

"You sound like a woman, dear," his wife said nastily.

Well, maybe he did have a headache. And maybe she was it. On the other hand, I had been choked once by a homicidal elevator operator and it gave *me* a headache.

Twinkie said to Emery, "I need a cup of coffee."

Bret spoke for the first time. "I need another Dramamine," he said.

I decided to go back topside. The wind and the spray didn't seem so unpleasant after all. Dangerous, yes. Unpleasant, no. But I should have moved faster.

I have mentioned that the waves came in cycles. When the really big ones hit the boat, they threw literally tons of water against the bow. We shuddered with every one. But at the minute I started toward the steps, the very mother and father of a wave must have crashed into the bow. At that instant, Greg had been handing Bret a Dramamine. Emery was crossing from the galley to the table to pour coffee for Twinkie in response to her rather peremptory summons. The impact of the wave on the port bow pushed Emery's feet starboard and sternwise, and he fell toward the table. I fell back, almost into his path. He kept a hold on the coffeepot, but the coffee itself kept moving, spewing out forward, over the dinette, over Twinkie, Bret, Greg, and the woven teak wall. Twinkie and Greg lurched up, Greg cursing, Twinkie screaming. The bottle of Dramamine tipped over, spilling white tablets everywhere, including into the puddle of coffee on the table. Lots of little white pellets rolled off onto the floor. Emery crashed forward, striking his chest on the table, then knifing over at the waist and hitting his head on the coffeepot. As I got up, Twinkie was patting her hair frantically. I think Greg was about to yell at Emery but had hesitated because he saw the kid was bleeding. For a moment we had a breathing space, and then

Bret, pale as a Dramamine, bolted to his feet a little too late and was sick—all over Twinkie, Greg, and the dinette table.

For a minute I fought an almost overmastering desire to turn around and run right back up on deck. But my feet, knowing their responsibility before my head did, were already walking me over to the sink for a towel.

I got Emery sitting at the dinette and checked him. He had cut his scalp on the metal edge of the coffeepot spout, and scalp wounds bleed a lot. I held the towel to it for a minute with just a little pressure, and when I took it away, the bleeding had slowed to an ooze. By the time I got done with this modest first aid, the picture at the table had altered. Twinkie had rushed, gasping, to the forward head. The fore head? The forehead? I was getting hysterical. Bret staggered weakly to the sink. Greg was standing indecisively in the space between the galley and the dinette, wiping his shirt with a towel. Of the four of them, he looked the least damaged.

"Help me clean up," I said, rising.

"I'm not an employee around here."

I had had it. "Listen, turkey," I said, "I'm not, either. But the kid is hurt and the place smells like a Chicago barroom after election day. I'm going to clean up. You just sit there and watch me if it will make you feel better."

Hell, he wasn't *my* guest.

He stared at me, but I turned around and went for a fresh towel.

"I can help," Emery said.

"No. You sit! Maybe you can help in ten minutes or so, when you stop bleeding." I passed my hand over my head and laughed. I was becoming giddy. I said, "You can help as soon as you clot."

Greg came up behind me and got a roll of paper towels out of the bottom cupboard.

"I'm a little upset tonight," he said by way of apology.

"Sure, I know. You don't get strangled every day."

In ten minutes we had done a fair job. The gorgeous blue plush carpet was wet and matted, the trash can was overflowing, and the walls were wet where the coffee had hit. Also, I think we had used every paper towel in the place. Compared to the usual shipshape room, it was a shambles. But it was a lot better than ten minutes before.

Twinkie came back, changed from top to bottom—in a black-and-green Black Watch plaid shirt, green pants, and believe it or not, emerald earrings. Bret came back essentially unchanged.

Emery said, "I'm all right now. I'll just polish up a little."

"I thought we did a nice job."

"Oh. You *did*. I just—"

"Don't sweat it. I'm kidding. Just take it easy. You've had an injury."

This time I made it up the stairs without incident. I met Daniel near the top step.

"I was coming to look for you," he said. "You were gone quite a while. Is anything wrong?"

"What could possibly go wrong?"

Our entire effective team was in the cockpit, Daniel, Belinda, and Takuro, and me.

"Don't we have an observer any more?" I asked.

"It's too dangerous," Takuro said.

Belinda motioned me to sit down near her. "We don't really think it's necessary," she said. "We've got three back here. One stands up, taking turns, for a longer view."

Takuro was at the wheel. "We quit," he said, matter-of-factly, "when I was washed overboard."

"What!"

"He was wearing his harness and he managed to hang on

to one of the lifeline stanchions," Belinda said. "Daniel got up there in a hurry and pulled him back aboard."

"There was no problem," Takuro said.

They seemed to take this very calmly, but my mouth fell open. I had already imagined being lost overboard in the dark, drifting, lost to the boat, the boat searching for me, but unable to see me . . . And in this rain and wind and heavy sea . . . Life preservers are all right, but how long would a person last in the cold water of Lake Michigan? What were the chances of being found, even when daylight came?

While I was engaged in these morbid thoughts, Takuro, Daniel, and Belinda were talking. Shouting, actually, but we were all used to that.

"We've been heading north and north northeast for over two hours now," Takuro yelled.

"Right," Daniel yelled back, and reinforced the words by nodding, in case the shrieking of the wind in the shrouds and around the mast had covered his voice.

"Think we should turn west?" Belinda asked.

"You worried about getting too near shore?" Daniel shouted.

Takuro said, "It's hard to tell how far east you wash." He meant that since the wind was from the northwest, we constantly were being pushed east.

"Will wouldn't like this," Belinda screamed into the wind.

"We must be north of Benton Harbor by now, but we can't really tell," Takuro said.

"Stay away from shore or small boats," Belinda shouted. "Will is always saying, stay away from the amateurs. People who don't know enough to run with lights."

"My sentiments, too," Daniel said. "Sure. Why not go west? It's a good easy reach."

"We'll roll a little," Takuro said. He laughed and added, "We'll roll a *lot*. But the boat is very well built." Belinda smiled. I worried.

Belinda took the wheel, and Takuro and Daniel went forward to operate the sheets. They looked back at her. She nodded and said, "Coming about," to me. But I didn't know what I was supposed to do about it, so I just sat there in a white-knuckled blue funk.

She brought the wheel around. The bow came up into the wind, hesitated a second, then swung across the wind and westward. The boom swung in response, from the starboard side, where it had been hauled rather close, across the deck with the sail snapping and popping when it reached luffing position, then out to the port side at about a forty-five degree angle to the axis of the boat. Daniel and Takuro tightened down the mainsheet to just the tension they wanted.

We were now broadside to the waves. The first wave was upon us, hitting the starboard side, throwing spray across the deck, washing past Daniel and Takuro and over the port side. We leaned far to port as we rode up the leading edge of the wave and leaned to starboard as we went down the trailing side. We rolled, but we didn't capsize. The weight of the keel held us down, held us stable against the incline of the wave. And now we started to run west, along the trough between waves. Of course, we did not stay in the trough long, for the next wave would run under us. But it was a different feeling, paralleling the waves.

Before, we had been pitching—cutting almost directly into the waves, going up in the bow, over the wave, and down, like a teeter-totter. Now we were rolling, going up on the starboard side, sitting atop the wave a second, then down on the starboard and up on the port as we slid down the wave. I wondered if I would feel less seasick.

I was carefully analyzing my internal feelings when I realized that I was standing knee deep in water.

"What's happening?" I shouted at Belinda.

"Nothing serious," she shouted back. "It's self-baling."

"What is?"

"The cockpit is above the waterline. Any water that runs in runs back out."

"Then why am I up to my ass in this wet stuff?"

"It's coming in too fast."

"Are we sinking?"

She laughed. Then she laughed even harder, and finally so hard she lost her breath and had to lean over and gasp a lot while Daniel put his arm around her shoulders and I held the wheel steady. Every wave that hit us from the right—sorry, starboard—shoved the boat sideways and therefore shoved the rudder and therefore tried to snatch the wheel out of my hands. I held on heroically until Belinda recovered.

"When the water washes in from the side instead of coming over the bow," she told me, "it fills the cockpit so full that it takes a little while to drain out. By that time another wave is coming over the side."

"Oh."

"When the water comes over the bow, most of it washes to either side of the cabin trunk and out over the sides and doesn't get back here."

"Oh."

Daniel and Takuro were closing the hatch that covered the companionway stairs leading down into the galley-dinette. They were shouting down the stairs as they did so, but I couldn't hear much. They were probably telling the folks below that the boat was not being scuttled and they were only trying to keep water from running down the stairs.

Suddenly it occurred to me: this must be battening the hatches!

◦ 12 ◦

Yes, you get just as seasick rolling as pitching.

The boat rolled and recovered, rolled and recovered, rolled and recovered.

While I was miserable, Takuro went below to get hot coffee and sandwiches for Daniel and Belinda. When he came up, battening the hatch after himself, I asked, "How's everything below?"

"Grim."

Twinkie, he said, had taken two sleeping pills Greg had given her. She was now sleeping in the bunk above Bill in the two-bunk aft dormitory. Mary was awake in the aft dormitory, sitting on the floor and checking Bill at intervals. Greg's throat was swollen and he talked like Jimmy Durante. Takuro didn't know anything about Will. The door to the fore dormitory was closed, so he was probably sleeping it off. No news from Chuck, either, so our berserk sailor was not murdering anybody. Emery was cleaning up. Business as usual.

He said it smelled worse down there, though, because it was closed up.

We were rolling wildly. Every wave swamped us from starboard. Even Daniel, Takuro, and Belinda were suffering. The preferred method was to quarter into the waves, not roll like this.

After an hour or more of being westbound, they decided to head north northeast again. Takuro estimated that we

were making about seven or eight miles an hour and therefore were seven or eight miles farther from land than when
we had turned. Belinda thought that was good enough.
Me, too.

I took the hatch cover off the companionway. Emery
yelled, "At last!"

So, at 4:00 A.M. we came about again.

I sat in the cockpit, useless, wet, cold, sick, leaning
against the coaming, just waiting for dawn and a better
world. Did people do this for fun?

Were we having fun?

Takuro said the waves were now fifteen feet high. Not as
big as ocean waves, he said, but because of the shorter distance across Lake Michigan, they came in quicker succession
than ocean waves. He was right. They came at you like
teeth.

The temperature had been dropping all night. Even in
my slicker, insulated by a life jacket and a sweater, I was
cold. And the cold made the nausea worse. Or the nausea
made the cold worse. Finally the rain quit, but the wind
blew the heat right out of any exposed part of the body. I
saw Belinda shove her hands under her armpits to warm
them after Daniel relieved her at the wheel. Takuro sat
hunched over, fighting shivers.

I volunteered to go get hot coffee again.

I had got up and was starting toward the hatch when a
sound like God's last trump struck. I couldn't imagine what
was happening. We were used to constant shrieking wind,
but this was like a thousand devils howling doom. I spun
around wildly, looking for a monster.

Bearing down on us from behind was a ship. A ship that
looked the size of a house—no, not a house, a whole high-
rise apartment building, a castle, a mountain! The bow
loomed over our port side, several times as high as our
mast, with a giant froth of white water rising like enormous
inverted waterfalls on either side of her bow.

I stood openmouthed for several seconds before my brain finally told my heart that since she was running alongside, she would not hit us. I wiped my hand over my face and looked again.

I could see the identifying numbers on her side, they were so large. I could see the superstructure in her rear coming toward us. And toward us. The ship looked so long, I thought it would never pass. There were lights on her bow and stern and in the superstructure windows. She was so tall, she seemed to lean out over us.

Then abruptly she came to an end. She diminished into the night, getting smaller and smaller, the lights growing closer together.

"Hang on for the wake!" Daniel yelled at me.

The wake struck us, stronger than the natural waves and from a different direction. It was a cliff of water from the west. It hit us and threw us up into the air and sideways. Then it swept away to the east and left us.

"That was close!" I said.

Daniel said, "Not really. Probably an eighth of a mile off, wouldn't you say, Takuro?"

"Yup. Easy."

Belinda said, "They knew we were here, from their radar. They hooted so we would be prepared for their wake."

"Oh," I said. "Spiffy of them."

"Well, a lot of freighters don't bother."

We huddled in the cockpit. There was a clamminess in the air that was more than spray from the bow, more than the accumulation of rain in our hair and water splashed on us. It was the clamminess of predawn. It was five-thirty in the morning.

Daniel held the wheel. His hair hung down wetly into his eyes, but he looked vigorous and alert.

I asked, "What do you see?"

"Look." He waved his hand generally forward.

I looked. It was dark. Waves rushed at our bow. I saw no ship, no lighthouse, no looming catastrophe. Then I thought—yes. The eastern horizon was a little, just a little brighter.

"Morning!"

"No."

"It isn't?"

"Morning's coming soon, but it always does this time of day."

"Well, what, then?"

"Cat, look at our sail."

The sail? It was just the same. Maybe a little less taut. Less taut?

The wind was going down!

Takuro said, "Thank goodness."

Daniel looked at him sharply. Takuro was quietly trembling. He had been hiding the fact that he was shivering, Lord knows how long, inside that loose slicker. Hypothermia!

Daniel said, "Belinda, please take the wheel."

She did. Daniel went to Takuro and peered into his face. His lips were bluish.

"I want you below immediately." He pulled the man to his feet.

"Go down, change clothes," Daniel said. "*All* dry clothes. Every single item! I'll give you five minutes to change, and then I'm coming down to look you over."

"Aye, aye, Doc," Takuro said, weakly.

"Tell Emery to get hot coffee or hot soup for him," Daniel said to me. "Whichever's quicker."

I relayed the message down the stairs.

The three of us huddled in the cockpit. Our eyes turned to the eastern horizon, where there was now a growing light. The wind was a little bit less strong, then a little less than that. Daniel looked closely at Belinda, trying to see whether

she was as cold as Takuro, but she was not shivering. She
had two layers of sweaters on. I saw a green turtleneck
sticking out of the top of her slicker and blue sleeves show-
ing over her wrists. She had prepared for the weather.
"You haven't checked whether *I'm* cold," I said.
"Yes, I have."
Know-it-all.
Just then Greg and Emery came up the steps. They wore
slickers, life preservers, and extra layers of clothing.
"We saw the condition Takuro was in," Greg said. "You
three are going below."
"Thank you," Belinda said gratefully. "We were about
done in."
Emery took the wheel. Greg checked the sail, the waves,
and the sky. "It must be down a bit," he said.
Emery said, "Not bad." He was happy to be taking the
helm. Small wonder. After a whole night of looking after the
ill, the injured, and the incurably crabby belowdecks, this
would be a positive treat.

Emery had tried to keep abreast of things in the galley, but
the sink was awash in mugs again. The place smelled awful.
It had been closed up half the night.
"First thing we'll do when it gets quieter," Belinda said,
"is air out."
Daniel took a look at Bret, whose head lay on crossed
arms on the dinette table.
"This one can wait. But we'd better check Will and Chuck
and Bill."
"I'll unlock Chuck's door," Belinda said. She fished out
her key. "I think," she said with a tired smile, "that Will
might prefer *not* to be checked."
Daniel and I went to the dormitory cabin next to the
master stateroom. Mary sat on the floor leaning back against

the bunk. She had probably been in much the same position all night. Bill was asleep.

"How's he been?" Daniel asked.

"He woke up about an hour ago and said his head ached. Every time he wakes up, he says his head aches."

"Was his vision normal?"

"I didn't ask. But he didn't say there was any problem other than—"

We heard a scream.

For a second the sound of that scream seemed all around us, not from any particular direction. Then there was a gasp and from the master stateroom a shrill voice said, "Oh, my God! No!"

Daniel straightened up.

"That's Belinda," he said.

◊ 13 ◊

Daniel and I ran, then jammed together in the master state-room doorway.

Chuck lay on his back on the bunk, very much as we had left him. His feet were toward us, and his head was toward the stern of the boat, so that we could easily see his neck. It was swathed in blood, like a bib. The ceiling above him was sprayed with blood. The wall next to him was sprayed with blood. There were rivulets of blood down the wall, drops of blood like rain over the bed, drops on the royal blue carpet near him. His chest was soaked in blood. On the floor was a bloodstained pillow. Another bolster pillow, equally bloody, lay next to him.

And standing near the bed was the beautiful and elegant Belinda Honeywell, holding the big roast knife from the galley. The knife was clotted with gore.

Daniel walked to her.

"I shouldn't—I shouldn't have picked it up," Belinda said, evidently referring to the knife. She moved it back and forth in a nervous kind of way, as if she wanted to get rid of it but it stuck to her hand. Then she dropped it.

"I shouldn't have touched it," she said again, mechanically. "That was very foolish."

Daniel took her arm and walked her to the door. I stood back to let them pass.

There was no blood on Belinda's clothing.

"Mary!" Daniel called. She came out of the dormitory room immediately. She must have been standing just inside, wondering, but not jumping in with questions. I liked her.

Daniel said, "Mary, take Belinda into the galley and give her a brandy, please."

"What—"

"Stay with her. Bill doesn't need you as much as she does right now."

"Yes, all right." She didn't ask anything else. Sensible young woman.

Daniel walked back to the bunk and put his fingers on Chuck's wrist. But it must have been as obvious to him as it was to me that Chuck had been dead for some time.

We locked ourselves inside with the key, which Belinda had left in the lock. I pulled it out and pushed it into the keyhole again. It made a metallic noise. When I turned it in the lock and the bolt slid over, there was a louder noise. But not so loud you could have heard it over a thunderclap. Daniel picked the knife up off the floor very carefully in two fingers and put it on the dresser between the berths.

We stood still and looked at the slaughter.

"You okay?" he said.

"Certainly. Bodies don't upset me." They don't. I can't say they make my day, but I did too much reporting of traffic accidents in my paying-my-dues years to be really squeamish.

"All right," he said, reluctantly. He obviously didn't believe me. "Well. Let's get started."

"Hold it. Why do we have to 'start' anything? Let's get the police."

"We may be four or five hours sailing time from the police. There's a lot of evidence that's going to evaporate if we don't record it."

Like the body temperature, for instance. He was right about that.

"True."

"So, listen, I'll stay with the body if you'll go get the thermometer from the medical kit."

I stood still. Thinking hard.

He said, "What's the matter?"

"You go get the thermometer."

He stared at me as if trying to read my brain. He looked angry, but that wasn't my problem. Finally he said, "Okay. Tell me what's wrong."

"What's wrong? I'm out in the middle of nowhere with people I don't know. They all know each other. One of them killed Chuck."

"I can see that it's difficult—"

"Difficult? It's not difficult at all. It's *dangerous*. For all I know, the reason they let me aboard in the first place was so I could be an independent witness. I never *did* really understand why they'd take a stranger along."

"Will isn't the type—"

"So I think maybe I'm being set up. You can't get Greg in here as a witness, even if you wanted to, even though he's a doctor, because he's the person most likely to have killed Chuck."

"You're jumping—"

"Plus, I don't really know anything about *you*. You gave Chuck the hypo. Maybe you want me here to witness your care in preserving the evidence. Maybe you killed him. Maybe you want me to go for the thermometer so you can get rid of some crucial piece of evidence."

"Christ! You really call a spade a spade, don't you?"

"I consider it my calling in life."

He put his hands on his hips. Probably he was waiting for me to suggest something or back down. Backing down isn't what I do best. I waited.

He walked to the door and unlocked it. "Mary, can you get me the thermometer from the medical kit?"

"His temperature is ninety-six point five degrees Fahrenheit," Daniel said. "So he was killed maybe over an hour ago and less than three hours ago."

I wrote it down. And the time. It was 5:45 A.M. "I thought body temperature wasn't reliable."

"It's reliable enough if you know all the factors. In the tables they say one degree centigrade an hour. Two to two and a half Fahrenheit. But with the factors here, I'd guess closer to two."

"Why?"

"Chuck was a big, chunky man. Large people lose heat slower. Also, it's humid down here. Evaporation speeds up heat loss. Humidity slows down evaporation."

"Duly noted."

We tiptoed over to Chuck again. We did not fear to wake the dead. We were trying to avoid stepping in the evidence—the blood droplets, which were everywhere on the carpet.

The body lay on its back. Daniel pulled up one eyelid.

"The cornea is filmed. Sometimes that only takes a few minutes after death, but it's usually longer."

I wrote it down.

Daniel said, "No, don't just *write* what I say. Look at it, so you can testify if you have to. Let's protect you and me both."

"He isn't very lovely."

"Look anyway."

I did. Filmed cornea. Right.

You haven't really lived until you've seen a filmy cornea. He took hold of Chuck's chin and moved it up and down. Now there was a disgusting sight. The head moved with the chin. I knew what that meant. Rigor had set in. The neck wound, however, gaped open and closed like a mouth.

"Rigor can start anytime from two to seven hours after death. And it begins in the face. It's here—" he moved the chin again. I wished he wouldn't.

"—and not here," he concluded, moving Chuck's limp arm and then his fingers, individually.

"Gotcha."

"Rigor may be a little early, but within the normal range."

He pulled up Chuck's shirt, revealing a hairy belly, formerly white with black hairs, now bluish in death. "See here?" he pointed. There was a faint purplish hue down on his back. "Lividity. The blood sinks after death. It's noticeable beginning anywhere from half an hour to three hours after death. After that, it gets more noticeable for a while. You don't have any other examples to compare it to, but you can tell how this looks."

"I've got that, too," I said dryly.

He straightened up and looked at me.

"Hey!" I said. "You don't have to work at it so hard. I was ahead of you anyway."

"What are you talking about now?"

"He died more than an hour ago and less than three. I already knew that."

"All right. I'm an easygoing guy. Exactly how do you know that?"

"Look at this." I leaned over to the wall and pushed at one of the drops of blood. One of hundreds.

I said, "See. It's dry on the outside and still soft on the inside. You try it."

He did.

"And it's also separated. See the clear serum on top and the clump of cells at the bottom?"

"Sure."

"If there's one thing I know, I know blood. Do traffic accidents, you know blood. Blood does two things: it clots and it dries. A drop of blood starts to separate in about ten minutes. Visibly. After fifteen or so, it forms a dry skin on the outside, like this one has. After about forty-five minutes, it starts shriveling from loss of water. But even after an hour, it's still jellylike inside. Like this one is."

"The humidity here would slow down the drying," he said.

"Right. But not the clotting."

"I knew that." He grinned. He did, of course.

"Sure. My point is *I* know. I know I'm not being conned on the other items."

"Great."

"Don't frown at me. I'm on your side, basically."

He said, "Good. So we know something that the police would never know if they saw the body for the first time this afternoon. He probably died—"

"Between three and four-thirty a.m."

"Mmm-mm. Not just five minutes ago."

"Which is also good," I said.

"Why?"

"I like Belinda."

"Yes. So do I," he said.

· 14 ·

As if by telepathic consent, we both went to the other bunk and sat down, checking first for blood spots. There weren't any.

"What're we gonna do now?" I asked.

"Lock the room and head for shore."

"That, obviously. What about asking people whether they saw anybody go in here during the night? While their memories are still fresh."

"Um," he said.

"If we have a killer on board, I'd just as soon know who not to turn my back to."

"Right."

"Why are you being so noncommittal?"

"It could be suicide," he said.

"Bull. Chuck thought he was the bee's knees. God's gift to the world."

"Look at his throat."

"Not again."

But I followed him to the body.

"Look at the wound," he said. "There are several cuts in the same spot. They're hesitation cuts."

Now, I knew what this meant. The idea is that a person who commits suicide, say, by cutting his wrists, makes a first fearful, hesitant cut, which doesn't do the job. Then he makes another. If he's going to go through with it, he finally gets his nerve up and goes deep enough to cut an artery. The same holds true for necks, as far as I know.

"If you find a corpse with one straight, successful slash," Daniel said, "you have a pretty good idea that it's murder."

"That doesn't mean a few cuts mean it's suicide. It could be an attempt to make it look like suicide."

"Too subtle. You're assuming we have somebody aboard who would know—" He stopped.

"Exactly. We do have people like that on board. Doctors. You and Dr. Greg Mandel. You'd certainly know how to fake hesitation cuts."

"Maybe."

"Or, how about somebody who isn't used to murder? Which most of us aren't. He creeps in during the night, scared, and makes a hesitant first cut. Then a little deeper. Finally maybe he closes his eyes and goes ahead."

"I suppose it's not impossible."

"And here's a third choice. Look at the wound. It almost looks like the killer drew the knife back and forth and back and forth."

"Yes, it does."

"Suppose it's somebody who really *hates* Chuck. Perfectly possible, I must say. He gets in here; Chuck is defenseless, and he *saws* him to death."

Daniel sighed. "Possibly."

"Plus, he's lying down," I said. "Suicides lie down if they've taken sleeping pills. But try to cut your throat lying on your back."

"Maybe he was sitting up."

"Check it out"

Daniel walked over to the body and with two fingers tipped Chuck's head to one side. The sheet under his head was clean. No blood.

"See? Died right there," I said.

"Mmm. Looks like it."

"And look at his hands. If he'd cut his own throat, the

hand that did it would be covered with blood. Both of them are just spotted, like the bed."

Daniel grunted. It was halfway to a groan.

"I'll tell you another one," I said.

"What?"

"You gave him a shot, and we watched him until he lost consciousness."

"Right."

"When we carried him in here, he didn't have a knife."

We stood at the master stateroom door. Pretty soon we'd have to go out and tell everybody.

I said, "I noticed the knife was missing a couple of hours after dinner."

"Maybe he stashed it here."

"Knowing we'd drug him and lock him in?"

"Maybe he staged the fight."

"Oh, *really!*"

"Maybe somebody left it here by mistake."

"Even less likely."

"And he woke up depressed from the fight, the drug, the drinking, and the knife gave him the idea."

"Daniel, are you serious?"

"Cat, tell me just one thing. Can you honestly say you believe there is none, zero, zip, no chance he killed himself?"

Well, he had me. It was improbable, not impossible. I said, "Ninety-nine point five."

"You're a hardhead."

"Me, in a nutshell. The probability is that somebody sneaked in here during the small hours. However difficult that seems. It's just not suicide."

"It could be."

"No, it couldn't."

Daniel sighed again. I sympathized. These were his friends, after all. He put his hand on the doorknob and said, "We'd better find out what everybody saw during the night."

*   *   *

We opened the stateroom door and had immediate proof that people in the galley could see it. Mary, Belinda, and Takuro sat at the dinette table, staring at us. The companionway steps were between us and them, but because they were open steps, like a ladder, we were plainly visible.

Mary had a pot of coffee and a brandy bottle in front of Belinda. Takuro was drinking from a steaming mug. He wasn't shivering anymore. He was chatting very, very casually with Belinda about the way the wind was going down, which told me he was trying to take her mind off what lay in the stateroom.

Mary handed me and Daniel both mugs of brandy-laced coffee before anybody could ask us questions. What a nice young woman she was!

I put the mug to my mouth, and my teeth chattered against it. What had happened to Chuck had made me forget I was chilled.

Then I noticed another thing—the coffee no longer sloshed from side to side in the mug, climbing away from me as I tried to sip it. I guess I had got used to drinking evasive beverages during the rough weather. Maybe the storm was over!

"Have you told them?" Daniel asked Belinda.

"Just the bare fact. I thought I'd wait and—um—see what you had to say."

Daniel said, "We've got a serious problem. I think we'd better get everybody together in one place. On deck, I think."

I stood on deck in warm, dry clothes—my other ones had been as comfortable as wearing wet cabbage leaves—waiting for everybody to arrive. The change in the weather was amazing.

The sky was the color of a gray pearl. It was almost daylight. The sun must be just below the horizon. The wind was down and only a gentle breeze held the sail out. Emery and Greg, who had not yet been told what had happened below, had raised the main from its reefed position to full.

We seemed to be making very little speed, but that may have been in comparison to the wild weather in the night. The wind did not shriek in the rigging. The waves ambled by as spent, dead rollers. There was no anger in them.

I was covertly studying Greg and Emery, wondering if either of them had killed Chuck. I asked, "When does the sun come up?"

They looked at each other in amusement. I had made a landlubber remark, I guess.

Greg said, "Today the sun is not coming up."

"Oh, very funny." Unless he had killed Chuck, it was unlikely he was making a statement of existential doom. "What do you mean?"

"Sorry. But it's not coming up any more than it already has. Dawn has happened."

"So where's the sun?"

He pointed low in the east, where the pearly glow was about the same as everyplace else. "Right about there, I would think."

Emery took pity on me.

"This is fog."

"Fog? Oh, fog." I looked around. The fact is, you can't really see fog, unless you see it against something else. At sea there isn't much else. I noticed there was no horizon. I looked up the mast, and yes, it got fainter toward the top. I looked at the bow of the boat, and it was grayer and less distinct than the deck nearer me. As I watched, a drift of thicker grayness passed by, and for a moment I could not see the bow pulpit.

"We were about to go down for a hooter," Emery said.

"A hooter?"

"A horn," Greg said. "You're supposed to sound a horn at intervals in fog. Say, if you aren't going right to bed, maybe you could go get it for us. Will or Belinda will tell you where it is."

"Uh—actually, they may be coming up in a minute."

"Why? Is something wrong?" Greg asked. "We heard a scream a little while ago, but with this crew, who knows. Could mean that Twinkie's neckerchief has fallen in the cocoa."

He had a way of talking about his wife that I didn't like. But since I didn't like his wife, either, I was in a very ambivalent position.

He didn't say anything else. Was that suspicious?

We stared at the fog. It was endless. You couldn't even tell whether the boat was moving forward or not. After a minute or two, Emery said, "I should be going below. They'll have the galley in a mess."

"It's all right," I said.

"And I should make up the used berths."

"*Most* of the berths," I said, thinking of Chuck's, "are in pretty good shape."

Fortunately, Will Honeywell came up the steps, blinking as he emerged into the light. He must have one hell of a hangover, I thought.

Daniel was right behind him. Then Belinda, Takuro, and Twinkie. There was a gap, then Mary and Bill together, Bill a bit pale, with a large bruise on his head. After half a minute Bret arrived, with the surprised look on his face of a man who finds that seasickness is not fatal. We were jammed into the cockpit.

Everybody watched Will. He stood on the deck, so everybody could see him. Vertical creases on his forehead and a constant flickering down of his eyelids against the light showed he had a fierce headache. His eyes were blood-shot. The way he compressed his lips after every few words testified to a dry mouth and throat. He didn't mention how he felt.

"Sorry for rooting everybody out of bed and getting you up here on a clammy morning. But it's quicker this way. Chuck Kroop is dead."

Emery gasped. Greg stared blankly. There were no violent reactions. Will went on.

"Belinda found him when she went in to check on him this morning. Daniel and Cat went into the stateroom immediately, made sure there wasn't anything to be done for Chuck, and made certain observations the police may want to know about."

Twinkie gave a little squeak at the word "police."

"Unfortunately, the circumstances are such that Chuck's death may be either suicide or murder. His throat was cut. I have asked Cat and Daniel to collect as much information as they possibly can before we get to shore. The more facts that are known about this, the fewer mistakes any investigators will make. So it is to everybody's advantage to clarify what happened."

Everybody but one, I thought. But of course Will would be hoping it was suicide.

"It will be a few hours before we make port. Belinda, after I went to bed, what was our course?"

Went to bed was one way of putting it.

"We stayed on your tack, just east of north, for about two hours," she said. "Then we thought we might be getting too close to land, so we did about an hour of west. After that we kept north northeast for the next two or three hours."

"Takuro, where do you think that would put us?"

"My best guess is thirty miles off the Michigan coast, with either Saugatuck or Holland as our nearest landfall."

"Fine. Thank you. Well, we don't know whose hands we'll be in—the U.S. Coast Guard, the Michigan State Police, the Ottawa County Sheriff, where Holland is, the Allegan County Sheriff if it's Saugatuck, or the Holland or Saugatuck municipal police. I have simply never had to know this sort of fact before." A wave of pain or chagrin spread over his face.

"The point is," he went on with a deep breath, "we don't know the qualities of these departments. I'm not running them down, we just don't know. But skills vary. Anyway, Daniel and I have sealed the cabin where Chuck's—where Chuck is. Sealed it literally with duct tape and locked it with a key. I fully believe that nobody here would be"—he looked at the faces—"violent. And therefore, I urge you to help Cat and Daniel record your observations while the facts are still fresh in your minds."

Very well phrased for 6:30 A.M.

In other words, good old Cat and Daniel would protect everybody against some ham-handed country sheriff.

"I think the best thing right now is for everybody to eat," Will said. "Emery should give up the wheel and start breakfast—"

"I'll help him," I said.

"Good. And I'll take over for Emery up here. I've slept. Belinda and the others who have been up all night should get some rest. Except for Cat and Daniel, I suppose."

I nodded cheerfully, but I heard the command inside the velvet tone.

Naturally, everybody started asking me questions. Emery remembered the missing knife and wanted to know if that was the one. Twinkie wanted to know what time he died. I'm not sure why. I told them what I knew.

Will said to Greg, "I'm going down for the horn. I'll be right back. What tack are you on now?"

"North. What little breeze there is has swung into the east."

"Let's try for northeast, then. We'll be more likely to hit Holland, and Holland's a bigger town." He headed for the hatch, right behind Emery.

Greg looked up. "It's going to take a while," he called.

Will halted. "Why?" Even as he said it, he looked up, too.

The sail hung utterly limp, like washing on a clothesline. The top of it was lost in fog.

"We're becalmed," Greg said.

• 15 •

Daniel said, "Then motor in."

"It'll take forever," Will complained. "And we may not have enough fuel."

Belinda said, "Wind'll probably come up soon from the southeast. Once the sun's high."

Will made a decision. "We'll eat first. We've all had a horrible night."

Emery fried potatoes and sausages and scrambled a couple of dozen eggs. Gee—what a pity he was a little too young for me to marry him.

I warmed the muffins and made coffee. Gave Will a mug of it to take up on deck. He was carrying a horn that had an attached canister of compressed air. A horn that blows its own horn. Vessels our size apparently are required to sound a four-to-six-second blast, followed by two one-second blasts, at least every two minutes in weather like this. Soon, we heard the first hoots of the horn. They sounded like mourning.

Everyone else must have thought so, too. They talked about anything else but Chuck. Anything else.

How long was the fog likely to last? Didn't you always get fog when the air cooled suddenly, because the water didn't? Would we get a breeze soon? Can you have breeze and fog at the same time? Believe it or not, Bret actually asked Emery how he got the scrambled eggs so creamy.

Emery looked bemusedly at the plate of eggs, as if they could just as well be fried spinnaker, and said, "Lots of butter."

Bill and Mary took plates up top, along with a plate for Will.

Oh, the sheer joy of being in dry clothes, warm, not seasick, and eating food! You can say what you want for intellectual pleasures. Give me food first every time. *Then* we'll talk.

Daniel and I did not sit together. For people who really didn't know each other all that well, we were estranged.

I noticed Belinda watching me. "Did I use the wrong fork?" I asked her. We were using sporks, those spoons with toothed ends, so I meant it as a mild pleasantry.

She smiled. "I'm sorry. I just noticed that was your seventh sausage."

"Gee, if I'd known you were counting—"

"No. I'm pleased. I was worried about you last night."

"It's her third muffin, too," Daniel said.

Emery poured me another cup of coffee.

Twinkie said, "Murder surely doesn't hurt *your* appetite."

Everybody stopped joshing.

My first thought was—is she just being nasty, or did she have reason to know it was murder? Plus, what was Twinkie really like? Was she simply an airhead? Was she really attracted to Chuck, or did she flirt with everybody because she couldn't help it? Was she trying to make Greg jealous?

It was impossible to read her face. For one thing, she had had another go at the Elizabeth Arden supplies. For another, somebody must have told her at an impressionable age that facial expression causes wrinkles. She had about as much expression as the Mona Lisa if Mona had been wearing purple silk and an amethyst choker.

I could have said murder didn't hurt her appetite for jewelry, but I'm too nice. Maybe she thought purple was semi-mourning. If so, the bright pink pants detracted.

Belinda said, "Now, Twinkie, Cat hardly knew Chuck. And as far as her appetite is concerned, she's been in the cockpit all night. She hasn't even slept. You did, but she didn't. The least we can do is feed her."

Twinkie shrugged. Not very graciously, but she kept quiet after that.

Emery was washing dishes. Belinda said, "You've done enough. Go get some sleep, Emery."

"I don't want you to do them, Mrs. Honeywell. You've been awake as long as I have."

"We'll leave them until lunch. We may even be in port by then."

"All right."

Daniel took a look at Emery's scalp wound. "Not bad," he said. He swabbed it with hydrogen peroxide. Emery mentioned that his chest was sore.

I said, "I think he hit his chest on the edge of the table when he fell."

Daniel felt around the rib cage.

"You may have broken a rib." He smiled at Emery. "No heavy lifting until we can get you to an X ray."

"Okay."

"Take an aspirin. Call me in the morning."

Emery went forward to the three-berth dorm, which the men seemed to be taking over. Twinkie and Belinda were going to use the two-berth dorm aft. Twinkie was already there. I wasn't going to get any sleep for a while, anyway, and I surely didn't want to sleep with a wet spinnaker or a corpse.

Before she went back to lie down, Belinda said, "In spite of what I told Twinkie, it's too bad nobody is really sad about him."

"About Chuck?" I said.

"Yes. Somebody—" her head drooped tiredly—"somebody ought to be sorry for him."

I caught Daniel's eye.

"Before you go to bed," I said, "could you tell us a couple of things?"

"Of course."

"When you found Chuck this morning, where was the knife?"

She shivered. "Lying on his chest—or maybe a little lower than that. On his abdomen."

I had my notebook out. Wrote that down. For just a flicker of a second I was worried about what would happen to my article. Would it be junked? Would I get paid anyway? Would I cover the murder instead? But I put it out of my mind.

"The knife wasn't in his hand?"

"Oh, no."

"Was his hand over it?" I asked.

"No. No, I don't think so. I shouldn't have picked it up. That was stupid."

"The handle's porous wood. Looks like it's been washed a thousand times. I wouldn't think it'd take good prints."

"It was stupid just the same."

I said, "Okay, it was stupid." She smiled. "How was it lying?" I asked. "Handle to the left or right? Sharp point of the blade aimed which way?"

"Um." Her eyes got that unfocused look people have when they're trying to picture something from memory. 'The handle was toward me. That would have been his left. It was across his body. Parallel to the belt line?"

"I see." Chuck had been right-handed.

"As far as the sharp part, I don't remember. Oh, dear."

Now she was remembering too vividly. She was shivering. I wanted to tell her to go to bed, but there was one thing more I had to know.

"You didn't move the body?"

"Move it? Good God, no."

That sounded true to me. Daniel looked at me, caught my assent, and said, "Go to bed now. Get warm. Sleep."

"Yes, doctor."

Daniel and I sat alone, finishing our coffee. There was still an air of constraint between us. I ate one last piece of muffin and stretched out my legs under the table. My foot kicked an object.

"What's this?" I reached under the bench.

It was one of the bottles from the medical kit. I put it on the table.

"Syrup of ipecac," I read.

"Where was it?"

"Must've rolled under the table last night."

"Let me see."

"Ipecac is an antidote for poison, isn't it?"

Daniel said, "No, not really. It's an emetic. It doesn't counteract any specific poison. It makes you regurgitate the stuff."

"Oh, well. We certainly don't need that. We've had enough—um—"

"Right."

"I'll leave it for Emery to put back."

"Never mind. I'll do it." He put the bottle in his pocket.

• 16 •

"All right," Daniel said. "You're mad at me."

"Not really. Disappointed."

"Oh, hell. What can I say? I'm reluctant—"

"Reluctant to admit we've got a killer on board."

"Well, sure! Point one: how did anybody get in there without being seen? Suicide is the most likely explanation. Point two: if somebody did it, who? These people are my friends. Which doesn't prove them innocent, but think about it. Will? He's a good guy. Good all the way through. Belinda is a darling. Very family oriented. Not flighty. Bill? You going to clap the kid in irons and sail to some port?"

"No, and while you're at it, I can't imagine that Mary cared enough about Chuck one way or the other to kill him. But she had the best opportunity."

"Takuro?" Daniel said. "He's a calm, sweet-natured, scholarly person. Bret? He's tried to be a good guest. He was sick, and he was trying not to upset everybody else. Greg's the most likely, but frankly, I can't believe it."

"I can solve your problem."

"How?"

"We'll pin it on Twinkie."

"You really dislike that woman, don't you?"

"I think she's vain, lazy, backbiting, snide, egocentric, nasty, and a tease. If you want to think I don't like her, that's your business."

"Oh, hell."

"You said that before." I stood up. "Let's get to work. Let's go find Mary."

"She's probably with Bill."

"No kidding. Well, that's okay with me. If they wanted to cook up a story, they've had all night to do it."

Mary's feet were dangling over the bow of the motionless boat. Bill sat folded up next to her, his arms around his knees.

"What do you remember about last night?" Daniel asked Bill. Well, it was fine with me if he wanted to start with him. Why not?

"You mean after midnight, or when?"

"Say from when the boom hit you on the head."

"I saw stars. The next thing I remember is lying on the rug in the galley, and you were asking me questions. Silly questions—" he smiled—"like what day it was."

"Trying to tell how badly you were concussed."

"Sure. I know. Well, after that, there was a lot of fuss, but I couldn't raise my head to see. I think somebody stepped on me about then."

"It's possible."

"Then Mary and somebody helped me into a bunk. I'm not much use to you, I guess, as far as knowing what went on."

"Actually, we took you in quite a while later," Mary said. "You'd been out or dazed or something."

I said, "Okay. Now you're in the berth in the room next to the master stateroom where Chuck was. What did you see or hear after that?"

"Scraps. Somebody must have spilled something in the galley, because there was some yelling about cleaning up. Hey, that was you. You ticked somebody off about not helping."

Daniel looked at me with one eyebrow raised. I shrugged. "I guess I did."

"Then—I remember Mary whispering at one point. I was half asleep. She was trying not to wake me up. That's all I remember until this morning when Mom screamed."

"Okay," I said. Then, on impulse, realizing how little I knew about Bill, I asked, "You want to go into your father's business someday?"

"No!" He blinked at the loudness of his response. Probably his head still ached.

"Your dad want you to?"

"He *wants* me to, but he won't insist, if you know what I mean. He doesn't talk about it anymore. He used to say things like when I took over, I'd probably want to do modern furniture and lots of glass and so on. This was about five years ago. Now he doesn't. I mean, he can see I don't want to produce furniture. I worry about it. I mean, it's—um—been in the family so long, and I think it hurts him. But he's been—"

Mary said, "He's been really respectful of Bill's wishes. Not like a lot of parents. He treats him like a person."

"He wants me to do what I want to do."

"And what's that?"

Bill's face turned blood red. I don't often see young men blush. In my profession, I run into young rock stars with P.R. agents or young crooks who are slick as Teflon. Bill was about twenty, and probably shy, I realized. He had the kind of honesty that shy people often have: they can't make small talk. If they could fabricate some snappy answer, they wouldn't need to blush.

"I want to be a poet."

Mary said, "You are a poet."

"No, no. Not yet." He was very serious about this.

It occurred to me to say that poetry was not financially rewarding. Then I realized that might force him to admit he had a rich father, which in turn would make him sound like a parasite. I half believed Bill wouldn't mind bagging groceries for a living while he wrote poetry. But unlike most people, he would not have to.

My guess was he'd take over the business eventually and write his poetry in his spare time. Which would probably be less and less. Sad? Well, he was still one of the world's lucky ones.

"Mary," I said. "You were awake all night?"

"Yes. I don't sleep well in storms. And I was watching—" she made a wry smile and aimed her head at Bill—"this one."

"Did you see anybody go in the master stateroom after we put Chuck to bed?"

"No."

"Were you watching the door?"

"In a way. Not every minute, of course."

"Didn't you leave to go to the bathr—head?"

"Not during the night."

"Did you see anybody?"

"Twinkie came in late. Into our room. I think somebody'd given her a sleeping pill."

"Did anybody else come to that end of the hall at all?"

"Oh, Emery did once. To see if I wanted some coffee. He knew I was sitting up. He could see me from the dinette area. He went back and got me coffee with lots of cream and sugar in it. We were whispering because we didn't want to wake Bill up. Emery's really nice. It's kind of awkward, because he's about our age, and he works for Bill's dad and—I just don't like it if he feels he has to wait on us like a servant. It's awkward."

"I can see that. When he brought the coffee, he didn't go into the master stateroom?"

"No."

"Could someone have slipped past while you were checking up on Bill?"

"I don't see how. I guess a person could sneak by if my back were turned. The carpet is quite thick. But I was facing the door. Bill was asleep and I was sitting on the floor with my back against the bunk. That's what you want to know, isn't it?"

That was what we wanted to know.

Mary said, "Cat, is it true that Chuck's throat was cut?"

"Sure. We'd hardly say so if it wasn't."

"I know. What I really mean is, you wouldn't think anybody would choose that way of killing himself."

"No, you wouldn't."

Daniel said, "It has happened before." I gave him one of my serious looks.

Mary said, "But that's what must have happened, isn't it?"

"Suicide, you mean?" I said. "Why?"

"Unless he was killed right when you left him. Or when you went in this morning."

"We don't think so."

"Because nobody else went in there all night. Nobody at all. It's impossible."

Daniel and I walked back along the deck in silence. There were visible traces of the storm. Two of the lifeline stanchions were bent, one amidships and one where Greg had nearly gone overboard. The radar reflector still hung in the rigging, useful now because of the fog. The deck was slippery with water that had not dried and would not dry until we got some sun.

Greg and Will were in the cockpit. "Why haven't you started the motor?" I asked, surprised.

Greg said, "He's going to. He's been resisting. Took him fifteen minutes to work himself up to it. Sailors are purists."

Will said, "We don't carry enough fuel to drive all over the lake. Plus, it's not a fast way for us to get around. We're not built like a cruiser." He paused. "Well, we have to get poor Chuck—poor Chuck's—anyway—"

"Stop hoping for wind," Greg said.

Will turned on the ignition and the motor purred into life. It was reassuring to hear the throb below. There is something dead about a sailboat without a breath of wind, let alone with a body belowdecks. Idle as a painted ship—

Will let it warm a minute, then shifted out of neutral. The boat glided forward, turning due east, leaving a crescent-shaped wake that faded off into the fog behind us.

Then the engine died.

"What the hell?" said Will.

"Oh, just start her up again," Greg said. "It's damp down there."

Will started it again. For a couple of seconds. Then it died. After it died, we heard gulls calling overhead. We could not see them because of the fog.

Will tried the starter again. It whined, but would not start.

"Is it flooded?" I asked.

"You can't flood a diesel motor. It doesn't have a carburetor." Will tried it again. It choked and sputtered, choked and sputtered again, then died into a whine.

"That's funny," he said. "It just won't go."

· 17 ·

Diesel engines are not found on most sailboats, according to Will. Most use gasoline. In fact, most small sailboats use a gasoline outboard. Outboards are less troublesome generally than inboards, and of course, when your outboard gets cranky, you can just take it off and leave it with a repairman and go on using your boat without power.

Naturally, an outboard on a boat the size of the *Easy Girl* would be ridiculous. Kind of like powering a stretch limo by mounting a Honda on the right rear bumper. But an inboard brings all kinds of complications. You need sound-proofing, which involves putting the engine down in an enclosed space somewhere and surrounding it with sound-absorbing material. Which makes it hard to get at. Then you need a shaft through the hull for your prop, and that means you can get leaks. Plus, you've got a permanently installed fuel tank and fuel lines. And naturally your internal combustion monster needs to breathe—you need an air intake and an exhaust.

Now, the gasoline engines used are mostly converted automobile engines. And they need an electrical system. The diesel doesn't, except for an electric starter. No spark plugs, for instance. It ought to be less temperamental than a gasoline engine.

So the question was: why wasn't it working?

The engine lived in the stern of the boat, under the cockpit. Will decided that since the sails were down and there was no wind, it would be okay for him to leave the wheel and for him and Greg and Daniel to take a look at the engine. As long as I sat there and blew the horn.

Will had been blowing it for an hour, so how could I complain? But it's boring. Blow a long blast, two short blasts. Wait about a minute and a half. Do it again. Wait. Do it again.

At first you feel like a kid playing tugboat in the bathtub, and it's fun. But it loses its novelty rapidly. I started out looking at the sweep hand of my watch to time the two minutes between blasts. After a while, I found myself looking at my watch and forgetting where the second hand had been when I first looked. Was this, I wondered, the first or the second time the stupid hand had swept past twelve?

For a while, I decided to toot my horn on every even minute. 7:52. 7:54. 7:56. 7:58. 8:00. There was a certain amount of excitement generated by blowing the horn on the exact stroke of 8:00 A.M. I felt like the night watch for a city: "Eight o'clock and all's well."

Of course, all wasn't well. Still—

By eight-fourteen that thrill had worn off. I stopped looking at my watch. I just waited a while, then tooted my horn. Was the Coast Guard going to be tooling around out here, giving tickets for inept whistle blowing? Come to think of it, let 'em. Let 'em show up, give us a ticket, tow us to port, and take over the body of Chuck Kroop.

And let me get off this floating house party.

No such luck.

After listening to gobbledygook from down in the bilge for twenty minutes, I lost patience and called: "How you doing down there?"

A head popped up with its hair matted. Daniel.

"Not too well."

"What's wrong with it?"

"Might have had some water forced into a wrong spot during the storm. There's a lot of pressure generated when waves crash into a boat."

"You don't have to tell me!"

"Acts like there's water in the fuel."

"Shouldn't the fuel lines be ready for that? I mean, the manufacturers don't expect the boats to spend their whole lives in a room at the McCormick Place Boat Show."

"That's the question all right."

Daniel pointed at the horn. I had missed a couple of blasts. I blew the damned thing.

I said, "So—did somebody sabotage it?"

"I don't know."

"Wouldn't that put him in as much danger as the rest of us?"

"We're not in *any* danger. It just delays us. You can sail all over the world in an unpowered boat this size."

"Oh." I thought about it. "It just delays us."

I didn't like that very much, either. Daniel might have agreed with me, but he didn't say so in words. He climbed out of the engine hold. "I'm going to wake up Takuro," he said. "Maybe he can do something. You keep blowing your horn."

With Takuro consulting on the internal combustion question, it was pretty crowded down there. Greg and Will got out and let Daniel and Takuro have a go at it. Bill and Mary came and peeked in, but Bill didn't claim any knowledge of engines. He volunteered to go and fetch tools. Mary finally said she was going to get some sleep, even if she had to sleep under a wet spinnaker, and Bill said that somehow or other he would get the spinnaker out of her way.

I had a sudden idea. The engine mounting space backed up to the aft wall of the master stateroom. Maybe there was a way through! I edged over to the engine well and looked in.

Shoot! Another great idea that had no foundation in fact. The wall between the space where the motor lived and the master stateroom was smooth, featureless, continuous white fiberglass. Which, now that I thought about it, made sense. You wouldn't want your elegant master stateroom even to have a chance of leaking in engine fumes.

Greg took over the horn. Greg, in fact, was a changed man this morning—helpful, cheerful, courteous. If I could have proven him clean and reverent, I would have given him our Boy Scout Fog Survival merit badge.

Tools were passed down. Tools came clattering back up again. There was talk about an awful lot of water in the bilge, which didn't upset the sailors, as far as I could see, but to landlubbers like me is only a step away from sinking. To me the very best thing a boat can do is stay dry inside.

There were commands to try the ignition and commands to stop trying the ignition. There was a long period of silence. Takuro asked for a bottle or jar. I got one from the galley. Daniel got a piece of hose from the cockpit locker. I waited, listening to our horn and looking out at the endless fog. Somebody coughed in the engine well.

Finally, Daniel and Takuro climbed out of the well and slammed the top. This restored the floor of the cockpit.

Daniel said, "No go."

Takuro held up a bottle of diesel fuel. "I think there's water in the fuel lines."

"Well, we can survive without it," Will said.

Takuro said, "Sure. I think I'll go back to bed."

There's a big difference psychologically between having an engine and not using it and having an engine you know is not working. Maybe there shouldn't be, but there is.

"Probably get a breeze soon," Will said.

Daniel said, "Maybe."

"Never saw a really long calm," Will said.

"Oh, not more than a day or so."

"All right, all right. You win."

I asked, "What are you two talking about?"

"Using the radio. I know Will doesn't want to call for help—"

"Never have before."

"But this time is different."

Greg said, "I'll take the horn and the wheel both. There isn't a thing moving out there anyway."

"And I'll go below," Will said, looking sick, "and call the Coast Guard."

"Try it again."

"I was," Daniel said calmly.

Will was not so calm. "Try clicking this off and on, then."

"Will, that's not going to help. We could try kicking it, too."

"We've never had any problem with it."

"Let's get the front off and see."

The radio was built into the wall behind a panel of woven teak, which of course matched the rest of the woven teak belowdecks. It was a complicated radio, with commercial stations, weather and Coast Guard bands, and telephone.

There was a screwdriver in its own little drawer under the tuning panel. Nothing but the best. Daniel rotated the screws and pulled them out of the panel. I think he thought Will was too shaken up to hold them, so he put them in the little drawer.

Carefully, he pulled the panel off to get at the innards.

It rattled.

As the panel came away, flecks of solder, pieces of wire, and a piece or two of plastic fell out on the blue carpet.

We gaped at the scrambled guts of the thing.

After a moment, Daniel said, "Well, hell, Will. You didn't want to call the Coast Guard anyhow."

Emery had napped, risen, washed the breakfast dishes, then made a meal that will sound inappropriate for lunch in July. But on this particular clammy, foggy day it was exactly right. He had baked all the potatoes left on board. He broiled steaks to order. There was sour cream with or without chives for the potatoes, and butter, though we were beginning to run low on that. There was hot coffee, hot tea, and hot cocoa. He made a green salad, and that was the only thing that was not eaten to the last bite.

Everybody aboard snarfed it up as if it were their last meal.

All of the living, that is.

There was a definite pall over the party. Belinda, Greg, Emery, and I cleaned up. Then Greg, who had been awake all night and manning the cockpit all morning, went to bed. Bret took a turn at sounding the horn while Belinda sat at the wheel.

Daniel and I decided between us that I would sleep for an hour, then he would. The other one was supposed to keep generally alert for whatever.

The rest of the crowd was at loose ends. Twinkie had a deck of cards out and was playing solitaire, having asked Greg to play gin and having been told he was going to sleep. I think Mary went back to bed. I headed for an upper bunk in the three-bed dormitory, the one I had disliked when I first boarded the boat. I was too tired to be fussy anymore.

I borrowed a sleeping bag off the floor and slithered into it dressed. I mean, we were into serious survival action here. The bag was as cold as the rest of the boat, but I counted on body heat to warm it up.

I fell half-asleep thinking of the corpse on board. Suddenly, the whole master stateroom popped into my mind, as clear as if I were looking at it. There was a hatch in the ceiling of the room! It was there for light and air and I suppose for dumping sails down, like the hatch in the bow. I supposed it could be opened from outside, like the one in the bow.

Could somebody have opened it during the night, slipped down into the master stateroom, slit Chuck's throat, and climbed out again?

As I fell asleep, I could almost picture a shadow sliding through the open hatch. Somebody thin—

Daniel shook me awake. I was in his sleeping bag, and he would take it over. It was time for me to get up.

"Any developments?"

"Nothing. Oh, yes. One big piece of news. Twinkie actually volunteered to blow the horn."

"Brave of her. How long did she last?"

"Fifteen minutes."

"Everybody is becoming public spirited, aren't they? Have a nice rest."

I decided to walk the boat like a cop walking a beat. I could cover the whole boat in four minutes without rushing.

Emery was in the galley wringing his hands. Or coming as close as any twenty-year-old kid these days is going to come. What he was actually doing was standing in front of the open refrigerator, looking inside and pounding one fist into the other palm.

To cheer him up, I said, "Discover a body in the cooler?"

He jumped a foot. "What?"

"I meant, what seems to be the trouble?" I rocked up and down on the balls of my feet, imitating a London bobby.

He was either too upset to notice or he hadn't seen the same movies I had. He said, "I gotta get to a grocery store." I had not realized this was our major problem. I thought a dead body in a berth and a sabotaged motor and radio was it. I said, "Why?"

"We're practically out of food."

"That can't be. I saw tons of it."

"We ate it. Oh, there are a few odds and ends. We've got lots of champagne. But we were figuring to be in Holland or Saugatuck by breakfast today. I mean, you're never that far from someplace when you're out here. I mean, you wouldn't be that far from anything if everything was the way everything usually is—"

"I understand. Don't go on. You couldn't anticipate this. Do you think the Honeywells are going to blame *you?*"

"Oh, no! They told me the itinerary, after all. And they're very nice people." His voice trailed off.

"You're worried."

"Well, they might wonder—I could have put some hamburger in the freezer. But they're *very* nice people."

He started pounding one fist into the palm of the other hand again.

"Don't think about it. Maybe a breeze will come up and we'll all get seasick."

"Oh, the Honeywells never get seasick," he said. Then he had misgivings about how that sounded. "I wouldn't want them to, I mean. They've been very decent to me. Hell, they're really very nice people."

"Emery, did you see anybody go into the stateroom where Chuck was during the night?"

"No. Nobody."

I left him. Since he was so distressed, I did not make the other cheering remark that crossed my mind. The one about it not being necessary to turn cannibal yet.

• 18 •

Bret, Twinkie, and Greg were playing cards at the dinette like one big happy family. I nodded to them as I went by. Greg said, "Want to be dealt in?"

"Thanks, but no. Maybe later."

Up on deck, Will Honeywell sat alone in the cockpit. He wasn't even touching the wheel. After all, he wasn't going anywhere. He picked up the horn and sounded one long and two shorts. "I'll do that," I said, taking the horn.

"I think we're just about to run out of compressed gas."

"Then what do we do?"

"Then we sit here and hope nothing runs into us."

"Well, the other ship should have a horn."

"Yeah, but we can't move. If it can't tell we're here and it's coming toward us, we can't get out of the way."

"We could bang on a saucepan with a spoon."

"Say, there's a bell someplace below. We could ring that."

Great! We would become a leper boat.

I was blowing the horn, pausing, blowing it again, and getting plenty bored, looking at my feet, when I noticed a strange thing. I was casting a shadow.

"Will!" I said. "Look!"

He must have been dozing—small wonder—when I spoke, because he jumped and looked out at the water.

"No," I pointed up at the sky. "Look!"

The fog was still there, but it had taken on a brassy glow.

At the zenith was a round, glowing, pale yellow disc, no brighter than a moon.

"The fog's burning off!" Will said.

I looked at my shadow again. It was fuzzy before; it was less fuzzy now. I tooted my horn again, this time with verve, if you can imagine verve in one long and two shorts. On the second short I got half a short. I blew it again and got half a splutter.

"It's gone."

"And we don't need it," Will said.

"Now that's the kind of coincidence I really enjoy."

Awareness of the sun's coming out had spread through our gallant crew. Everybody made for the deck. There had been a graveyard feeling to the cold boat, plus being trapped below with a corpse was dampening by itself.

Speaking of dampening, all the wet clothing came out on deck with the people. Emery started it, bringing out towels and dishrags to dry. Within a matter of minutes, the entire lifeline all the way around was festooned with sweaters, slickers, shirts, towels, pants, socks, rags, and even a couple of sleeping bags. We looked like a Chinese junk on washing day.

And speaking of the dead, there was another curious example of human behavior. When the sun came out, it quickly got warm on deck. But nobody put on a bathing suit. There were shorts and cutoffs and pants, and people lay in the sun on towels, but no swimsuits. I think a kind of respect for the dead was operating.

There was still no breeze, but the mood aboard was a hundred percent better.

I woke Daniel after giving him nearly two hours of sleep. I wanted to have a serious talk with him, but it was hard to find a private spot.

The deck was full of people, but even below wasn't very private. Conversations in the galley or dinette carried right

up the companionway stairs. Even a conversation in the forward cabin would be heard by anybody lying near the hatch
up on deck.

But of a bad lot, the forward cabin seemed the best. We
tightened down the hatch cover and closed the door.

Daniel flopped onto a V-berth and pushed back until he
leaned against the anchor-line locker which formed the very
front end of the cabin. I sat on the same berth, facing him,
leaning back against the aft wall of the room.

The red-white-and-blue spinnaker lay neatly folded on the
other bed, on top of two white sails.

"You're right," Daniel said. "It's time to be systematic."

"Okay. Personnel. Besides you and me and Chuck, there
are nine people on board: Will, Belinda, Bill, Mary, Greg,
Twinkie, Takuro, Bret, and Emery."

"Right. And some of those are unthinkable as killers."

"Let's do physical possibility first and worry about psycho-
logical possibilities later."

He smiled. "You think anybody is capable of doing almost
anything."

"Not quite. But I think I don't know what people will do."

"Realistic."

"So—ingress and egress." I told him about my vision of
somebody slipping in the hatch.

"We can check it. At least whether it opens from outside.
I have to admit, I don't remember that. Still—it's so close
to the wheel. Somebody would have noticed. Will, Belinda,
Takuro, and I were at the wheel most of the time."

"Can the wheel be lashed down?"

"So that it would sail without being attended? You're
thinking one of them—one of us slipped down and killed
him during the night. Or two of us. Or three of us. While
you were below."

"Who knows?"

He nodded rather grimly. What could he do? What could

I do, for that matter? I liked Daniel. But if he was a murderer, I'd better find out before I got to liking him too much.

"Now, what about the key?" I said. "If the hatch doesn't prove out, then somebody went in the door. You had a key. Belinda had a key. I had a key."

"And Belinda said she left one in the galley drawer."

"Right. But that lets out people who wouldn't have known it was there."

"Bret."

"That's all?"

"Well, Cat, Takuro was the designer. He may always have had a key. Twinkie and Greg and Bill and Mary have been sailing on the *Easy Girl* before. Maybe Belinda always leaves the keys in that drawer. She got them out of that drawer, remember?"

"Hell. You're right."

"I think," he said seriously, "we'd better see if any of the rest of them remember somebody going into the master stateroom."

I've known people like Twinkie before. She's got to act like she knows more than she's telling. She's got to say things in secretive, tantalizing ways. She's got to make herself sound important. She's got to flirt.

She's got to be the most boring person in the world.

"I'll make a deal," she said.

Daniel said, "What about?"

"Tell me all about what happened to Chuck."

"It won't be much more than we've already said. His throat was cut. The knife was found on his body. He was lying in the berth where we had put him, and there was no indication that he'd moved since we laid him down there."

"What time?"

"What time did he die? Most likely between three and four-thirty in the morning."

"No booby traps?"

"You mean, like a knife that sprang out of the wall and sliced his throat? No. There was absolutely no indication of anything like that."

"And if I'm not mistaken," Twinkie said, "you people had locked the door."

"Yes."

"Then I guess you *do* have a problem."

"Okay. You said you'd tell us what you remember."

"Fair enough. I wasn't looking down the hall every minute."

I said, "It would sound odd to me if you said you had been."

She glared at me, then dismissed me. "I am quite sure, though, that I would have noticed if somebody went into Chuck's room. The stateroom. Because I would have thought, that's all we need now is to let him out."

Daniel said, "Right."

"Emery went to the room where Bill and Mary were once. Then he went back a minute later with coffee. I did *not* see him go into Chuck's room.

"I left the dinette twice when I wasn't feeling well. So anything could have happened while I was gone. Except— wouldn't you think that even if I was gone when somebody slipped in, I would likely have been back when the person slipped out?"

I said, "Yeah."

She continued to talk to Daniel, not me. "Plus, I was gone a little while after an unpleasant incident occurred. Bret is so embarrassed this morning."

"Not his fault."

"No. Well, that's it. Now, if I think of anything else, I'll be sure to let you know. Daniel, you should come out on deck. You could use some sun; you need a little more color in your face."

"Later, Twinkie. Could you send Greg down?"

"Of course. Just like a movie. What fun!"

*   *   *

Greg flapped his large hands and pulled his bushy eyebrows together. "What I remember of the evening, huh? Well, it could hardly be what I've forgotten of the evening. Silly way of putting it. Hmm. I'm wandering.

"Well, after you chucked Chuck in the bunk, Daniel—by the way, I wasn't very gracious about all that. Sorry. Let's see, Twinkie held the ice on my neck and Mary took Bill to lie down—"

He went on in some detail about the evening. His recollections were more specific than Twinkie's, but no more helpful. He knew who'd had coffee and who'd had cocoa and remarked on the fact that Emery had not sat down once until he crashed into the table. But he didn't remember anybody going to the master stateroom. Emery took coffee to Mary, yes. Stateroom, no.

"I'd have noticed if I thought somebody was going to let Chuck out. I can tell you that! Then, with Bret cleaning himself off in the galley and Twinkie in the head and Emery sitting on the floor bleeding, Cat here got a little sharp with me. Which was absolutely justified. I was being unpleasant."

"You had cause," I said.

"No, I had cause to feel nasty. I did not have cause to take it out on people who weren't to blame. While I'm apologizing, let me say that I felt nasty because of Chuck, but the reason I didn't get up to help with the cleaning up was— you know how it is when you've been angry. During the fight I was just so damn furious! And after you've lost your temper and cooled down, you feel completely wrung out."

Daniel and I made agreeing mumbles, but I wondered, was Greg claiming to be so wrung out as a way of saying he was too exhausted by then to have killed anybody?

"Was this the first run-in you've had with Chuck?" Daniel asked.

"No. Not exactly. But the first that came to blows. He's been hanging around Twinkie more and more. I realize that half the problem is that she lets him. He doesn't understand, though. Didn't understand. Twinkie was just having fun."

"You mean teasing him?" Daniel said. "Toying with him?"

"In a way. You know how she is, Daniel. I sometimes think half her trouble is that she gets bored so easily. She's very quick-witted. Very bright. She gets bored. Then she tries to shake things up, one way or another."

Well, in my work I've heard lots of excuses—

"Sure, that could be it," Daniel said judiciously. "After Cat barked at you—"

"Cat wouldn't let Emery work while his head was bleeding. After a while Cat went back on deck, and then a little later you guys yelled down that you were closing the hatch while you tacked west. During all that time, I never saw anybody go down the hall to the master stateroom. Later you opened the hatch and Takuro came down for sandwiches. Twinkie went to bed. I gave her a sleeping pill. Bret and I sat at the dinette. Emery messed around in the galley, and we finally talked him into sitting down. It was very, very rough. I could imagine the kind of beating you people were taking on deck."

"At the dinette," I asked, "who faced toward the stateroom?"

"At first we were moving around some. After Twinkie left, Emery, Bret, and I just sat around. I was facing the stateroom all of the time after that, because I didn't get up. Emery sat next to me. We let Bret sit by himself on the other side of the table so he could get up in a hurry if he needed to."

Daniel said, "Okay, then. I guess that's it."

Greg stood up. "Daniel, I've been thinking. Most of the evening there were at least four people in the galley area. Even after Twinkie went to bed, there were three of us. If one of us had gone to the stateroom door, the others would have known it. Who's going to be stupid enough to walk in and kill Chuck, knowing there are several people who will surely see him either going in or coming out? And he'd have had to walk past the door where Mary was, too."

"Well, that's the whole question, isn't it?" Daniel said.

"It's impossible."

I said, "Um."

"Anyhow. Hmm. Have I been any help to you?"

Daniel and I spoke simultaneously.

He said, "Yes."

I said, "No."

Bret had been so sick that he wouldn't have noticed if a green sea monster had slithered down the companionway steps, broken into the stateroom, swallowed Chuck whole, burped, and left by way of the forward hatch. He admitted it.

"I was mainly trying not to disgrace myself," he said. "I felt so stupid, an elegant woman like Belinda up and running the boat, and there I was sick as a dog and worthless."

He didn't remember Emery's taking coffee to Mary.

But he did remember that Emery was sympathetic to him. "People who don't get seasick aren't very sympathetic to people who do. Emery brought me water and Dramamine."

"Who was unsympathetic?" I asked.

"Chuck. He came down for something or other just before the fight and saw that I wasn't feeling too well. He said, 'Try acting. Make believe you feel well.' Do you suppose—maybe he meant it as a real suggestion. Power of positive thinking. That sort of thing."

"Who else?"

"Well, Twinkie said I should 'fight it.' As if I wasn't trying. Of course," he added with a trace of satisfaction, "that was before she got nauseated herself."

*   *   *

"It's not that I want to pry," Takuro said. "But if you really think we've got a killer on board, I'd like to know. After all," he said with his head cocked, "we're all in the same boat."

Daniel laughed. I said, "I couldn't have expressed it better."

Takuro said that he was on deck continuously after the fight, except when he went down for sandwiches.

"When I went down for the sandwiches," he said, "I certainly did not go into Chuck's room."

"What were the others doing?" Daniel asked.

"Sitting around the dinette looking green."

On impulse I asked, "How do you feel about Chuck's death?"

Takuro sighed. "I would like to be more—to feel that I would miss him more. I'm sorry he's dead, and I'm sorry he died quite young. I've worked with Chuck for many years. I've designed furniture for him for a long time. He wasn't easy to work with. He was a man of inadequate serenity."

Will remembered nothing after yo-ho-ho and a bottle of rum, and he wasn't sure which yo-ho-ho was the last he remembered.

I told Daniel what Emery had said about not seeing anybody go into Chuck's room. Emery was, by far, the person aboard most likely to have noticed, because he was always watching to see whether one of the Honeywells' guests needed something.

We looked at each other. Less antagonistically than before. We got up, opened the cabin door, and strolled up the stairs.

The sun was low and copper-colored. The water to the west looked like hammered brass. There was neither cloud nor breeze in the sky.

The cocktail hour had come once again to the *Easy Girl.*

• 19 •

"But *why*," said Twinkie, "is there no food?"

Belinda rolled her eyes up.

Twinkie said, "Don't you people *plan* these things? Don't you people realize that winds are not at your beck and call?"

"We thought we'd be in Holland this morning," Belinda said patiently. "The steaks you had at lunch were the emergency rations. Anyway, there is some food. There's a small amount of tuna fish salad. You can have mine."

"Tuna?" said Twinkie. "*Gawd!*"

"And all the champagne anyone could possibly want," Emery said eagerly, trying to make things better.

"I'm just curious," Greg said. "How much champagne is there?"

"Four dozen bottles," said Emery.

Twinkie gasped, "Four dozen bottles! Why, you could practically distill it and use it for fuel! Why so much champagne? Couldn't you use the same space for extra food?"

Emery looked hangdog, but Will jumped into the conversation, using his chairman-of-the-board manner. Now that I was getting used to Will, I realized this meant Twinkie was not behaving well, according to his standards.

"Fresh food is perishable. Champagne properly cared for, is not. What's more important, western Michigan is one of the prime fruit and vegetable growing areas of the world. Especially for blueberries and raspberries and peaches this time of the summer. We get the best quality produce shopping at the farmers' markets there as we go."

"Well, it doesn't seem to have worked out very well this time."

"Things have worked out even worse for Chuck," Will said grimly.

Emery said, "Plus, we have *plenty* of caviar!"

I saw Greg put his hand on Twinkie's shoulder. "There's something unpleasantly let-them-eat-cake about this conversation," he said. "I'll tell you what. I'll be brave and live on champagne and caviar this evening."

My wounded article on sailing with the rich popped into my mind. Could I use this? Was there any hope at all of getting a coherent piece out of this mess? What was I going to do?

There was an odd, manic restlessness about our crew as evening came on, and I don't think it was just the champagne. Although champagne is strange stuff. Actually, champagne and caviar wasn't really all we had. There was flour, some condiments, and a few staples. There was also some soda pop, brandy, rum, bourbon, vodka, liqueurs, tea, cocoa, and coffee left. I made up a brandy and coffee, the sedate version of mixing uppers and downers.

There was also some Cheez Whiz, which goes well with a modest little Armagnac.

The natives, as I was saying, were restless. The whole, long, dreadful day had done something to their nerves. Plus, we were looking out at a lot of nothing. The lake was dead calm. There were no clouds. Darkening blue above, blue below, and here we sat.

An occasional seagull cocked his head at us and went on. We saw a freighter in the distance once, but we had no way of hailing it, it was so far off.

Greg, with his new cheer and in his new role as master of festivities, organized a combined poker and sundown party on deck. The sun sets slowly here in midsummer, and the deck stays warm until the last rays are gone.

"Everybody get out coins," he said.

Will, Greg, Bret, and I were the players at first. Daniel and several others were taking a second nap.

"I don't think I can afford this," I said. When playing with the very rich, it's good to make it clear beforehand exactly where you stand.

"Just penny ante!"

"Well, all right, but I reserve the right to quit while I'm ahead."

"Think you're gonna be ahead, huh?"

"Sure I will."

Greg dealt five cards. I had a pair of deuces, and deuces were not wild. Will asked for one card. Bret two. I wanted three. I got a pair of fours and a queen. Hmm. Greg took none at all.

Two pair. I bet a whole nickel. Will folded, having probably hoped to fill a straight or a flush and failed. Greg raised a dime. I called.

And won. Greg had nothing at all and was trying to bluff me out.

I hadn't figured Greg for a bluffer. The sun sank to the horizon while I parlayed my winnings into more. Will was also winning, but slowly. He had a quiet, conservative strategy and never bet big bucks except on sure things. I learned not to try to bluff Will. Bret lost. He hadn't the head for it. He kept trying to read facial expressions rather than concentrate on the odds. But that's actors for you.

Greg won big and lost big, and on the whole tended to lose over time.

It was ten o'clock when the sun finally went down. Immediately it got chilly. We played a couple more hands, but the darker it got, the colder it got. When I noticed I was not the only one warming the unused hand under the other armpit, I suggested we go below.

By now there were several empty champagne bottles lying around on deck. I cleaned up a couple as we went down. We left a half-full one with Bill, who was sitting in the cockpit waiting for the wind that never came. He probably wouldn't drink it.

There was a caviar-and-champagne party going on in the dinette, so we sat on the floor to continue the game. At ten-thirty I said I had to go wake Daniel.

"Quitting while you're ahead," Greg said.

Bret said, "You can't do this. I'm $4.78 in the hole."

Will said, "Good businesswoman, Cat."

"Think of it this way," I said, scooping up the coins. "It's only fair to redistribute the wealth a little." I'd netted $5.92.

"Right," said Will. "Keep communism at bay a little longer."

Takuro took my place.

Daniel and I replaced Bill as cockpit watch. It was now very dark and very, very quiet on deck. The boat rode slowly up and down the most gradual of swells. You got more motion, and I'm not kidding, in an apartment high up in the swaying John Hancock Building in Chicago.

"Are yachting trips often this dull?" I asked, referring to the lack of motion.

"Last night wasn't dull."

"Last night was calamitous."

"Think of all you're learning."

"What am I learning right now?"

"How to sit still, I guess. No, seriously, usually they're fun."

"I had fun. Really, I did. Up to—um—about nine or ten last night. Are we going to get a wind soon, do you think?"

Daniel took my hand. "Not until morning would be my guess."

"Then why sit here on watch?"

"In case. If a breeze comes up, somebody has to know it.

If another boat came close, we'd signal for help with the
flashlight."

"What would they do? Tow us in?"

"Might. If it was a pleasure boat. Commercial boats don't.
If a freighter came by, it probably wouldn't even slow down.
But she might radio the Coast Guard if we sent up a flare."

I started to laugh.

"What's so funny?"

"Oh, I was just picturing Will's face. How he'd feel being
towed in to port by some little cabin cruiser."

Daniel had not released my hand. I stood up, pulling it
away in a moderately natural manner.

"We've got a good opportunity to check the hatch cover,"
I said. "Nobody's watching."

"All right."

I had to admit, with the hatch right there at the back of
the cockpit, it would have been hard to open it and harder
still to slide in without other people in the cockpit seeing.
Daniel was looking at the setup skeptically, too.

"Cat, even if somebody was alone at the wheel last night,
they couldn't have left the wheel without the boat going out
of control."

"They could lash it in place with something."

"What?"

"I'll figure that out later. Since it couldn't be suicide,
and since nobody could get in the stateroom door, it *has*
to be this."

I was fumbling with the screw-down latches shaped like
wing nuts that held the hatch cover tight against water leaks.

"Oh, all right," Daniel said. He unscrewed the two on
his side.

"Logic," I said. "This is the only possibility left."

I pulled up the hatch. It went up about four inches.

"Pull up on your side," I said.

He did. It went up about four inches, too.

"Come on. Try harder."

"Wait a minute."

He got the flashlight out of the cockpit locker and shined it inside at the hatch cover bolts. They ended directly below the frame, their ends covered by their own wing-nut latches. The hatch could be pushed up from below or pulled up from above. But only four inches. Plus, stapled to the frame was screening to keep out bugs.

"It's just for ventilation, I guess," Daniel said.

I was aghast. "Yeah. Gee. I suppose they never put any sails down into the master stateroom. They don't need it bigger."

"Nobody could get in there."

"Don't rub it in."

"Nobody with a head wider than four inches."

"I know! I can see that!"

◦ 20 ◦

In the galley, Twinkie was winning at gin. At first, I thought it was just plain luck. Then, after a while, I thought maybe she peeked at other players' cards when they didn't hold them close enough to their vest. Finally I decided I had been unfair to the woman; she was simply good at it.

Greg certainly wasn't. But he was cheerful.

"Champagne," he said. "You're getting low."

Emery proudly produced a box of saltine crackers he had found hiding somewhere. "You can spread caviar on these," he said.

Greg said, "Think of it as hardtack biscuit."

Will was watching Greg. I watched Will watch Greg, wondering what he was thinking. Will was in a rough position. He had to behave soberly out of respect to Chuck, and at the same time, he must have wanted his guests to have a reasonably good time.

Half an hour passed. Nobody seemed to want to go to bed.

"I've produced a midnight snack," Emery said proudly.

Groans from the group.

"Not more caviar!"

"Not Cheez Whiz sandwiches!"

"Cheez Whiz fondue?"

"Cheez Whiz à l'indienne?"

"Cheez Whiz à la grecque?"

"Watch out for Bret. We'll have Cheez Whiz à la whoops."

They laughed their way to the counter, where Emery was pouring warm brandy over a stack of crepes. He lit it and blue flames played all around.

"Good heavens!" said Belinda. "Crepes suzette."

Emery said, "We had flour and some eggs left. And lots of Cointreau."

"I'm not surprised about the Cointreau," Greg said. "The boat is a floating bar."

People grabbed for plates and forks and crepes.

To my amazement, Twinkie offered to go up and relieve Takuro at the wheel so that he could come down and have the last two crepes. With Greg cheery and Twinkie willing to pull her own weight, I could hardly have been more surprised if we got a breeze.

The gin game broke up. People were restless. Mary and Bill found a set of dominoes someplace. They invited the rest of us to play, in the nicest manner possible, but they were so obviously happy with each other's company that nobody had the heart to accept their invitation.

Greg went up on deck to take over the wheel from Twinkie. Belinda, Takuro, and Emery cleaned up the galley. People wandered around, too restless to sleep. They were as unsettled by the lack of motion of the boat as they had been by the violent motion the night before. They would take a turn around the deck, then come down and poke around the dinette and galley. I almost offered them one of my books.

After a while, Bret started singing. I think he did it first out of boredom, humming a tune to himself from their musical comedy. But then Takuro said, "Sing the other one. The cute one."

Bret laughed. "That isn't quite enough description."

"No. I know. I can't think—is it 'I Wish I Had a Way with Words'?"

It was. Bret sang it. He used a light Irish accent, and when he finished, everybody applauded.

"It's not one I sing in the show," he said.

It was probably the association with the Irish accent that led Bret to start singing "Danny Boy." After the first verse Mary joined in, with as pretty a soprano as I have ever heard. Bill sat there and glowed as she sang.

The old words drifted sweetly around the boat. They did not sing it as a dirge, but it was mournful. It made me, and the others I'm sure, think again of Chuck's death. It was a sort of farewell.

When they were done, no one applauded. We all sat still. Finally Bret said to Mary, "That was really *good.*" It was genuine praise, one singer to another.

Mary blushed.

Then Bret lightened the mood by singing "Inka Dinka Doo" in the manner of Jimmy Durante.

"Where's Twinkie?" Will said. "She'd enjoy this."

"Probably fixing her makeup," Greg said. He got up for a new supply of champagne.

Belinda took over the wheel-watching.

When the next song ended, Daniel and I went up on deck to exercise our muscles. It was cold, and the stars were hard and sharp. We stepped into the cockpit to see Belinda. She said hello, but her voice was not as cheerful as usual.

"What's the matter?" Daniel asked.

"Oh, the night, I think," she said. "It's eerie, just floating here. No landmarks. No motion."

It was that. The blackness was endless and the water made hardly any sound.

"I've been thinking too much," she said.

"About what?"

"Everything. What if we were stuck here for days? No food, no—"

"*If* we were," Daniel said, "we'd survive. No problem. We've got water, water everywhere out there, and it's all drinkable. Now, if we were becalmed on salt water—"

"If you're going to be becalmed, this is the best—" Suddenly, she covered her face and sobbed.

I put my arm around her shoulders. "What's really bothering you?" Daniel sat on her other side.

"It's such a horrible idea. It's—if we did have to stay here a long time—it's summer; it's warm in the days, at least." She shuddered. "I mean, we've got a body down there—it's been nearly twenty-four hours already."

I said, "Oh, I see." Decomposition. Rot. Stench.

Daniel said, "That simply won't happen. The weather is too changeable in Lake Michigan. We'll get wind."

"I know—"

"Belinda," he said, seizing her shoulders, "put it out of your mind. *It won't happen.* You're getting morbid, and that's not like you."

He sent her to bed. Ordered her to take two aspirins. Really. He said aspirins have a mild tranquilizing effect.

"Well," I said after a couple of minutes staring at the black, silent water, "it's no wonder she's at the breaking point. She's been carrying a lot of the load around here."

"You've been pretty gallant yourself."

I was startled. "What do you mean?"

"You were terrified last night, but you hung in there."

"It was a terrifying night. Everybody hung in. What was the alternative—walk to shore?"

"It wasn't just the night. You're terrified of water."

"I'd rather we didn't—"

"Don't get huffy. You're entitled to a phobia or two. My point is, you helped out where you could and you took everything the night could throw at you."

"Umm."

"Listen, I don't want to sound stupid here, but you're not married, are you?"

"Nope. Nor divorced, either."

"Committed to somebody?"

"I have two current significant others. Mike is a lot of fun. He's wild. And he has serious problems. John is very considerate, and very sedate."

"And very dull."

"Not exactly. Conservative. Hell, I don't know. He wants to get married. Commit."

"And you don't."

"Not right now. I don't want to make a mistake."

"You're afraid of making a mistake?"

"Hey, skip the pop psych. I have a pet parrot, Long John Silver, and I've been able to make a commitment to him! Are *you* married?"

"No. And never have been."

"I would have thought—" I stopped myself.

"You would have thought at my age I'd have been married. But you don't want to ask how old I am. I'm forty-nine."

"What are we doing here? Are we making the first moves toward a possible relationship?"

He laughed. "Are you always this direct?"

"Mostly. Are we?"

"Maybe. Would you back away?"

"Maybe not." My mind came up with one thing that had given me doubts about him. "Tell me honestly, do you really believe that Chuck killed himself? With the amount of Valium you gave him—and remember, you wanted to be sure he wouldn't attack anybody the rest of the night—could he possibly have got up and found a knife and cut his own throat?"

Daniel looked at me just a second or two. He didn't want to answer. I said, "Come on."

"No. I don't think so."

"You know what this means. We've got an impossible murder."

"Either that—"

He stopped, but I finished for him.

"Either that or Mary is involved. She couldn't have missed seeing somebody going in or coming out. Probably both. The distances are just too short down there. Either she saw whoever went in and is covering up—"

"Mary wouldn't do that."

"—or *she* was the one who went in."

"Wait a minute. Imagine her trying to do it. There were a dozen people on board, and not more than four of them were ever up on deck. Most of them never even went to bed. They were milling around in the dinette area, less than ten feet from the door. Emery was around all night. Greg was sitting at the dinette. And Twinkie. And Bret. The companionway stair comes down the center, I know, but it's an open stair without risers. You can see right through it. The lights in the galley, dinette, hall, dormitory room, and the stateroom with Chuck in it were on all night." He paused and then added with perceptible satisfaction, "It is impossible for anybody to have gone in there."

"Unless all of them did it."

"As a team? Bret's virtually a stranger. Emery an employee. He doesn't have any reason to murder Chuck. He doesn't have that much loyalty to the Honeywells."

"Hell." I agreed with him. But I was excited at the idea, too. An impossible murder in a locked room. The real McCoy. The true quill. Hot damn!

"Now, are we done with this for a while?" Daniel said.

"I guess."

He reached out and touched my hair. Just then Takuro came up the companionway steps. "Relief crew!" he called.

In the galley, Emery was rummaging around, hoping to find food he might have stored and forgotten. Bret asked to be allowed to man the cockpit watch.

"It's absolutely dead calm," he said, "so I can't possibly screw up."

Will chuckled and said go ahead.

"There isn't anything else left to go wrong anyway," he said.

Greg was the most restless of all. It was now 2:00 A.M., the best time in the world, or maybe the worst, to be restless. I saw him going into the head, then the forward three-bunk cabin. Then he walked through to the aft two-bunk cabin.

He came back into the galley faster than he had left.

"I was wondering," he said in a strained voice that did not suit the casual words, "whether any of you have seen Twinkie?"

"No, why?" said Will.

Mary said, "She's probably gone to bed."

Takuro was coming down the stairs. He paused on the third step and stared.

Greg's face was white and he was breathing hard. "She hasn't gone to bed. I looked!"

Mary said, "Up on deck—"

"I didn't see her," Takuro said.

Will rose to this feet. "This is ridiculous. She can't have vanished."

There was just a hair's-breadth pause, where it seemed to me nobody breathed. Vanished? We were in limbo in the middle of nowhere more literally than I had ever been in my life. Vanished? Vanished where?

I walked fast toward the berths in the bow. I would have run, but I didn't want to terrify Greg. Will and Daniel and Greg were right behind me. The rest crowded after us.

We tore the fore dormitory apart. We looked under every sail, opened all the lockers under the beds. Nothing. Greg was gasping and wringing his hands behind us.

On to the three-bed dorm. Nothing, and nowhere to hide.

She wasn't in the head. Will and Greg pushed in together, getting into each other's way.

By the time we got back to the galley, Emery had every cupboard open, plus the refrigerator and the cold locker. No Twinkie.

Will and Greg passed us on the way to the two-bunk aft

dorm. Belinda lay on one of the bunks, sleeping like the dead. We all rushed in, throwing open the equipment locker under her bunk.

"What?" she asked sleepily. We pushed out again, but Mary stayed to explain. We heard her saying "What? What?" as we went.

This brought us, of course, to the door of the master stateroom. Behind it lay the bunk with Chuck's dead body, the blood on the walls and floor, and the master stateroom head.

"I don't think anybody has taken the tape off this door," Will said. "She couldn't be in here."

I said, "Somebody got in once before."

Greg didn't even speak. He just reached out and ripped off one of the strips of duct tape.

"Hold it," Will said. "We can't go in and mess up the evidence—wait a minute—you can't do this, Greg!"

"The fuck I can't!" Greg said, and went on stripping tape.

"You—if you go in now and later on somebody suspects you of Chuck's—of—" Will couldn't bring himself to say, "of killing Chuck."

"I'll go in," I said. "I'm not involved. I don't know anybody here. Didn't until yesterday, anyhow."

Will said, "She's right." He grabbed Greg's arm. "Okay?"

"Okay. Okay! But hurry!"

The tape was off.

I stepped into the master stateroom. It had been closed a full day by now. It smelled horrible. There are odors you can't avoid at a death scene—urine, feces, and in this case, blood. And now, twenty-four hours after the death, the slight, almost sweet smell of decomposition. It would not be long before it became eye-watering and stomach-turning.

Chuck's face had sunken in. The eye sockets were stained a darker purple. I didn't need to look at him long, though.

"Is she there?" Greg called.

"Wait a minute."

Breathing through my mouth, I opened the locker under the other bunk, not Chuck's. Twinkie was not there. I hardly thought she would be, if she were alive. She was not the type to spend the night in a room with a dead man.

But she could be there, dead. In a way, it wouldn't be entirely inappropriate for a killer to have stuffed her body in the locker under Chuck's body.

I forced myself to walk toward Chuck and open the locker under the bunk he lay on. Some blood had dripped down the side. I held my shirttail over two fingers and lifted the door, thinking maybe this would also avoid messing up fingerprints, if there were any and if they were important.

I looked in. And jumped back. But it was only some clothing of Belinda's, and a sweatshirt. The sweatshirt happened to be a light purple color, almost Twinkie's favorite amethyst.

No Twinkie.

"Come on!" Greg called.

I had to look in the head. Quickly, I walked to it and pushed open the door.

Nothing. Just bathroom and blank, blue tiles.

No Twinkie.

"She's not here."

I was out of there fast. Slapped the tape back on the door, while the others ran to the deck, clattering one after another up the companionway ladder.

I put the tape back on as well as I could, resolving to get a fresh batch as soon as we saw where we stood. Then I ran two steps at a time up the stairs after them.

All ten of them were standing around the deck in various places. The deck lights and running lights weren't strong, but they showed Will in the bow, Bill hugging Mary, Bret standing near the wheel, Takuro and Belinda leaning with half their bodies over the port lifeline, staring out, Daniel hovering over Greg on the starboard side.

The flat, obsidian-black water stretched off into eternity. The hard stars were still clear in the sky. They were reflected as tiny, sharp points all over the flat surface of the water. The flat unbroken surface of the water.

Greg began to shriek.

◇ 22 ◇

"Twinkie!"

The scream echoed out over the water and faded.

He screamed it again.

And again.

Will said, "Emery, get the flashlights."

"Get out the dinghies!" Greg yelled.

"It's too dangerous. And it won't help."

"You don't know that."

"If we can't see her with flashlights, she's—um—she's not around."

Will was throwing things out of the cockpit locker. He finally found a big, square, heavy-duty flashlight. He handed it to Greg. Greg jumped to the side and flipped the switch on. "Twinkie! *Twinkie!*"

"Keep quiet, now," Will said. "If she's out there calling to us, we want to hear."

We were silent. The beam swept back and forth so frantically, I almost expected to hear it swish as it passed over the water. But it didn't, of course, and no other sound broke the deep stillness.

Nothing, nothing, nothing. We held our breaths.

Then Greg jumped to the other side of the boat and swept

the flash back and forth. Emery came running up with three four-cell lights. Takuro, Daniel, and Will took them and wordlessly went to different stations around the boat and shined them at the water.

I thought, it's thirty miles to shore on the east, sixty miles to shore on the west, a hundred south and over two hundred north, and the boat was dead in the water. What were we supposed to do?

Greg yelled, "Twinkie, Twinkie!" and went on without waiting for a reply. Finally, when he got hoarse, he ran to Will, who was in the stern.

"We've got to take out the dinghies. We've got to look for her!"

Will put out his hand. "There's no use, Greg."

"Yes, there is. We haven't moved much. There's no wind. If she fell overboard, she can't be far away."

"She would have drowned," Will said, trying to put his arm on Greg's shoulder.

Greg pushed it away. "She might be wearing a life preserver. She might be unconscious."

"Greg—"

"She could be just out of sight. Floating. You can't just give up."

Belinda said, "Will, I think he does have to look. Even if only—for later—to be able to think he did everything he could."

"It's too dangerous. Plus, Greg's been drinking."

Daniel said, "I'll go with him."

"Let's go!" Greg said urgently.

Will was wavering.

"You've got two dinghies," Greg said. "We could cover more area with both of them. There may not be any time to waste!"

I could see that Will thought there was all the time in the world, but Takuro said, "I'll take out the other one."

"No, let me. I'll go, Uncle Greg," Bill Honeywell offered.
Bret and Emery both said they'd go, but Will said,
"Emery, you can't because of your ribs. And Bret, you don't
swim well enough. You two get out the dinghies. Daniel,
get four life jackets."

Greg said, "Hurry up! Hurry up!"

"I'm going with them, Will," Belinda said. He looked at
her for a second, then nodded.

People rushed up with supplies. Greg tore open the dinghy cover and pulled the self-inflator. The dinghy ballooned,
shouldering us aside like a growing giant jellyfish.

"Now listen to me!" Will shouted. "In the first dinghy
Greg will go with Daniel and Belinda. Everybody wears life
jackets. You two watch out for him. Emery, where are the
oars?"

"Right here."

The oars came in two pieces in order to store compactly
with the collapsed dinghy. Emery snapped them together.

"Takuro and Bill will go in the second boat. Each dinghy
takes two flashlights. *Do not* go out of sight of this boat! If
you once get lost, we may never find you!"

Bill had the section of lifeline amidships open. Greg
dropped his dinghy in the water and held onto its rope. Bill
rigged the ladder and Greg rushed down it, jumping into
his dinghy so fast he nearly swamped it.

"Greg, no matter how upset you are, you've *got* to do as
Daniel instructs you. Don't go beyond our lights. If a breeze
comes up and I call, get right back here! I'm not going to
lose any more people tonight, do you hear?"

"All right. All *right*. But hurry up!"

Daniel got in the dinghy. Belinda followed him down the
ladder. Emery handed down the oars, and Greg hastily
forced them through the canvas loops that served as oar-
locks. Takuro, meanwhile, was getting the second dinghy
ready.

Will's dinghies were nothing like kids' beach floats. They were the kind of thing you would want on your side if you had to abandon the troop carrier in the middle of the Pacific. The two of them could have easily held all twelve of the people who had started out on this trip, and knowing Will, I am certain he wouldn't invite more people than his lifeboats could accommodate.

These were eight feet long, blue on the bottom and yellow on the top, with solid thwarts you could sit on. They had several separate gas inflators, feeding several separate air cells, so that if you got a rip in one spot, there would still be plenty of inflated pockets to keep you afloat. It would have taken something in the Great White Shark league to make a dent in that stuff anyway. It was *heavy*-duty canvas overlaid with extra-heavy vinyl. I had helped Takuro lift the second one overboard, and it had to weigh fifty pounds.

With the second dinghy launched, Bret, Will, Emery, Mary, and I stood in the stern watching.

Will was very tense. Seeing him clench and unclench his hands made me nervous. After all, he hadn't paled at lightning, fog, titanic waves, or all the other crap we'd had to put up with. To see him stressed out was scary.

Plus, I understood the problem. If even a gentle breeze came up and pushed us along, would the people in the dinghies be able to row fast enough to catch up?

"I should never have agreed to this," he muttered.

"They can see the anchor light a long way off, Mr. Honeywell," Emery said.

I said "Anchor light?" thinking an anchor light would either be low on the deck or down in the water.

"The anchor light is on the top of the mast," Will said.

Silly me. Of course it was.

We watched the flashlights bobbing on the water. The darkness had swallowed the dinghies themselves. Beams stabbed out, catching the tops of almost imperceptible undulations of the water. The dinghies were separating now, to search on both sides of the *Easy Girl.* Both were at the outer limits of visibility.

"I should never have allowed this," Will said again. I suppose repeating himself was as close to screaming and handwringing as he ever got. If I ever got to land, maybe I'd have material for some kind of story or other. Lord knows what—the rich under stress? No, I wouldn't abuse his hospitality to that extent.

I told him, "I agree with Belinda. You had to let him go try it."

"I suppose you're right."

"He could have blamed himself for the rest of his life otherwise. And you certainly couldn't let him go alone."

"No, no," he said. He seemed to consider. Then he said "No," again.

Far out over the water, we could hear Greg calling Twinkie's name.

The flashlights on the dinghies were not much brighter than the reflections of the stars in the water. They were very far away. Will noticed it, too.

"Come in closer!" he yelled.

There was a moment's silence. Then Daniel's voice called, "What did you say?"

"Come closer! You're too far away!"

"All right!" It was Daniel. Nothing from the other dinghy. "Takuro! Bill! Do you hear me?"

"What, Dad?"

Bret said, "Let me do this." Then he boomed, *"Come closer!"*

Bill yelled, "Okay!"

Will wiped his forehead. He was sweating and shivering at the same time. What a nightmare this must be for him, I thought. From his point of view all of it was his responsibility.

"This better?" Daniel called. They were not much closer. Greg must be resisting. Will and Bret were about to answer when Mary screamed. I looked around. I couldn't imagine what had happened.

A freighter was bearing down on us from behind.

In the five or ten minutes we hadn't been looking south, this leviathan had been closing on us. We saw the bow rising up and up.

Surely it had seen us on its radar. Surely the watch on her bow had seen our lights!

Yes! When I looked closely, I realized that they were not aimed dead at us, but slightly east of us. They would miss us by several hundred feet. They probably had seen us on their radar miles back.

And then my blood went cold. They would have seen the boat. They would not have seen the two dinghies bobbing out there in the darkness, low in the water and invisible. Even if their lookout caught a glimpse of their flashlights at the last minute, there was no way to turn a freighter of thousands of tons.

Will was aware of it at the same instant I was.

"Oh, God, no!" he screamed.

When Will screamed, it terrified me. He was my lifeline.

I ran to the bow pulpit and clutched it and stared back at the freighter. It was nearly upon us. Now I could even hear the hiss of its bow slicing through the water.

Will yelled, "Emery, get the flares!"

At the same time, Will was throwing flares out of the cockpit locker. He pulled the self-igniter on the first one, and a long, red flame shot into the air.

"Emery, hurry up!"

Emery ignited a second. What were they doing? It was too late to stop the juggernaut ship. But then I realized he was planning ahead in the midst of his terror. If someone was hit, if someone was hurt, there'd be more chance of survival if the freighter had at least called the Coast Guard.

Emery had the distress rocket launcher in hand. He paused, touched off something, and red fireworks arched up and exploded.

The ship was passing now. There was no chance to look for the dinghies. At least they were not together. If one of them was hit, the other would survive.

That was when I noticed Mary. She had fallen to her knees next to the cabin. Her eyes were fixed approximately where we last heard shouts from Bill. Her hands were pressed over the lower half of her face. Either she was praying or keeping herself from screaming.

The wake hit us then. I clung to the metal of the bow pulpit as the deck rose and plunged under my feet. That wake must have hit the dinghy on our port side before it hit us. Would they survive that, even if they hadn't been run down?

Behind me there was a sizzle and a whoosh as another rocket shot up and burst far over the boat.

"Light another!" Will yelled. It rose and burst and the water turned blood red in its light. I walked back from the bow to stand with Will.

The freighter was past, diminishing in size.

We waited, too afraid to call. We heard a voice. But it was from the other side, starboard.

"Where are you?" Will shouted.

"Over here." It was Daniel's voice. He was rowing toward us, Greg and Belinda holding flashlights. Belinda's trembled.

"Are they all right?" Daniel called.

"Where is Bill?" I heard Belinda ask.

Will said, "We're looking." The dinghy with Greg, Daniel, and Belinda was close enough now so that we could see them.

"Go around the other side. About a hundred yards off—" Will choked and stopped.

"What?"

Bret got out his stage voice again and bellowed, "He says go around the other side of the boat and go out about a hundred yards!"

"Oh, God," Will said, so softly that only I could hear him, "let them be there."

We had only the one big flashlight aboard. When Mary came to the side and stood leaning against the lifeline, I handed it to her.

We didn't see anything. The wake of the big ship had vanished, and the water had closed flat and dark over its trail. Daniel, rowing hard, swung the boat around our bow and made for the dark water. Belinda was in the bow sitting next to Greg. One hand was over her mouth. The other pointed the flashlight forward like a sword of light. Greg, next to her, held his flashlight in two trembling hands and moved it back and forth over the water.

Then we heard a distant cry. Daniel's dinghy was drawing away from us, and we couldn't tell right away who was calling. We heard it again. It was a distressing sort of sound, clearly from a human throat, but without words. A choked shout.

A couple of seconds later, Daniel called, *"We see them!"*

Will whispered, "Ask if it's both of them. Quick."

Bret had already thought of that. "Both of them?" he shouted.

We waited.

"Just a minute. Yes!"

I wondered why Will himself hadn't called out and turned to look at him. There were tears running down his cheeks. I don't suppose he could have spoken loudly.

We waited some more. Lights bobbed around. There was shouting, cursing, and long periods of silence. We leaned against the lifeline, straining to see. And couldn't see, of course. Bret didn't call again. We knew they were doing what they could out there.

Finally Daniel's voice said, "Hello?"

"We're here," Bret yelled.

"They're in our dinghy. The other one's swamped. Heat some coffee and get some dry clothes ready."

Mary gasped and ran below. Emery handed me his flashlight and followed her.

"The bow wave rolled us over," Bill said. "Just rolled us over like a cork. Upside down."

Takuro said, "They never saw us."

"Then we were caught under the dinghy—" Bill said.

"Actually," Takuro said, "we were just a few yards out of

their path. After we were rolled, the dinghy and everything
got sucked under by their wash."

"Get below," Daniel told them. They were both shaking.
It was the aftermath of fear even more than the cold. I could
hardly imagine how it must have felt to be in the direct path
of a freighter as high as a ten-story building and plowing
right at you.

Belinda was holding Bill's shoulders and only let go so
they could go down the companionway single file.

Will, Greg, and I were left on deck. We hauled the dinghies up out of the water. A heavy job. The one that was
run down by the freighter was upside down and the other
had a lot of water in the bottom.

When we got done, they both lay on the deck, blue bottom side up, like sagging jellyfish. I looked over to the
north, where the freighter had gone. The lights on its superstructure were still partly visible, just disappearing over the
curve of the earth.

"Do you think they saw the flares?" I asked Will.

"I don't know."

"Will they radio the Coast Guard if they saw them?"

"Oh, sure."

"So what do you think?"

"By the time we got the flares off, they were going away
from us. They look ahead, not back."

"But if even one of the crew was watching—"

"That's right. We can hope."

Greg had been just sitting there, listening to us, maybe,
but not saying anything. He didn't show any interest. Daniel
came back up and noticed him immediately.

"Greg, let's go below. I'll get you some brandy, or—"

"I'd like to sit here." He said it pleasantly enough, but
he meant, leave me alone.

"You think you have to watch—"

"Listen, Daniel," Greg said. "I'm not being stupid. I know there isn't any chance now that Twinkie's still alive. If I needed anything to prove it to me—I thought I had got my own nephew killed just to—just to—prove it to myself. But I'm going to stay here. If I went to bed, I wouldn't sleep. I'd be thinking all night there might be a voice out there, calling me."

"Oh, God," Will said.

"And, excuse me, but I don't feel like eating when I think that Twinkie—Twinkie's body is sinking to the bottom of the lake."

Nobody said anything.

"Will," Greg said, "how deep is it here?"

"Christ, Greg, *don't!*"

"I can look it up on the goddamn chart! Why make me do that?"

Will said slowly, "I suppose—I guess where we are here, it must be around three hundred and fifty feet."

◇ 24 ◇

"Hey!" I caught Daniel Silverman in the galley about half an hour later. "Are you ready to talk?"

"Talk?"

"I mean are you ready to take this seriously now? We started out with twelve people. We're down to ten. Do you have a magic number where you get worried? Eight, maybe? One? I mean, we're into serious crisis time here, if you ask me."

"I agree. I just don't see what we can do about it."

I was pissed. "We're stuck here. Either you help me or I'll go on doing this myself."

"Oh, all right. Let's go up on deck to talk."

I had spent that half hour asking people questions. What they remembered about the evening. I'm not sure their answers helped any, but it sure beat sitting around thinking about Twinkie, sinking into the cold and perpetual dark of Lake Michigan. Lying on the sandy lake floor—

Well. Don't think about it.

We went up on deck. Four in the morning and becalmed is definitely not a fine time to be on a yacht. It was dark here and quiet as ever. Greg was sitting at the wheel, and he didn't seem to want to talk. Can't say I blamed him.

Daniel and I wandered up to the bow.

For just a moment I asked myself whether this was wise. For all I knew, Daniel himself was the killer. He'd had as much chance as Belinda to kill Chuck. Which is to say not much, but then we didn't know how it was done. Should I put myself alone up here in the dark with a potential killer?

With Greg largely catatonic, sixty feet away in the dark? No help at all.

For that matter, maybe they were all in it together, and now they would polish me off. No, that was paranoid. They needed me as a witness, if anything.

In the last analysis, you *have* to go on your own instinct. I just plain didn't believe Daniel was a killer.

But I wasn't ready to die for that belief. I did the minimum—didn't let him get behind me as we walked up and sat on the deck in the bow.

"Tell me about Twinkie and Greg," I said.

"Twinkie and *Greg*? If anything, I thought you'd want to know about Twinkie and Chuck."

"That's not as important, really, is it?"

He thought a moment, then nodded as if he were forced

to agree. He said slowly, "I'm afraid that anything I could say about the situation can be interpreted wrong."

"Try me."

"Greg is an old friend. I've known him since medical school. You haven't seen him out here as he really is. He's compassionate and scholarly—not at all money-oriented, whatever you thought of Twinkie. Greg's father was very rich, and then when Greg was about ten, his father lost all his money. They went through a rough period, I suppose, where they lost touch with their friends. And then his father made a new fortune in commodities. The man was a genius, in a way. But Greg never seemed to have cared one way or the other." He thought another few seconds. "See, if I say he was terribly in love with Twinkie, you'll think that her flirting with Chuck would drive him mad and he'd kill them both."

"He could have."

"So could the rest of us. And if I say that he'd become disillusioned with Twinkie or fallen out of love, you could think it was because of Chuck, and he hated them for it and killed them both."

"Give me more credit than that. Tell me this: suppose they had a dispute. Say Greg wanted to go to a movie and Twinkie wanted to go dancing. Which would they do?"

"Go dancing."

"Which of them was better at business matters?"

"Oh, Twinkie, no doubt about it. People all assumed that he set her up in business when she started the Twinkle, Twinkle Boutique. You know, give the little woman something to do with her spare time. But it wasn't like that at all. Twinkie conceived and planned the whole thing. And she didn't jump into it impulsively, either. She spent *two years* looking for the right location, negotiating a lease, talking to suppliers to get the best prices, and she worked in a jewelry shop to learn the ropes before she ever opened the store. She had the best location and the best interior decoration. And she was doing really well."

"That's funny. She never seemed very energetic on this trip."

"Oh, Twinkie had plenty of energy. Twinkie was very bright. But Twinkie did what Twinkie wanted to do."

"It wasn't very bright of her to take up with Chuck."

"Cat, I don't think she had taken up with Chuck in any sexual sense. She was a tease. You don't understand her. She thought she was livening things up."

"I do understand. There are a lot of us who were systematically brought up by our mothers to be teases. Prettied up and packaged, but not supposed to be touched." I sighed. For a moment I pictured Twinkie lying on the sand under three hundred feet of water, still wearing her jeweled necklace and earrings. I felt sorry for Twinkie. Now.

"Still," Daniel said, "teasing came naturally to Twinkie."

"And anyway, if Greg believed—"

"If Greg believed she was having an affair with Chuck, it didn't matter whether she actually was or not. As far as what Greg might have done."

"Hell," I said.

"Let it go."

"What do you mean?"

"I know you're feeling guilty because you didn't like her. You didn't like her and now she's dead."

"All right, so I feel a little guilty. Oh, shit. You know, Daniel, you're pretty empathetic."

"I'm just a sensitive kind of guy."

"But I'm following this up anyway. Let me tell you what I think happened to her."

He groaned. "Can't we leave this to the police?"

"No. We're stuck out here. Figuring out our killer is the best defense I can think of."

"I can't argue. Go ahead."

"First, she couldn't have been simply pushed overboard. She'd fall into the water and start screaming. It was a quiet night. We'd all have heard her."

"Hit her first, then, or choke her."

"Right. My guess is the killer hit her on the head with a champagne bottle and then quietly lowered her over the side. Choking her would take too long. She might kick and make noise or break free. It would be dangerous."

"Actually," Daniel said, "the whole thing was dangerous. Any one of us might have come up the stairs. Or we might have noticed her missing immediately and remembered who was on deck with her."

"It was only dangerous up to a point. It's not true that we would have noticed her missing immediately. We weren't checking up on people. The only person who might have gone looking for her was Greg, and he was really blitzed on champagne. Even when he did go looking for her later, it took him fifteen or twenty minutes before he realized that she really wasn't aboard."

"That's true. People were wandering around all night. If they didn't see her, they'd think she'd gone to bed."

"All right. I've been talking with people. Let's put it together. Bill was at the wheel about ten o'clock. I took over from him at ten-thirty. Emery about eleven. Twinkie about eleven-thirty. Greg about midnight. Will at twelve-thirty. Belinda at one. You and I relieved her briefly at one-fifteen. Takuro at one-thirty. And Bret at two a.m. It was while Bret was at the wheel that Greg found out Twinkie was missing."

"And could have been missing for a long time."

"Right. But not hours and hours. Twinkie took over the watch from Emery. Therefore, Emery couldn't have killed her because Greg would have noticed nobody was at the wheel when he went up."

"Emery couldn't have killed her *then*."

"Okay. Right. But after Greg came Will, Belinda, and

Takuro. For any of them to have killed her, she would have had to go back up during their watches. And why would she? That makes Greg the most likely, when he took over for her, doesn't it, Daniel?"

"Hold it. Did anybody see her after Greg's watch?"

"Greg says he did."

"Oh, wonderful."

"But a couple of the others think they did," I had to admit.

"Such as?"

"Bret thinks he noticed her in his audience while he was singing. He's not sure, because he says champagne goes right to his head."

Daniel thought that over. "But you know, a performer habitually watches the audience. It's second nature to them."

"I admit that. And Will thinks he saw her come down the companionway stairs at one point and go to the head," I said. "Then later he thinks he saw her going back up again."

"Much later?"

"He's not sure."

"But it's still a strong piece of evidence, Cat. Tell you why. As far as I know, the first time she went up on deck in hours was when she went up to take watch. So if Will thinks she went up twice, the second time had to be later, and that lets out Greg."

"Not quite. She could have come down at the end of her watch and gone back at the end of his watch. He could have killed her then."

"So could any of the people on watch after him."

"Will, Belinda, Takuro, and Bret."

"Right."

"Daniel, what do you think about the killer being a person who was not at the wheel? She goes out on deck with some-one and they walk up to the bow. It was dark, like it is now. Greg can't see us when we're sitting down like this, unless he stands up. The killer could just have been careful to keep low. He hits her on the head and lowers her quietly over the side."

"I don't think it works. Whoever was at the watch would remember two people going forward and only one coming back. It was very boring at the wheel—"

"Wait! I've got it! Twinkie and the killer come up near the end of somebody's watch. They stay at the bow. The relief watch comes up. If the previous watch doesn't say to the new person 'Twinkie and X are in the bow'—and why should he?—then the killer knocks her unconscious and lowers her into the water quietly. After a while, the killer strolls back along the deck, says, 'Cold evening, isn't it?' or some such thing to the new watch, and goes below. The first watch doesn't know that anything is wrong. Neither does the second watch. How's that?"

"Cat, that's absolutely brilliant! And I never thought of it. That's amazing!"

"Amazing that you never thought of it? Or amazing that I thought of it? Your compliments leave a little to be desired."

"Let me try one on you."

"Shoot."

"Twinkie comes up on deck alone. She goes to the bow. The watch changes and the new watch doesn't know she's there. She slips into the water, swims away from the boat, and drowns. Nobody would know."

"Why would Twinkie engage in this rather eccentric behavior?"

"Because she killed Chuck and is afraid she'll be found out."

"Unfortunately, she wasn't going to be found out. Nobody was."

"Or she's feeling remorse."

"No, Daniel. Twinkie might think she was justified, or clever. Not remorseful."

"I was afraid you wouldn't like it. I can't say I'd believe it, either. Have you given any thought to why Twinkie was killed?"

"Of course I have. She saw the killer go in the master stateroom door."

"I don't think so."

"It's obvious!"

"I don't believe it. Mary would have seen him, too, either going in or out."

"Unless the killer is Mary."

"Mary is *not* a killer," Daniel said.

"All right, genius. What then?"

"I think she figured out the murder. Figured out how it was done."

"*Figured out how it was done?*" I jumped to my feet. "When you and I can't? Twinkie! That's impossible!"

Daniel laughed. "Cat, your humility is an example to all of us."

"Well, really. I mean, she didn't even see the body and we did."

"Remember when we interviewed her? She asked a few intelligent questions that nobody else did about what had happened to Chuck."

"I don't believe it. I *don't* believe it!"

• 25 •

"Takuro is a stockholder in Chuck's company," Daniel said, when I pressed him to talk. "And he designed furniture for Chuck. For some of his best-looking stuff. There's a parallel between working with fiberglass and plastics in boats and in furniture. The techniques are transferable to a large extent. What the materials can do and how they react to stresses."

"All right. Tell me how Chuck and Takuro got along."

"Quite well, I think."

"Would you expand on that?"

"Oh, hell, Cat. You know what Chuck was like. There are lots of people like him. They think making any stupid ethnic remark is the same thing as humor. In fact, I sometimes thought if Chuck had a genuine sense of humor, he might be an attractive person."

"He'd be a *different* person."

"Yeah. Right."

"So you're saying Takuro resented Chuck's remarks?"

"I don't think so. I think Takuro felt sorry for Chuck. He knew Chuck was just that way. He did it to everybody. Racial jokes. Ethnic jokes. The women's movement has been a positive field day for him, as far as jokes are concerned. Chuck was one of those people you cringe to go into a restaurant with, because you know he's going to say horrible, heavy-handed, condescending things to the waitress."

"And Takuro—"

"Didn't seem to mind. He wasn't as patient when Chuck

tried to withhold credit for some of Takuro's furniture designs. It wasn't that Chuck didn't want to pay him, although Chuck always paid the least possible. It was public relations. See, Chuck wanted people to think his *system,* the way he set up his corporation, including the design department, was absolutely great. He didn't want to admit that he got designs from an outside specialist. But Takuro's were so much better— Because Takuro was a stockholder, he wanted the company to do well, whether he was credited or not. So Takuro was kind of stuck."

"Was he angry?"

"Takuro doesn't get angry. Lately, he had Chuck sign a contract that called for crediting Takuro for the designs, before he would submit the designs."

"Nice guy, Chuck."

"He had his rough edges. But he was a good man with a balance sheet. He could eliminate fat in a manufacturing process like nobody else. He wasn't the visionary he thought he was. He just happened to be making furniture with synthetics because he could get them cheaply. Plastics first, then fiberglass, now acrylics and all the new polymers. Just then a huge market opened up for low-cost furniture. It ran away with him, his success, I mean. He was a poor kid, and when he had money, he felt he had to spend it in visible ways."

"Okay, what about Bret?"

"As a killer? Impossible, Cat. He hasn't any motive."

"Let me give you a motive for him. Tell me this: did Bret want Chuck to produce the movie of *Off and On* instead of Charisma Productions?"

"How would I know what he wants?"

"Think. You're a young musical comedy actor. You've just made a big hit on Broadway. Somebody's going to make a movie of that hit and you're going to star in it. It's your big chance at film. Given the cutthroat nature of the industry, it may be your first and last chance. Which person do you want to handle the movie—an established production company with access to the best directors and the best distribution facilities, or a manufacturer of cheap furniture who lucked into a Broadway play and now thinks he's going to be Sam Goldwyn?"

"When you put it that way, I agree."

I said, "They may fail at this movie and lose serious money."

"Okay. But Bret didn't know where to get hold of the stateroom key."

"As far as we know."

"As far as we know. And then there's still the question of Twinkie," he said. "If I'm right, and she'd figured out how the murder was done, why go to Bret? Blackmail? Bret didn't have any money and Twinkie had plenty. Why would she tell the killer what she'd guessed?"

"Simple. To tease him. Twinkie was a tease."

"Let's say Bret didn't have a key and couldn't get one. Eliminate him. Say he couldn't have killed Chuck. And Mary, Bill, and Emery couldn't have killed Twinkie."

"Why not?"

Daniel said, "Because they had deck watch *before* Twinkie was pushed overboard and didn't go back up. As far as we know. If Twinkie went up to meet the person on deck watch, which is what I'm beginning to think happened, then the killer would have to be Greg, Belinda, Will, Bret, or Takuro, because they had later watch."

"And you have to eliminate Belinda, Takuro, and you, because you three couldn't have killed Chuck. You were on deck all night."

He turned his head toward me when I included him as an initial suspect, but I was in no mood to cater to Daniel Silverman.

"Not Takuro," he said. "He went below once."

"Oh. Yes. And about three-thirty, too."

"So if we eliminate them, and Bret because of the key—
for the *moment*," he added, seeing that I was about to
object, "and assuming there is only one killer, that the same
person killed both Chuck and Twinkie, that means the killer
is Greg, Will, or Takuro."

Well, it seemed thin to me. But after all, from the point of
view of character, they all seemed unlikely killers to me.
Will was not only what used to be called a real gentleman,
but also a truly considerate person. And Takuro was another
gentlemanly man. Considerate and industrious. Greg was a
more difficult case, because he had been so close to Twinkie
and so angry at Chuck. But he seemed a man of peace, and
I'd grown to like him.

The others? Bill was a gangly kid, gentle and modest. Mary
was bright and devoted and, as far as I could tell, completely
without reason to kill Chuck. Belinda was not just stylish but
warm, the sort who anticipated your needs so skillfully that,
as a guest, you felt you were causing no trouble.

Bret? A bit of a show-off, but what actor wasn't? It didn't
make him a killer, or even deceitful. He helped out when
he could. Emery? Would Emery resent a man like Chuck,
rich and boorish, pushing him around? Would he hate him
enough to kill him?

When I went below, Emery was still at his place near the
sink in the galley.

Everybody else, except for Greg, was in the dinette-gal-
ley-dorm area. Staying in groups. Small wonder. Go off with
somebody and you might get killed.

Bret sprawled across the table with his head down, sleeping. Probably wouldn't feel safe alone in a room. I had asked
Will whether there were any firearms on board. He said
not, but naturally he hadn't searched his guests' bags. It
wouldn't be courteous.

Emery polished the counter and polished the counter, then polished the stove for a change of pace. Then he polished the counter again.

"What's Will gonna say when he finds out you've worn the finish off?" I asked.

Emery grinned in a sickly way. "I don't understand it," he said. "They're all nice people."

Just what I was thinking. I said, "Yeah. All except somebody."

He looked at me as if I were a life jacket that had sprung a leak. What could I have said? That we'd just had two rather grotesque accidents?

I poured a mug of coffee. "Would you like me to spill some so you'll have a real spot to clean up?"

Emery smiled. "You're nice. You at least try to make jokes."

"*Try* to make jokes? That *was* a joke."

"I meant—"

"I know. Don't sweat it. I'm just kidding. Do you ever think maybe you're too inclined to think everybody is nice?"

"Yeah. I guess. Only—who isn't?"

"Who isn't what?"

"Of these people. Who isn't nice? Ms. Marsala, who's killing us?"

Wishing the sun would come up is about as useful as wishing the tides would stop rising and falling. But I couldn't have been the only person aboard wishing for dawn.

Greg was asleep in the cockpit. I said to Daniel, "Good news. Breakfast will be hot buttered champagne and Cheez Whiz caviar fondue."

"Great. I'll take two."

"You should take a nap."

"I did earlier. Why don't you take a nap?"

"Frankly, I'd be too scared. Plus, I slept yesterday afternoon."

"We'll make land today," he said.

"I hope."

"And turn this over to the police."

"What if they brush it away? They could call Chuck a suicide. And Twinkie, too. They could decide Twinkie killed Chuck and then killed herself in a fit of remorse."

"They're competent people. You don't have any right to assume they'll screw up."

"Tell me this, Daniel. Are they gonna give a lot of weight to what we tell them about these people's personalities? If we say Twinkie was too self-satisfied to kill herself, are they gonna just say, 'Okay, you knew her and we didn't,' and Chuck the same. They say Chuck killed himself, and we say hell no, he thought he was wonderful, and they say since nobody could have gotten in, he *must* have killed himself, and what then?"

"Well, what then? Can *you* prove any different?"

"Not yet."

"You want us just to sit out here while you think?"

"No! Somebody else might get killed. What I want to know, Daniel, is whether you really *want* this case solved."

That hit him. I'll say this much for him—he didn't give me a hasty answer. And he didn't try to fool me or put me off. He took a minute and then said, "I don't want it solved if it has to be solved at any cost."

"What does that mean?"

"Chuck was not the most valuable member society has ever produced. I felt sorry for Twinkie, but I didn't really like her. I have—yes, I'm ambivalent about hunting down the killer if it was somebody pushed beyond what he or she could endure."

"You can't mean that! Whoever it is could kill again."

"But suppose that's not true? Suppose it's over?"

"We have to *find out* or we can't know that."

"Once you find out, it could be too late."

"People need the truth."

"The truth will set you free?"

I said, "Yes. Or put it another way. Lies and cover-ups can endanger you."

We sat, unspeaking. I couldn't believe that he really meant what he said. Now, I had to admit that the police might be able to handle the case. Even though I felt I had a better grasp on the personalities and the physical possibilities on board. All right, maybe that's carrying self-confidence too far, but jeez! You basically have only yourself to rely on.

But to say we shouldn't even try?

"I feel sorry for whoever it is," Daniel said.

And that I could understand. Didn't agree with it, but I understood it. Somebody aboard right now must have gone through hell this trip. First desperation and rage. Then blue blanked-out resolution to go ahead. Then horror at what he or she had done. Then terror that Twinkie suspected. Desperation again.

What would the killer be feeling now? Despair?

Yes, I could understand.

There were footsteps on the stair. Takuro.

"I've come to watch for the sunrise," he said. "I'm going to regard it as symbolic."

"Well, pull up a piece of deck," Daniel said, "and sit down."

We sat and stared while several minutes passed. Then my numbed brain told me that I had been staring at a pinkish glow in the east. Dawn!

"You timed this pretty well, Takuro."

"Well, naturally. I looked at my watch. It doesn't pay to come out at midnight to watch for sunrises."

It was as if the whole sky had taken a breath and smiled. The vault over our heads, so close when it was dark, grew larger and warmer. A shaft of light ran up from a sun that was still below the horizon. The shaft caught invisible water vapor in the air, revealed itself as a shimmering path. There was another, then another, making a half star at the horizon. Then the sun itself rose.

But the horizon was a continuous circle of emptiness. There was no other boat anywhere, not even a discourteous freighter. The water was unlived-upon. It had closed over the events of the night before. The stars were gone from the sky and there was no cloud.

We were alone.

I turned to Daniel and Takuro, expecting to find them similarly cowed by the emptiness. They were both staring at the water. They got up together, moved to the edge of the deck together, and looked down.

I did, too. "What is it?" I said uneasily, expecting to see the body of Twinkie Mandel.

"Look," said Daniel.

"What? At what?"

"That."

"Where? What?"

"It's a swell."

"Daniel, maybe it's-a swell," I said, pretending an Italian accent, "but what's a swell?"

"Look at the water. You see that slow undulation? That's a swell."

"And what does a swell portend?"

"It's sort of a spent wave," Takuro said. "A swell means that someplace fairly distant there's a wind blowing. This swell is coming from the south."

"What does a wind somewhere else do for us?"

"If it's just sprung up, the chances are very good that it'll eventually reach us."

"Oh!"

I looked over to the east. I could almost remember how land used to feel.

· 26 ·

The sunshine woke Greg. He sat up, looking somewhat re-
freshed, and instantly I realized that he'd forgotten what had
happened. You could see awareness pass over his face. It
ate away the light in his eyes, weakened the line of his jaw.

In that moment, I knew he had not killed Twinkie.

Greg stood up and scanned the whole horizon, turning
around until he had seen all three hundred and sixty degrees
of water. It was empty for us. It was emptier for him.

Takuro and I were shy with him. Daniel was quicker and
kinder. He went to Greg and put his arm around him. Greg
mumbled something at Daniel.

Daniel said, "No. Whoever did it must have knocked her
out first. He couldn't have risked her calling for help. It
would have been quick and painless."

"I hope you're right. I just keep imagining her swimming
and swimming, trying to keep afloat—"

"It's not possible. She probably didn't even know she was
in danger."

Greg rummaged in the cockpit locker and found a pair
of binoculars. He went to the bow pulpit and put them to
his eyes.

"It's hopeless," I said.

Daniel said, "Yes. But the kindest thing is to let him
do it."

Takuro had been staring at the mast. "I think we should
run up the distress flag," he said. "In case a boat comes by."

Daniel agreed. They got it out. It was an orange flag with

a black square and ball. Takuro took it to the mast, hooked
it on, and I pulled it up. Just as we were doing so, Will
Honeywell came up the stairs, his face crumpled from sleep.
He stood with his arms hanging loose and looked at the
distress flag.

"I've never used that," he said sadly. "It's never even
been unfolded before."

And there we sat. The sun rose farther into the sky, as it
always does. Some tiny puffy clouds formed to the south.
We were out of coffee. Emery brought up a tray of champagne, caviar, Cheez Whiz, and crackers. Everybody stared
at it blankly. They probably wanted to scream, "Oh, please,
no more champagne; no more caviar! I'll confess! Just don't
make me eat this!" I was wondering whether I could catch
a fish on a ball of Cheez Whiz, but I didn't want to ask
because it would sound like a slur on Will's hospitality.

I was starving. Finally I spread some Cheez Whiz on a
cracker and pushed caviar on top. Maybe later I could make
a hot drink with champagne. Yuck!

People wandered up to see the day. They were a dispirited
crew this morning. And no wonder. They were also casting
quick little sidewise glances at each other. There was a tendency for them not to turn their backs on each other, too.

Can't say I blamed them.

While I ate, I was racking my brains. Since I was certain
Chuck had been murdered, it must have been physically
possible for somebody to have killed him. All I had to do
was think of how.

Will's face was so hangdog, he was so obviously thinking
that he had provided a floating graveyard instead of a pleasant weekend, that I said, "Hey. It's not your fault."

"Thanks, Cat. But still—"

"I've learned things about boats I'll always be glad to

know, Will. I'm almost half—well, maybe a quarter—of a sailor now."

He produced a smile that looked normal. "Cat, for whatever it's worth, and whether you're glad or not, I'm glad you came along."

It was 10:00 A.M., and the gloom and mutual suspicion was denser than fog, when I saw Daniel look alert. He jumped to his feet. I expected anything from a body in the bilge to an airplane dropping food packages. But what I saw was good. Will, Takuro, and Greg noticed it the same time I did.

The distress flag was fluttering sideways from the mast.

Hot damn! We had a breeze!

Four of the five of us broke into a cheer.

Will dove for the cockpit, a man rejuvenated.

"It's south!" he hollered. "Daniel and Greg, I want the main up. We're going due east on a starboard reach. Cat and Takuro, you get that goddamn distress flag down. We can make it in faster ourselves than anybody could tow us."

We jumped to obey. I was gratified that Will had included me as if I knew what to do, even though taking down the flag was really a one-man job. In half a minute Greg and Daniel had the main up. The breeze was not strong yet, but the thrill was.

The sail filled and tightened. The *Easy Girl* answered to her helm again and swung east into the morning sun.

Our cheers had alerted everyone aboard. Some must have been half-asleep. Some were just hiding out. Pretty soon they were all out on deck. Every face turned forward with eagerness and hope.

Every face except Greg's. I saw him looking backward at our wake, staring at the spot we left behind.

*   *   *

All the tempos are different on a living sailboat responding to the wind. It breathes and moves in its own style. The hull creaks as it answers the stresses of the waves, and the breeze makes faint singing sounds in the rigging.

The swell that had preceded the breeze now turned into gentle waves. Will stayed at the wheel. He talked with Daniel about putting up the jib, but they didn't seem to get around to it. For one thing, most of our able-bodied seamen had gone back below. To sleep. Relief had made them aware of how tired they were.

Emery had been the first one to show exhaustion. He stared happily at the full sail. But he sagged on his feet. Will ordered him to go take a nap. This reminded Bill, Mary, and Bret of how tired they were, and they went below, too. Daniel said, "Sleep at least two to a room."

They were aware, of course, that there was a killer on board. But now that there was a breeze, they believed they'd be on land soon and maybe it would all be over.

My guess was that in a day or two, when they were rested and less numb, they'd be more worried than ever about what had happened. Who was the killer? One of them. Most of these people had to deal with each other on a daily basis, some for the rest of their lives. This wasn't a peccadillo they could just go home and forget about.

Unless, of course, I could figure it out.

Belinda, Takuro, Daniel, and I went below for tea and caviar. If I never see another fish egg, I won't feel deprived.

We settled around the dinette. Belinda took a breath and hesitated. She wanted to say something. Finally she did.

"I'm sorry about this. It was supposed to be a relaxing time for you, wasn't it?"

Takuro took her hand. "Please. What I'm happiest about is that I was here to help out. Don't apologize."

He's in love with her, I realized. I'd half noticed it before. I said, "Listen, when somebody asks me how my first sailing experience went, I'm going to say *unforgettable*."

That got her to smile. But not for long. "It was Chuck and Twinkie's last trip," she said. "I can't stop thinking about that."

We sat there, the four of us, in companionable silence. We'd been through so much together that we'd didn't need to make social chitchat. In that respect it was rather nice.

I was thinking about the first murder. How was Chuck killed? Understand that, and Twinkie's death should be no puzzle at all.

Takuro, amazing man that he was, was not tired. He went up to relieve Will. Will came down the stairs a few moments later looking ten years older than when we left Chicago. But before the breeze came up, he'd looked twenty years older. He flopped into the dinette and poured himself a mug of tea.

"Wind's about eight miles an hour," he said. "Nothing spectacular, but it's picking up."

Daniel said, "Not bad. How far out do you think we are?"

"Takuro guessed thirty miles off the coast last night. By now maybe ten or fifteen." He turned to me. "At about five to seven miles out, we should start seeing land."

We were rolling gently in the waves. The condiment shelf over the dinette, which was hung on pivots, moved back and forth like a child's swing, hypnotically.

"When do you think we'll get in?"

"Couple of hours, maybe less."

"Wow!" I said. "In time for dinner!" I realized that wasn't very gracious. "Oh, hell. I'm sorry."

Belinda and Will both smiled. "We realize," she said, "that refreshments haven't been very exciting the last day or so."

"You know what I don't understand?" Will said.

"What?"

"Who ever stocked the Cheez Whiz?"

Belinda smiled, but Will said, "No. I'm really curious. None of us ever liked the stuff."

"And we're certainly not going to like it after this."

"So where did it come from? I certainly didn't put it on Emery's shopping list."

"Believe it or not, dear, it was Bill. He said he picked up 'a bunch of it' at the store because it was cheap."

"Don't knock it," Daniel said. "Without it we'd only have had caviar."

I got up to heat more tea water. As I squeezed past Daniel, the boat gave a sudden lurch. I was flung sideways against the galley cabinet and hit my head. But I didn't drop the teapot.

Takuro yelled down from the deck: "Are you guys all right? I dropped my mug and lost the wheel for a second and broadsided the waves. Bad seamanship."

"I'd better go up and relieve him," Belinda said. "He's got to be tireder than he looks." She picked up her wide-brimmed red sun hat and mashed it securely on her head.

Will said to me, "You're not hurt, are you? I can*not* stand another injury to anybody."

"No, I'm fine," I said. But I was thinking furiously.

Takuro came down the stairs. "See? One little mistake and they replace you."

I warmed the water. I was getting to be pretty good at small boating tasks. My brain was ticking over. You can feel an idea coming, sometimes. We were at a thousand RPM and rising.

"I think I'll go up on deck and get some air," I said.

Everything made sense. In a horrible sort of way.

I climbed the stairs. The sun was shining brightly and it was getting hot. Belinda waved. It had been sensible of her to take a hat. I sauntered over.

"Hi," she said.

I said, "Two kinds of motion, basically, on a boat. Pitch." I paused. "And roll."

Belinda reached for her hat and sent it over the stern into the water. As I glanced back, she pushed me over onto the slippery transom. I grabbed for the lifeline as she seized my ankles and swung them sideways off the boat.

I flailed wildly and got hold of her arm with my left hand, pulling her over with me. She was overbalanced anyway. She went past my head into the water. I hung by my right hand from the lifeline stanchion, but the water was up to my thighs and it sucked hard at me, trying to pull me under.

I slipped a little lower.

◇ 27 ◇

Belinda was in the water, but Belinda could swim. If I lost my hold, I might splash and dog-paddle for a couple of minutes, but I'd sink fast.

The boat was slowing. With no one at the helm, it swung up into the wind and lost power. But momentum would carry it for a while. I clutched at the lifeline stanchion with both hands and gripped hard. It was pencil-thin and cut into my fingers as my weight and the sucking of the water pulled on me. It was slippery, polished metal. I knew I couldn't hold on long.

My clothes were wet now, adding weight. My shoes were filling up with water. I couldn't hold on. I had to, and I couldn't. Where was Daniel? Where was Will? They must have noticed the change in the motion of the boat!

My hands, screaming in pain, lost their grip. I fell into the water. Water closed over my head. It was green and smothering. I paddled madly with my hands. I tried to kick with my legs, but the Levi's and shoes made my legs worse than useless. They were pulling me down.

Dog-paddling, I struggled to the surface.

For an instant, as I tried to see through the water in my eyes, I was afraid to look around. I believed I would see open water and the boat vanishing in the distance. Abandoned.

What I saw was the life preserver sailing over my head. It landed five or six feet behind me, and its yellow nylon line was right next to my shoulder.

I grabbed the line. They started to reel me in.

Belinda had vanished. I stood on deck wrapped in a blanket while the others ran back and forth, changing course.

Takuro yelled to everybody to keep clear of the boom, which was swinging across the deck. We were bow into the south wind. Will whipped the wheel around to head west to go back to where Belinda had fallen overboard. At first the *Easy Girl* did not respond. He swung the rudder full right then full left, backing and filling, until finally the sail caught wind. The bow came west and the sail stood out starboard. Will was puffing and panting, as if he'd run a four hundred meter race.

Takuro's head went back and forth between Will and the sail, agonized. He wanted to know what had happened, but he knew this was no time to ask. And he had to watch the mainsheet.

Will said in a strained voice, "Don't haul it in too close. I don't want to pass her."

Daniel strained forward over the lifeline, binoculars to his eyes.

Everybody else was coming up from below, even the ones who'd been asleep. Bret, Emery, Greg, Mary, and Bill crowded to the stern, asking Will what had happened.

He only said, "Belinda's overboard."

Bill turned pale and climbed on the cabin to see better. "How far back was she?"

Nobody answered.

"When did she go in?"

Daniel said. "Just a couple of minutes ago."

We'd been heading east when Belinda and I went overboard. Now we'd gone west several minutes. We should be right about at the spot.

"Maybe we passed it," Will said.

We came about into the wind and headed east, slowly, with the sail not hauled close. We were a little south of our previous westbound wake. Will probably thought that the south breeze might have pushed us north of where she went in.

"I'm going to climb the mast," Takuro said.

Will automatically answered, "No, it's too danger—" but the words tapered off and hung there. Takuro had shinnied up, hand over hand. His knees were clamped to the slippery metal. The sail on the side of the mast made climbing difficult. But once when he slipped, he grabbed it and held on.

Near the top, maybe fifty feet up, he stopped and clung, scanning the water.

He said nothing. Nobody asked. We knew he'd call if he saw her.

We continued to run east.

After a while, Will yelled, "Coming about!" We sailed west again, maybe a little south now. It was hard to tell. It was trackless out here.

Will and Greg stood shoulder to shoulder. Emery stood nervously holding a big white life preserver to throw to Belinda if we found her. Bret looked just plain stunned.

But Bill really worried me. He kept trying to ask Will what had happened. Then he grabbed the binoculars away from Daniel. Bill's eyes seemed to sink into their sockets farther and farther the more time passed with no sign of Belinda.

For Greg it must have been all too much like the search for Twinkie.

We turned east again. Suddenly, Takuro screamed, "Stop!"

Will threw the wheel over and the sail luffed. Takuro pointed past the port bow. We rushed to port as the boat drifted. Just below the surface, floating lazily, was a wide-brimmed red sun hat.

The water was clear and greenish, like gelatin, reflecting sunbeams down into its depths. We could not see the bottom.

We could not see Belinda.

We tried. And tried and tried. While I went below and got into dry clothes, they sailed back and forth in a tiny compass, going just far enough in one direction to get up enough momentum to come about. When I got back on deck, they were still trying.

Will was white. Bill was in tears. Takuro slid down the mast and then clung to it as if his shoulders were shrieking with pain.

They had pulled the hat aboard with a gaff, but we never saw any sign of Belinda.

Emery was at the wheel now. His face was limp with incomprehension. Greg sat on the deck with his bony length folded up, arms around his knees.

And finally Will called off the search.

"Dad! No. We've got to keep looking!"

Will said, "Where?"

He went and put his arm around his son's shoulders.

"We've been over and over the spot," he said. "This is the right place. It's been an hour. She's gone."

"Noooo!" Bill howled.

Will held him. "She's gone," he repeated.

"She can't be! Mom's a great swimmer! She *can't* be!"

Mary and Daniel both moved toward Bill. Will was obviously hesitating between honesty and kindly deceit. Finally he said, "Daniel threw the life preserver overboard immediately. She never tried to reach it. I think she swam down, Bill."

So they had both got on deck fast. Maybe they had seen everything that happened.

"Why? That's crazy!"

Daniel and Will exchanged glances. Will nodded.

Daniel said, "She had just pushed Cat overboard."

Will said, "Daniel and I came up from the galley, because Daniel thought Cat looked—looked as if something important had just occurred to her." His voice got hoarse and he stopped. Daniel continued for him.

"We saw Cat speak to Belinda as we came up the stairs. Then Belinda tossed her hat back over the stern, and when Cat turned to look at it, she pushed her over. Cat grabbed at Belinda and they both went in. It happened so fast, we couldn't get to them in time."

So Daniel had saved my life.

I said, "She intended to sail on a quarter of a mile or so, then throw the life preserver over and tell you all that I fell

in reaching for her hat. She knew I'd sink before you ever
got back to me."

Bill stood stunned. He couldn't really absorb the meaning
of what Daniel was telling him. Greg did, though.

Greg said grimly, "Why would Belinda do that?"

There was a silence.

If ever I've seen a pregnant pause, this was it. Nobody
said a word, but the people shifted places. Mary went to
Bill and threw both her arms around his waist, holding him
tight. Daniel put his arm over Will's shoulder. Will's head
was high, but he was suffering. Bret and Takuro watched
quietly.

Emery held the wheel, but we weren't going anywhere.
The sail luffed. *Easy Girl*, with her weather helm, was bow
into the breeze.

They were looking at me.

"Belinda pushed me overboard because I had just done
the same thing Twinkie did. I told her how she had killed
Chuck Kroop."

The silence drew out for half a minute. Then Mary said,
"I'm taking Bill downstairs for a brandy." Will nodded, as
if he should have thought of that himself, but Mary wasn't
waiting for approval. She shepherded Bill out of there fast.

I was extremely relieved. It was hard enough talking
about this in front of Will, even though I thought they both
had a right to know. Let Bill take it in slowly, and if he did
it without me, that was okay, too.

Will, with a voice like sandpaper, said simply, "Now
tell us."

"Twinkie had figured it out, and she went to Belinda while
Belinda was at the wheel last night to tease her, and to
hold it over her, I think. Belinda must have hit her with a
champagne bottle and lowered her over the side. Daniel

and I came up a few minutes later. Belinda was still shaking. She made up a story about being upset because there was a body on board and it might decompose."

Greg suddenly ran forward, leaned over the lifeline and was sick. The rest of us stood around and waited. We were all too drained to react much.

Greg came back. He was the color of a lake trout, but he was able to walk.

"But she *couldn't* have killed Chuck," Takuro said. "She was on deck all that night."

"That's true," I said. "And Chuck was killed about three-thirty. Belinda was on deck. I was there with her. But nobody else could have done it, either. You could hardly find a door more constantly in view of a lot of people. There were at least four people in the galley almost all that time. And Mary was watching from the dorm room. And nobody could really be sure that Bill wasn't awake, too. Unless several of you were in collusion. And Emery isn't related to any of you, and Bret is new here, so that didn't seem likely."

"Nobody went in the door?" Will said.

"No." I hesitated. "Do you really want to hear this?"

"*Of course not*," he said. More quietly he added, "But I have to."

I could understand that. In fact, I felt that he was like me. It was better to know. It was always better to have the facts. Ducking truth is dangerous in the long run.

"Belinda had been the last to see Chuck. We put him to bed about midnight. She went back in for a few seconds to turn on the light, she said, in case he woke up. She couldn't have killed him then. The blood was too fresh in the morning. In the morning, she was also the first person to see him."

"So she killed him in the morning?" Greg asked.

"No, by then the blood was half-dried. That couldn't be faked. I wondered whether she had left some trap or some device, but there was no place to put it. So what did she use? Twinkie figured it out first, and I only wish she'd told one of us."

I glanced at Greg. He wouldn't catch my eye.

"Belinda killed him between three and four a.m., while she was on deck. What kinds of forces entered that room? Air? Heat? Cold? I got the answer this afternoon when Takuro lost control of the wheel for a second and I hit my head. Gravity. We had been sailing east, with the wind from the south, and the waves were broadsiding us. When he lost the wheel, we swerved upwind. Because I wasn't expecting it, I lost my balance. I realized that a boat in high waves has basically two motions, pitching when it's moving at right angles to the waves, and rolling when it's paralleling them. There are mixes when you're quartering waves, but those are the basics. That's what I said to Belinda."

"I don't understand," Greg said.

I said to him, "Would you get me a knife from the galley? And two dinette cushions?"

He did, without asking why. The others just stared. I took the two cushions and laid them on the deck, wedged the knife handle between them, crosswise to the axis of the boat. I looked around. "Can I have your scarf?" I asked Greg. He handed me that, too.

We were wallowing, the sail luffing, Emery at the wheel. "Turn so that we cut into the waves," I said.

I wet the scarf in water from the deck, then rolled it tightly into a cylinder and put it under the knife. Emery brought the boat up into the wind and we began to pitch. The bow went down, then up. Knife and scarf stayed in place.

"Now turn ninety degrees."

He brought the boat around so that we were parallel to the waves. We began to roll, leaning over to one side, then to the other. The heavy, wet cylinder of scarf began to roll one way, then the other, under the knife. Very slowly, a tiny cut appeared.

"A head and neck would move back and forth more freely," I said. "And the roll was much, much more violent that night."

They gazed at the four objects, horrified.

"Let me tell you what Belinda did. By midnight we were heading north, cutting directly into big waves that had formed before the wind went more to the northwest. Virtually all of our motion was pitching. We'd come over the back of one wave, plane down into the trough, then ride up the next. Stern down bow up. Then bow down, stern up.

"Belinda had wedged Chuck in place with heavy bolster pillows even before we left the stateroom. After we had left the room, she took the long, heavy roast knife from under her slicker and laid it over Chuck's neck, with the sharp edge down against his throat. Then she wedged the handle firmly between two pillows and left.

"The bunk, and all the bunks, are along the long axis of the boat. As long as the boat went on pitching, Chuck wouldn't roll much and the knife wouldn't move much. His bed would go down at the foot and up at the head, then down at the head and up at the foot, like the boat.

"But a little before three a.m., Belinda claimed we were getting too close to the coast of Michigan for safety. She decided to head due west for a while. So we turned west. And when we turned west, we broadsided the waves.

"For an hour, it was almost pure roll. The boat would tilt far to port as the wave hit us. Then the wave would move under us, and we'd tilt far to starboard. This was the worst motion of the night. It flips mariners out of their beds.

"Down in the stateroom, Chuck's head and neck had started to roll back and forth. Under the knife."

Somebody drew in a hissing breath. I think it was Will, but he gave no outward sign.

"Of course, there was only the weight of the knife itself to press down. It was a heavy knife, but the process took time. Little by little the knife cut down and finally it reached the carotid artery.

"Belinda, of course, didn't know how long this would take. We held west for an hour, then turned northeast again. For a couple of hours.

"Then it was morning. Belinda went in to check on Chuck and 'accidentally' picked up the knife. She knocked one pillow to the floor and probably spread the other pillows around, too, to make things less obvious. It would take so little time, she could accomplish it while she was screaming."

Will asked, "How—" he stopped—"how could she know it would work?"

"I suppose on an earlier trip she experimented. Locked herself in the stateroom saying she was sick and tried it on a beef roast."

"Oh, my God," he said. He was remembering something.

"And if it hadn't worked," I said, "it wouldn't be a disaster. If Chuck woke up, he'd be confused from the tranquilizer. He'd probably have knocked the knife off onto the floor before he even knew it was there. If he woke up with a small cut on his throat, none of us would have believed he hadn't taken the knife in there himself, no matter how much he protested. And if Belinda went in the next morning and found the knife on the floor and Chuck alive and asleep, all she had to do was either 'find' the knife or hide it. No one would care. In other words, either the murder would work, or the preparations would be unnoticed.

"If it worked, she assumed we'd think it was suicide. She didn't know the stateroom door would be under such constant observation. She had planned that it wouldn't. I think she put a drop of ipecac on the Dramamine tablets. I also think she hadn't expected as violent a storm. Ordinarily, some of the people would have gone to bed.

"Naturally she had to be the one to check on Chuck in the morning, but that was no problem. What was vital was for us to swear she hadn't left the deck all night. Having me along as a completely unrelated observer was important for that. I had wondered why they invited me. She may have asked Daniel on the trip so as to have a doctor who could swear to the time of death. Greg might confirm it, but he was too involved for his word to be unimpeachable.

"She knew there was a storm predicted. She knew that Will loves storms and drinks rum. Therefore, she knew she would eventually be at the helm.

"I guess that's all."

Takuro spoke for the first time. My heart went out to him, he was so obviously tormented, but his question was practical.

"Why did she want to delay us getting to port? Why screw up the motor and destroy the radio?"

"I'm guessing, you know. But I would think she might have thought a careful autopsy might see that there were many, many little cuts on the neck. It might seem like *too* many. I think she hoped that by delaying as much as possible, the drying of the cut itself, plus decomposition, would make it hard to tell. She was more or less right, I would think."

"Probably," Daniel said.

Will asked, "How did she stop the motor?"

"When we were leaving Michigan City, I think she faked finding the engine difficult to start. Clicked the key on and off, I suppose. Later, she and Emery took the cover off and went down to look at it. She was carrying a cup of coffee. Probably she poured it in the diesel fuel. That could be checked."

"But it went on working."

"We put up the sails within a quarter of a mile. Wouldn't there be enough fuel for that in the line?"

I looked at Takuro. He said, "Yes. Plenty."

Will said, "But I don't see—it all depended on getting Chuck so enraged he had to be sedated. How could she possibly count on that?"

"Will, Chuck *did* have a terrible temper. If he once got mad, making him worse wouldn't be hard. And he and Greg have had words before, haven't they?"

"Not an actual fight."

"She got them both cooped up on a boat with Twinkie. Belinda let us think, quite casually, that Chuck invited himself along this weekend, but that wasn't true, was it?"

Will said, "No. I heard her ask him."

"Twinkie could be counted on to tease them both. Bret only added to the volatility. Then Belinda skillfully kept Chuck and Greg apart until the moment she wanted the fight to happen. I didn't see how she did it because I was on deck at the time. What did she do, Greg?"

In a whisper, he said, "We were both in the galley. I got up for coffee. She said something about how two grown men ought to be able to get along together. Naturally, he said something sarcastic. My God. She was my sister!"

"But *why*?" Will said.

"Money. She was afraid your business wasn't doing well. Haven't you been having problems?"

"We've had to close a division. But we'll make it back. We're conservative."

"She couldn't be sure of that. You'd net one point two million dollars from the sale of *Off and On*. Wouldn't that help?"

Will nodded. "It'd help a lot."

"But Chuck wanted to produce. Belinda thought he'd screw up and lose instead of winning. I think she was right about that, too. He knew nothing about movies, and he thought he knew so much about everything that he wouldn't take advice."

"We could live perfectly well on a lot less—"

"Will, I had heard that Greg's father had lost his money when Greg was ten or so, and they went through a rough time before he made it back. I didn't realize then, but that meant Belinda, as Greg's sister, also had a father who lost his fortune. She was a little older. A teenage girl losing her friends and position—that would stick in her mind. She was very frightened about being without money. And not for herself so much as for Bill. She knew he was no businessman and didn't want to be."

There was a long pause. I could almost hear Will's mind searching for something good to say about Belinda.

"So she killed herself to save Bill and me the embarrassment of a trial."

It could be. Or to save herself. Who knew? It wouldn't hurt to let him think so.

Tears were running down Takuro's face. The rest of them stood around like funereal manikins—sort of an illustration for "L. L. Bean Goes to a Burial at Sea."

Then Emery said, "Look."

There was a thin line of rosy beige and green on the horizon. The sand dunes and pines of western Michigan.

· 29 ·

The authorities kept us in Holland three days while they took statements. And fingerprinted and photographed the *Easy Girl*, probably. I stayed away from the harbor.

I took a motel room in Holland, as did most of the rest of our crew. Will wanted to pay for my room, but I said no,

Hal Briskman would pay for it. Hal would be *so* pleased. I had nightmares the first night. Water was sucking at my legs, pulling me under. I woke up sucking air and gasping. It's happened every night since.

I phoned John. Asked about my parrot.

"Long John doesn't miss you at all," he said.

"Certainly he does."

"Nope. I've been feeding him roses—"

"John! They're *basted* with insecticide!"

"No, they aren't. They're from my mother's garden."

"Oh. Plus, you told me you'd feed him a balanced diet."

"He gets birdseed for dessert. Are you keeping out of trouble?"

"Sort of."

"That bad, huh? Long John said, 'Water water everywhere and not a drop to drink' today."

"He did not. Birds don't say W."

"Did so."

"I'll be home Wednesday."

"I'll be here," he said in a tone fraught with meaning. Pointed. Urgent. Pushy, even, you might say.

Tried to call Mike. He wasn't at home. I thought of trying to call him at the paper; it's never a good idea. It makes them notice if he's been missing for days.

I rented a typewriter and got on with the story. The press was all over us about the deaths on the boat, so I didn't feel I had to cover that. After several false starts, my story came out as "A Landlubber's Guide to Sailing, or What Can Go Wrong on Water."

I virtually never do a first-person article. Ninety percent of journalism school is learning to write without ever using "I," "we," "us," or even "you." Which is difficult. But this time it was an antidote both to my training and to the events of the last three days to do a humorous piece on all my misconceptions about sailing, about learning the hard way, and what it's really like.

Forget the question of how the rich live on board. Forget Hal's question: What is class? It didn't seem to fit. What sounds like a good idea to an editor isn't always so hot when you try it in black and white.

Daniel and I went to lunch at the Dutch Village and ate Dutch cheeses on dense, moist, Dutch rye bread.

The second evening he took me to dinner at The Sandpiper, facing Macatawa Bay.

"I get the feeling we're splitting up before we've begun," he said.

I said, "You saved my life, Daniel."

"Your next word will be 'but.' "

"No. You're a genuinely empathetic person. I watched you anticipate all the times when people needed help or support, and you were always right there. I'm truly sorry that it doesn't seem to quite work between us." And I meant it.

"Just because you think I wanted to cover up Chuck's death?"

"I didn't say cover up—"

"I would have handled it differently, that's all."

"Why? Why were you so *eager* to call it suicide?"

"I thought Mary had done it."

"Oh."

"To protect Bill from losing his inheritance. She was the only one who had a chance of slipping into that stateroom."

Oh, swell. "And then what? Would you have let her go free?"

"I would have got her into therapy. Blackmailed her into therapy if I had to. Do you think putting people in prison does anybody any good?"

"Sometimes. This is a pointless argument. What I think is that you have to tell the facts the way they are. Let truth make its own way in the world."

"So tell me this." His face was set and a little angry.

"Shoot."

"If not so much had hit the papers about the murders on the *Easy Girl*, or if the story as it came out had been less accurate, would you have written one?"

"A story about Belinda?"

"Yes."

Honesty compelled me to say, "It would have been hard. I wouldn't have wanted to hurt Will's feelings."

"It would be hard to put in everything?"

"Yes."

"How is that different from hiding truth?"

"Well, for one thing, I'd probably have wound up putting everything in once I started. Within space constraints, of course. I'm not any good at intentionally glossing over facts."

"You *think* that you'd have been brutally honest if you'd had to write the piece?"

"Facts are facts."

"But can you swear you wouldn't have tried to spare his feelings?"

"Not exactly."

"Well, I guess we'll never know, will we?"

"No. We'll never know."

For a farewell scene, the Greyhound bus depot in Holland, Michigan, doesn't make it. It's as unlike the end of *Casablanca* as you can imagine. No mist, no fat-bodied airplane starting its propellers. In July, not even any trenchcoats.

It's really just a counter inside a party store. Outside there's a bench and a phone booth. In fact, the only really bizarre thing about it is that the phone book in the booth has all its pages.

Daniel had brought Will to say goodbye. He was staying with Will on the boat and would help him sail it home later.

Somebody at Bay Haven Marina, by the way, had offered to sail me back to Chicago. This person owned a forty-footer, so I'd have been crowded, being used to greater luxury. I told him I was grateful but particularly enjoyed the comfort and elegance of a Greyhound bus.

The bus originated in Grand Rapids. It was two minutes late.

Will took my hand and said, "I'm glad you were aboard."

"You must wish I hadn't been. Maybe nobody would ever have known what happened."

He thought seriously about that for a minute. Obviously, he had been worrying that thought for several days. Finally, he said, "And what if one night, two or three a.m., I woke up and suddenly realized by myself how it had been done and that Belinda had done it? And there's Belinda sleeping next to me. Can you imagine a worse hell?"

"No. Not easily."

"Cat, how did you know Belinda and I weren't in it together?"

"You would have covered for her at several points. Especially, you would have delayed Daniel when he wanted to go up on deck while she was pushing me overboard."

"Oh." He looked shocked for a second. Half-relevantly, he said, "Well, I've still got Bill." Daniel put his hand on Will's shoulder.

The big white-and-blue bus pulled in, lumbering as if it were pregnant. The window in the front said CHICAGO. Fumes, mess, noise, muggers, and crowds had never beckoned so strongly.

Will took my hand. I was staring into the eyes of a man who had lost his wife, whose brother-in-law was prostrated by sorrow, and who looked forward to months of helping his son recover from shame and grief.

He said, "I hoped you'd have a happy time this weekend. I'm sorry it turned out so badly for you."

Now that's class.

Glossary of Nautical Terms from Cat Marsala's Notebook

Aft: To the rear.

Amidships: Toward the middle of the ship.

Auxiliary: The gasoline or diesel motor. I think they're trying to express the notion that wind power is primary.

Battening the hatches: Closing the hatches down and fastening them, usually with cleats.

Beam reach: Tacking with the wind abeam, that is, coming directly toward the side, or perpendicular to the long axis of the boat.

Beating: Sailing against the wind, or tacking.

Berth: What on land would be called a bed.

Bilge: The bottom of the boat.

Bilge water: Water in the bottom of the boat. Real sailors seem to think some bilge water is perfectly normal.

Binnacle: The case in which a compass and sometimes a light are kept on board ship for use by the helmsman.

Boom: A horizontal pole attached to the bottom of the mast, used to keep a sail stretched out.

Bow: The front end of the boat.

Bow pulpit: A point at the very front of the bow where a small metal railing makes a U-shaped place you can stand.

Burgee: A flag of identification, usually triangular but sometimes swallow-tailed.

Cleat: a piece of metal or wood, often shaped like a flattened T, to which ropes are fastened.

Coaming: A raised edge, like around a hatch, to keep water out.

Chop: Small, broken waves.

Cockpit: In a car they would call it the command module. The place where the person stands at the wheel and steers, usually sunken and surrounded by a coaming.

Come about: Turn the boat in order to go on a different tack.

Companionway: What on land would be called stairs.

Deck: What on land would be called floor.

Dinghy: A small boat, sometimes even an inflatable life raft, used for chores or for a lifeboat.

Fore: To the front. The opposite of aft.

Galley: On land this would be called a kitchen.

Halyard: Rope for lowering or raising a sail.

Hatch: An opening in a boat big enough to pass a sail or a person through. Some are like doors; some are more like skylights.

Head: What on land would be called a bathroom.

Hull: The shell or frame of the boat.

Inboard: Short for inboard motor, one built into the boat.

Jenny: A nickname for Genoa, a type of jib.

Jib: A triangular sail, smaller than the main sail, usually fixed in the front, designed to catch extra wind. Those balloon-shaped colorful sails are also most likely to be jibs.

Keel: A heavy dagger-shaped piece, often of metal, under a boat to keep her steady.

Lifeline: A line running through metal uprights all the way around the boat about waist high, intended to keep sailors from falling overboard. The nautical equivalent of a railing.

Lifeline stanchions: Thin metal poles with a hole at the top through which the lifeline runs.

Loudhailer: A voice amplifier. In the old days, a kind of megaphone. Now they are battery-powered.

Luffing: Turning too close up into the wind. This causes the sail to shake and the boat to lose power.

Mainsail: The main sail, of course.

Mainsheet: The rope that goes to the mainsail.

Mast: The big stick in the middle that holds up the sail.

Masthead: The top of the mast.

Outboard: Short for outboard motor, one not built into the boat.

Pitch: The plunging motion a boat makes when it tilts down in the bow and up in the stern, then up in the bow and down in the stern.

Port: The left side of the boat as you face front.

Porthole: A round window in a boat.

Reach: Strictly speaking, a tack, but when the wind is at approximately a right angle to the axis of the boat. In other words, you call it a reach when you're not trying hard to go upwind.

Roll: The swaying motion a boat makes when it leans over to one side, then over to the other side. Almost as annoying as pitching.

Rollers: Large, heavy waves.

Rudder: The flat piece hinged vertically at the back of the boat that is controlled by the wheel for steering.

Run with the wind: Sail with the wind behind you, kind of the opposite of tacking.

Running light: A light you're suppose to have lit whenever you're moving at night, usually high on the mast. There are also red and green lights at deck level.

Safety harness: Straps that tie to a sailor or his life vest and clip on to some part of the boat. The idea is to keep him or her from going overboard.

Sheet: Not a sail, as you might think, but a rope running to the lower corner of a sail.

Sloop: A sailboat with one mast.

Spar: A pole, mast, boom, gaff—in other words, almost anything on a boat that's long and rounded and wooden.

Spinnaker: A large triangular sail that is attached to a boom opposite the main boom, used mostly when running with the wind.

Starboard: The right side of the boat as you face front.

Stays: Ropes or cables used to support a mast. On land these might be called guy wires.

Stern: The rear end of a boat.

Swamp: When the boat fills with water and sinks. An outcome strictly to be avoided.

Swells: Large, rounded waves with no crests.

Tack: As a noun, the direction the boat is going. As a verb, to cut diagonally across the path of the wind, so that you can sail zigzag into the wind.

Thwart: Any crosswise brace on a boat, like the seat in a canoe, and by extension the direction in a boat that a thwart might go.

Topgallant: A sail placed above the topmast and below the royal mast on old sailing ships. No, the *Easy Girl* doesn't have one. Just kidding around.

Topside: On deck.

Turnbuckle: A really clever metal sleeve with threading at both ends that goes in opposite directions. Attached between two threaded rods or wires, it can be turned to tighten or loosen them.

Wallow: A condition in which the boat washes around clumsily without direction. Definitely a bad idea.

Waterline: The level on the hull to which the surface water is supposed to come and above which it ought not to go.

Weather helm: One that tends to turn toward the weather or wind. The opposite of a lee helm.

Wheel: On a car it would be called the steering wheel.

Whisker: A spar, usually near the bow, used for holding the jib guys or wires farther out from the boat.

Winch: A drum with a crank that aids in winding up rope or wire.

Yawl: A sailboat with two masts, the shorter one in the back.

Chicagoan Barbara D'Amato is the author of several mystery novels, including *On My Honor*, which was nominated for an Anthony at the Bouchercon World Mystery Convention in London, 1990, and musical comedies that have been produced in London and Chicago. She has worked as a carpenter for stage magic illusions and an investigator in criminal cases. She teaches mystery writing to Chicago police officers. Her first Cat Marsala novel was *Hardball* (Scribners, 1990). She lives in Chicago.